Phoen

IRISH SHORT STORIES 2000

Pass me on when
you've finished
reading me

Healthy
Planet

www.healthyplanet.org

Phoenix **IRISH SHORT STORIES 2000**

edited by David Marcus

PHŒNIX

First published in Great Britain in 2000 by Phoenix, a division of

The Orion Publishing Group Ltd
Orion House
5 Upper Saint Martin's Lane
London, WC2H 9EA

A CIP catalogue record for this book is available from the
British Library.

ISBN 0 75381 111 1

Typeset at The Spartan Press Ltd
Lymington, Hants
Printed in Great Britain by
The Guernsey Press Co Ltd
Guernsey, C. I.

ACKNOWLEDGEMENTS

None of the stories in the following pages has previously appeared in print.

'Charlie Barley', Copyright © Fred Annesley, 2000; 'Berkeley's Telephone', Copyright © Harry Clifton, 2000; 'Strange Fruit', Copyright © Macdara Doyle, 2000; 'Out of the Ordinary', Copyright © Brendan Glacken, 2000; 'Mother's Day', Copyright © Patricia Hickey, 2000; 'The Ghosts', Copyright © Fred Johnston, 2000; 'Great Bus Journeys of Dublin', Copyright © Paul Lenehan, 2000; 'Where The Sun Doesn't Shine', Copyright © Martin Malone, 2000; 'Waking the Jew', Copyright © Aidan Mathews, 2000; 'The Break', Copyright © Fiona O'Connor, 2000; 'Loose Head', Copyright © Tommy Frank O'Connor, 2000; 'Canticles', Copyright © Mary O'Donnell, 2000; 'Her Blood Dripped into Grass', © Cóilín O hAodha, 2000; 'This Game', Copyright © Bridget O'Toole, 2000; 'Talking to My Father', Copyright © Deirdre Shanahan, 2000; 'The Whaler', Copyright © Joe Sheerin, 2000; 'Harbour', Copyright © Howard Wright, 2000.

CONTENTS

INTRODUCTION

With this, the first of the annual *Phoenix Irish Short Stories* anthologies to be published in the new millennium, one might ask what important changes in and/or for the Irish short story have taken place in, say, the final fifty years of the last century. There have been four major developments.

Firstly, there was, from the 1960s on, the new liberalism which helped to bring about the emasculation of the censorship laws and so removed virtually all the taboos that had prevented Irish writers from dealing with many of the fundamental themes of daily life, or, if they did deal with them, prevented Irish-based readers from reading them and drove a number of the authors to emigrate.

Secondly, and probably stemming to a large extent from the aforementioned new liberalism, many Irish women took up their pens, enriching the short story and bringing to it experiences and insights beyond the power of male writers.

Thirdly, the growth of short story competitions encouraged many who might otherwise never have written, and as a result the form benefited from the discovery of excellent new talents, as the biographical notes for this anthology attest.

Fourthly, contemporary Irish short story writers, along with Irish novelists, have been noticeably reducing their reliance on permutations of country, creed, and nationality for their material, a trend which the razing rather than the raising of walls and borders, accompanied by the spread of cheaper air travel, fostered.

The foregoing are the pluses. Minuses? The big one, carried over from the second half of the last century: readership stagnation. Not that there aren't, both in Ireland and Britain, publishers who regularly include anthologies and single-author collections in their list – Phoenix House, the publisher of this annual collection, being one of the foremost. But more are needed if sales are to make the short story more attractive to book publishers. Can anything be done about that? I don't know. But I do know one thing which hasn't been tried. There are annual prestigious awards with the attendant media publicity for books of almost every conceivable category, but none for a collection of short stories. If the main publishers in Ireland and Britain combined to launch such an award, each contributing according to its means, the expense would be shared, but the results, given time, could benefit all. And if the publishers themselves are reluctant to do the spadework, what about the Publishers Associations of both islands? Is there a story doctor in the house?

DAVID MARCUS

MACDARA DOYLE

Strange Fruit

This is how it happened.

The next day El Jefe awoke with an enormous orange placed skilfully inside his cavernous eye socket by Lynch, the cunning manservant.

Horrible weight on his right eye. So heavy it pressed the lid shut. A bad bruise, he said on waking, but wouldn't turn to lie on his side for fear.

He recalled stumbling some hours earlier through endlessly spread furniture, following an evening with Alex and rivers of imported (probably smuggled) whiskey. Fucking Lynch left chairs and obdurate tables scattered askance around the room. Unable to find the lightswitch, the Father of the Nation attempted a struggle through the obstacles, until a heavy blow to the hip sent him curling to the floor, damning Lynch to a slow, painful death.

He wasn't certain, but thought vaguely there had been another blow – to the eye – as he lay mouthing imperial vengeance upon furniture-makers throughout the land. That was all. Lynch must have tucked him in.

He had. And once the withered fuck was flat, the cunning manservant had carefully placed a heavy sweating orange inside the furious eye socket. A fresh vivid weight gently pressing the eye closed.

With his left he could see little: huge shadows that blurred beyond the ridge of his nose. There was colour, warm and verging maybe on red. The same vague hue that had first interrupted the vision of his father, before sucking the life from within him. And now a hulking shadow closed his eyes in fright.

By mid-morning he knew a tumour had come to destroy him.

As it had destroyed his father. A thing that had swelled in the darkness as he'd lain stupefied, farting happily on his back.

His eyes never opened again. Instead, he learned to discern shadows that skulked across his eyelids. Roaring when appropriate. Matters of state were decided thrice-weekly by the bedside. Devoted ministers he heard slither to their seats. How long now?

At first they sat far forward in earnest that they might be seen. But within a week El Jefe had issued edict Number 4002. Made them sit a full three feet back to stop his face drenching with the lickspittle.

By the bedside this solemn (sometimes sniggering) council plotted the historic course of the nation. Studied the plans for making war on unsuspecting neighbours, as drawn up with regularity by generals grown bored with the peace. None dared even aver to the fact that El Jefe – Father of the Nation, protector of the weak and a fine golfer at that – lay prone with a bright, ripe, orange cosy in his eye socket. Madness too was within his power. If he so desired it.

But Minister Buenaventura Delaney – Flowering Plants & Big Trees – worried at the bright fruit. Worried whether such produce might fall within the remit of his ministry which, even after ten years, he remained decidedly unsure of. He'd wanted Faxing & Photocopying. Had insisted that this new ministry be called into being for the sake of the nation, his anxiety fostered and nurtured by overheard conversations among foreigners at the resort bars. He'd even sent for the manuals. But El Jefe refused. The army needed guns, the generals better uniforms. Other urgencies. He heard later that the money went to the man they called El Hombre. A national matter.

Still he worried at the bright fruit softening in the heat.

Often discussion lapsed. Times when the most daring plans for war seemed dull from repetition; when even an ingenious scheme to attract more tourists by adopting two crossed golf clubs as the symbol of the nation (Delaney suggested a young girl) failed to excite the vision of this solemn council. Times when El Jefe slept and saw comfort in memories of Martha. When the historic course of the nation meandered. And when Minister Olivio – Maps & Instruments of Measurements – rose up hard on the hind legs of his chair, huge and dextrous hands in the lamplight causing bunnies and harum-scarum monsters to erupt on the broad wall behind.

On one such dry afternoon, Minister O'Brien – Domestic Animals – reached out to peel the succulent fruit. Educated abroad, as was the tradition among his class, he had displayed some cunning with the nation's books. New columns and categories metamorphosed overnight. Old, insistent problems were disappeared among the footnotes and the nation brought to brusque health by an adept pen. Men from overseas came with briefcases and more clever pens. The nation now a wonder abroad, it was announced, as was the custom, on Independence Day.

Olivio was quick to dissuade, touching O'Brien's vacant wrist in time to stop him lifting the orange from its obvious comfort.

And so it went.

None could recall whose idea it had been. In later years, Olivio was to insist the proposal had nothing to do with him. Buena-ventura Delaney too denied all knowledge. But O'Brien said it had all been the fault of Minister O'Farrill – Electrical Goods. He made this claim many years later to an intent and, as he soon discovered, remarkably gullible doctoral student. And related how this history had been constructed. And of his own heroic role. And watched as the young student wrote it down as he said it. Like the anxious press did also.

There are too many cows in the country, El Jefe declared one brilliant afternoon. And they are eating all the grass. And the tourists are choosing other countries instead, countries like ours was before the cows made it bare and unpresentable, Lynch said El Jefe said. And he – O'Farrill – was to find a solution to this problem of the cows. And had twenty-four hours in which to do so, O'Brien said Lynch said El Jefe said.

O'Farrill promptly retired to the nearest bar, confident that a bout of fevered drinking would yield at least one remarkable solution. He was joined by Delaney. And then Olivio. Twenty-three-and-a-half hours later the three ministers emerged. It is said today that early on in their session they conceived a scheme of astonishing ingenuity, which they very sensibly committed to paper for safety. But in the justifiably frenetic celebrations that followed, the paper with their plan was mislaid. All O'Farrill could remember of the plot was that it somehow involved the man they called El Hombre. Crucial, insisted Delaney, the man they called El Hombre was crucial. Olivio swore later he had seen Lynch in the bar.

The entire Cabinet, it is said today, was fifteen minutes from summary execution when O'Brien spoke up. Began to outline what he knew to be a simple, but brilliant scheme. A plan formulated during his long years of education abroad, as was the tradition among his class.

A country cannot be modern with cows, he said. Such clumsy beasts interrupted the march of the nation. Literally. So all the cows in the country would be given to the man they called El Hombre, he said, watching all the time the Jefe with the orange nurtured in his eye socket.

And the man they called El Hombre, he said, would in turn sell these extraneous beasts to backward countries where the cow was still prized. This would make the man they called El Hombre very rich. Richer perhaps than the nation. And the presence of such bounteous wealth in their country would be a source of great pride, prestige even. It would please the men from overseas with briefcases. More men like the man they called El Hombre would come. And they too would bring their riches. Because money could only feel comfortable in the presence of more money, he said.

In time the nation would be richer than all of its neighbours. And with this wealth would come the finest of foods, the best of wines, the most conspicuous of consumables. All to be packed happily along the shelves of the hospital-white hypermarkets that would be called naturally into being with their coming. And the cinemas. The marbled cafés. The centres of long leisure. The highways black like coal. The plans for war.

El Jefe, his right eye now permanently weeping from the small but insistent quantities of acid seeping into it, was stunned from the simple brilliance of it all. Certainly, he never spoke for one full minute and fifteen seconds afterwards. Olivio counted the steady clock-ticks from the corner. Then he raised an arm and words struggled on his tongue.

All leaned forward quickly lest they be judged wanting in respect, none more so than an eager O'Farrill. Gladdened of the opportunity to tighten his arse and fart. Olivio's spectral creations submitted to the persistent lamps.

El Jefe, it is said today, spoke only three, maybe four words.

'Is it big?' it was said he said.

'Yes,' immediately replied O'Brien, and continued, 'With the money that will be brought by the men like the man they call El Hombre' – momentarily he wondered at the source of this strange title, a valorous deed in youth, perhaps? A personal matter? – 'the nation will be rich. Immeasurably richer, more important abroad, than our neighbours. Even our neighbours combined.'

Olivio meanwhile stared hard at O'Brien's head, seeing how the skin around his temples flexed with the anxiety of speech, and his hair did not. Yes, he said, nodding. El Jefe is right. It is a wig.

And Delaney looked long at the enormous orange placed skilfully inside El Jefe's cavernous eye socket by Lynch, the cunning manservant. And wondered if anyone in his ministry knew the slightest about such things. Certainly it was big, the biggest he had seen.

And then, bored, El Jefe let his head go limp, nearly turn on the pillow. The enormous orange rolled up, almost out of its socket. Lifting, it went hesitant at the lip before tumbling oversized back into expected comfort. And he dreamt again of Martha and wondered if Alex had known. And he dreamt too of O'Brien and his strange obsession with fucking cows. The nation, he decided, needed a war.

Lynch, sniggering, interrupted to say the meeting was over and Olivio sucked his cheeks in coarse anticipation of the centres of long pleasure to be constructed throughout the land.

*

Three days later El Jefe was murdered in his bed. The killers, it is said today, were agents of the man they called El Hombre. Before murdering the Father of the Nation, the killers had gently removed the strange and enormous orange placed skilfully inside his cavernous eye socket by Lynch, the cunning manservant. Almost black and rotting all over, it had left a stain. A dark, deep stain verging maybe on red. Waking momentarily, El Jefe briefly knew sight again, before the pillow pushed hard down on his face. Horrific weight on his lungs. So heavy it pressed them shut.

Martha.

Twelve hours later, on the imperial balcony a weeping O'Brien publicly acceded to the will of the people knelt below and bent his head to let the heavy sash encumber his slim shoulders. Following the celebrations, his faithful ministers retired with a choice selection of the nation's young females to a recently opened centre of long pleasure.

And the man they called El Hombre, having rid the nation of backward cows, retired abroad to a wealthy country where his enormous riches would have comfort and company. And Lynch, the cunning manservant, busied himself putting the furniture in order.

This is how it happened.

HARRY CLIFTON

Berkeley's Telephone

How many times have I rushed up these stairs, hearing my own phone in the depths of the building, feeding my key into the door on the first floor landing while imagination ran ahead of me into the realms of wish-fulfilment – surely this is she, surely this is it – only to have it ring off just as I reached for it! To have it ring off, and the silence I live in now come back on me like a blow from a boomerang, and slowly, oh so slowly, to hang up my coat in the old absence of urgency, half-wondering, perhaps, would it ever blurt into life again and challenge me as in the past. And an evening ahead of me like this one, alone in my own head.

In the distance, trills, obligatos. A piano, a cello, somewhere in the building. The faint yelling of an infant, just woken for its evening feed. A man swearing, who has just dropped something. Tones of voice, reproachful, consolatory. Outside, the blazing klaxon of an ambulance passing away. That at least, by way of a future. Or do I imagine it too? And as for Anna, who will not be coming back, was she anything more than a figment of imagination also? Yet I still feel her as a lack, and not simply because she brought in money. God knows how she stood my hysterical demands, on several planes of existence, as long as she did, across half the continent of Europe, unless I invented her myself in the first place. Anyway she is no longer a reality, and life must go on. I understand. That is the way things happen. I understand, because I am a philosopher.

'An answerphone,' she said to me, on the day she finally snapped. 'That would solve all your problems, the abstract as well as the practical. Not to mention the imaginary.'

It was her parting shot, and it remains a strong argument even yet, though I have done nothing about it. Efforts of will are

beyond me altogether now, as my inner attentiveness strength-
ens. Unquestionably, though, it would have quelled my terrible
rush up the stairs on evenings in the past, though rarer and rarer
now as fewer and fewer try to get through. How many of us are
hiding from each other, I wonder, in this city of cities? For that is
what Paris has become for me now – a paradigm out of Plato, a
city of cities. But as to Anna's suggestion, an answerphone,
though satisfactory in some respects, would carry snags. How
many for instance, confronted by that disembodied voice at the
other end, that bleep and then the toneless darkness that is and is
not a listening silence, hang back, and in the last analysis hang
up? How many at the listening end, terrified by the bleeping
otherness of that contraption, hang back under threat of an
unwelcome voice, before picking up or leaving the receiver? Here
we all are, in a vast electromagnetic field called Paris, playing cat
and mouse with each other. Can any of us ever be sure who has
hovered out there, on the brink of an ultimate communication
with us?

   'I will have to think about it some more,' I remember answering
at the time.

   'Well don't hurry,' she muttered, bundling her stuff into a
suitcase. 'Another two thousand years of European thought
should sort it out. After six rented apartments, at least I will
leave you with a telephone. That's progress.'

   As I said, I am a philosopher. But let me qualify that at once. I
qualified in philosophy, a long time ago, in the city of Dublin,
among spoiled priests, a diplomat's daughter in jodhpurs, two
would-be businessmen and the son of a drunken commissioner for
oaths. And, of course, the gorgeous Anna. For three years we
listened, an ever-diminishing audience, to the history of ideas.
Little enough rubbed off on the others, for they have all been
roaring successes. As for Anna and myself, having jettisoned all
but our precious Berkeley in a secondhand store on the quays, we
set off to piece together the conceptual map of Europe. Where
haven't we pitched our tent, over the past ten years, attempting,
at the back of our minds, to unite the ideal with the real? I am the
ideal, Anna is clearly the real – which is why, unfortunately, we

have parted. And now, so long after saying goodbye to all but my Berkeley, back the books have come to haunt me. Womanless, jobless, alone in a strange, strange city, I have at last become a philosopher.

'I'll go mad if I don't telephone someone,' I remember her saying one day, at the start of our wanderings. We were then, I think, in Italy.

'Remember Joyce,' I said from behind my desk. 'Sending a letter, getting a reply the same day. Keep faith in the written word.'

'In this place?' she shot back. 'It's worse than Tibet. Lend me some change for the callbox across the road.'

I watched her shapely figure, through the window of our studio, crossing the hot asphalt in the lamplit darkness, to hover with the others at the callbox. Like her, they were believers in communication. Every day, they waited in line to have a word with mothers, brothers and cousins twice removed. She would hover there a long time.

'What do we need all this distance for?' she asked when she finally came back. Sweating, beginning to undress.

'It gives us perspective,' I said, watching her body unsheathe itself. 'On our false society, our empirical selves.'

In fairness to Anna, I too was beginning to lose faith in the great Idea we had come there to seek. For the spread of pre-Socratic consciousness up from the Aegean was not all that it might have been, when seen through the cheap glass portals of a joint called the Academy of Learning, where we earned our keep through evening classes. If you see men in green, ignore them, the myrmidon who ran the place told us – it's only the police. If you see men in white, shut up shop fast – it's the tax inspectors. For the Academy of Learning ran on transient intellect like ourselves, and a clientele with a short memory for where its money went. At a stretch, Heraclitus might have understood it. You never stepped in the same classroom twice, though you always got your feet wet. Men off the night-shifts, on the run from domesticity. Middle-aged women dressed like panthers, twiddling silver pens. Local cuckolds tapping at the windowpane, asking after absent wives.

Spumante bottles popped, and dolci were broken open. Cars came and went, discharging the dissolute of the region. All who were fleeing reality, including ourselves, fetched up at the Academy. At night, when I locked up, cars were still rocking in the parking lot.

'Philosophy my eye,' said Anna, down to bra and panties. 'They're at it like rabbits around here.'

'When in Rome,' I said, rising from my desk and melting with her into the bedroom. For she could still get through to me then.

My watch sweats, a fine fuzz of condensation under the glass. What time it is I cannot now make out, but thank God, it is getting late. The sounds are changing, diminishing, here inside the building where a great quietness reigns, and out in the rain-drenched street I came in from ages ago. The only other clock, the one on the wall, has registered ten minutes to two for the past week and a half, its pendulum hanging, a black metallic drip, under a dead mechanism. If I had an ounce of energy, I would get up on a chair and set it going again with a simple flick of the finger. But I have better things to consider. For instance, the *esse est percipi* of Berkeley. Here I am, in the depths of a building, no one to know if I am alive or dead. Well might it be said of me, then, that since nobody sees me I don't exist. I haven't existed since I was kicked off that homecoming bus an eternity ago. Lights, the sea of faces looking at me, the brief altercation over non-payment of fares, which God knows, I have stopped doing for ever since money became scarce. I have it all in my head, like an abiding vision. One minute zooming along in the social band-wagon, the next booted unceremoniously into nothingness. And the rest of them, solid citizens, barrelling on to their eventual destinations, suspending their terrors and disbeliefs – getting on with their lives, as the saying goes. But where do they go, or what do they dissolve into, those solid citizens, when the door closes behind them and they are alone in the night?

'If you had an ounce of faith in that machine,' Anna advised me one day, 'and stayed on the line, someone might amaze you by coming up with a job.'

'It's the Fantasias,' I confessed. 'They frighten the living daylights out of me. Five minutes in musical limbo while others are in there somewhere, considering my fate.'

'I'm fond of them myself,' she said. 'Especially the embassy ones, when we ring for bail-out funds. If it wasn't for the coins running out, I could listen to them forever.'

'Watch out,' I warned her. 'Greater philosophers than you or I have vanished down that particular black hole.'

'Personally,' she said, 'I know the difference between a machine and a human being.'

I forget, now, which telephone box that particular conversation took place in. As it was all about employment, it must have been after we moved to the north of Europe again. A succession of images, as on a moving train, opens up instantly. Glimpses of winter-bound border stations in the small hours, the train stalled between states and time-zones, the passengers pouring out to use the phones. Shouting into mouthpieces, fishing in their pockets for loose change, trying to steal a march on the hours. A flurry of night-time snow under sodium light, with the crows hopping upwind, feeding on scraps, from tie to railroad tie. And myself watching, contented for a moment in that suspension of everything. For only upon entry to a given city did my frenzy begin again, my telephone hang-up, as Anna bargained for some job in a pharmacy we could actually see across the road. A slushy subzero street at dusk, our sense of exclusion deepening, in Munich I seem to remember. Or London in summer, the Bank Holiday coming up, the offices shutting, and the one public telephone occupied by a man telling his life story. And getting through eventually, but too late. A chain of telephone calls and missed connections, of fallings-through to the darkness in between, the darkness I am sitting in now, with the clock stopped and the dogs of the neighbourhood barking, territorial, making more sense to each other than the pair of us ever did, to each other or anyone else.

'Do you know what this is called?' she would say to me in despair. 'This is called falling through the net.'

True, the telephone on the street had by now become our operational base. Smashed kiosks with the wind whistling through them in winter, burgled coinboxes, boiling plexiglass ovens in summer, where we waited for return calls that never came, or were swallowed up in traffic-noise. Only today, zigzagging aimlessly through the streets of Paris, I came upon one ringing and ringing unanswered in a void, and watched it in a trance, as all those years came back to me. Yes indeed, we had taken the open-plan concept of office-work to its logical conclusion and still things weren't moving. But I obstinately refused to have a telephone in any flat we then inhabited. Misapprehension was for the street. Indoors, we would exist only for one another.

'You're going mad,' she said to me gently, stroking my hair as we lay together in bed. 'Either that or you're the purest Cartesian who ever lived. Even Descartes would have found a way out of his own head by now.'

'We'll just have to go to France then,' I gasped out, choking back sobs. 'The home of Rational Enlightenment. Will we give it one last try?'

'Fine,' she replied, kindly but firmly. 'This time, though, I insist on a telephone.'

Mind you, the telephone we ended up with is nothing to write home about. A piece of white plastic, modern design, already quite obsolete. Nothing to the cordless wonders people in the streets and apartments around here bark into. A world of digital interconnectedness had already outstripped us, solipsists that we were. The phone purred, I left it alone in sheer terror. Anna picked it up and listened, there was nothing at the other end, and she hung up. Again and again it rang – the same listening silence and the click when she yelled into it.

'The boundlessness of the infinite,' I said. My worst fears were being confirmed.

'Or the dirty old man on the metro. He follows me home most evenings.'

By day, to keep us in rent and square meals, Anna went to work in a tourist agency. It was her looks that had got her the job, they told her quite frankly. That, and her telephone manner. Every afternoon at exactly three o'clock, she got in touch with me at the flat. Exactly three o'clock, for anything either side of that would have had me in the usual anguish as to whether to lift the receiver, leave it off the hook, or go out altogether and miss the one call that might solve everything once and for all. The only way I could calm myself was by imagining that everything, as Berkeley had said, was cancelled behind me when I went out – null and void, a blank. There was nothing there for anyone to get through to any more. I was carrying it all in my head.

'That much at least is true,' Anna sighed, tapping my skull at the end of another day.

The last straw, I am afraid, was the destruction of our love-life. For if there was one thing, up until then, that could bring me down from my mental stratosphere, it was Anna in the flesh. Diogenes himself would have crawled to the entrance of his tub to get a better look if Anna's legs, instead of Alexander's, had blocked out his light. I remember with gratitude our vast matrimoniale in Italy, not to mention the calisthenic beds of Bavaria, and even at a stretch the one-and-a-half-person numbers in London, designed for the prevention of pleasure between the tenantry of whatever welfare hotel or rented room we ended up in. No, the rocket of philosophy, threatening burn-out, had a point of touchdown on a warm mattress. Until, that is, the calls started getting through to me – the wrong numbers, the ringings off, the shrill interruptions in the middle of love-making, destructive of what little instinctual life was still left to me after ten years' headbanging against the ever-receding wall of philosophical scepticism. For whether or not the telephone actually rang, I was now in a permanent panic, trapped between waiting for it, answering it or unhooking it and losing the critical call that would pull us through. Thrown back on ourselves we lay there in a hag-sweat, desperate. It was then, as a last resort, that Anna magicked up the Deus Ex Machina of the answerphone.

'That way,' she clutched at my throat, her eyes bulging, 'we lose nothing. We make love and the calls come through and all are recorded. All right?'

'But philosophically . . .' I began.

'Philosophically too!' she shrieked. 'Can't you see the genius of the thing? No more wondering, while you're away from it,

whether this flaming hole-in-the-wall actually exists or not. For if
a call is logged in our absence, surely to Christ that is a sign, when
we come back to it, that the whole building hasn't evaporated in
the meantime. An answerphone, you imbecile, is the true and
absolute refutation of Berkeley everyone has been waiting for.'

I was taken aback. Imaginatively, I could see it all in a flash.
Someone putting a call through to what Berkeley would describe
as a void. No human answer, but a message left, and therefore
when the tenants of that space came back, the trace of something
actually having happened in what otherwise might be pure
absence. And then, by deduction, the whole place coming
together again, solid and real and to be leaned on – the bed
where we slept and made love, the tiled kitchen where we ate, the
clock on the wall that whirred automatically every ten minutes,
and yes, even the telephone.

'What if someone called,' I asked her, 'and left no message?'

'It would register anyway,' she said. 'You would hear a click.
You would know someone had been there.'

'But what if no one called?' I persisted. 'Wouldn't our place only
exist then, if somebody tried to get through on the phone?'

'You don't want to believe me, do you,' she said bitterly, getting
up from bed and starting to dress. 'It's not only your mind, it's
your will that's diseased. Philosophy has ruined you.'

But I was thinking. If we left this room, this cell of a flat, this
building, and went around the corner, not only would everything
be blotted out, as Berkeley had said, but the answerphone too,
with its disembodied voices speaking in a void, would be gone
as well. There was, in fact, no elsewhere for the voices to come
from or arrive at and be recorded. They were all there already,
jabbering away in the depths of my own head. The voices that
would rescue me or condemn me for ever. How could I ever come
back to an answerphone when there was no leaving or coming
back in the first place? And this woman with the lovely face, who
now was shouting at me from what seemed a great way off, had I
not created her also?

'I will have to think about it some more,' I heard myself saying.
It was then, I remember, she threw the two thousand years of

European philosophy at me like a piece of domestic china, and began to recede for ever from my life, into a small tearful figure bunched over whatever bundle of transient possessions was left after ten years in search of absolute truth. In philosophy, I knew then, there can be no real dialogue.

'I'm headed for Ireland,' she spat at me, slamming the door behind her. 'I believe it still exists, at least on the map.'

Maybe. Maybe not. But one thing is true. Between the mind and the body, the self and the other, the state and the individual, there is a dark well to trip and fall into, like Thales of Miletus with his head in the clouds, while Thracian maids like Anna, all health and realism, have a laugh at his expense. I am at the bottom of one such well. All around me, in this darkened building at the edge of the city, others sit at the bottom of theirs, all of us staring heavenwards at the same star, or the same lights of the same passing car. A hundred-year-old woman, deaf to everything, who lives behind the wall. A long-dead man who is still receiving letters. I will not be answering the telephone any more, let alone installing an answerphone. But the voices inside me, twenty-five centuries of them, grow stronger all the time. And what they say to me is this. Keep faith with the written word, and leave the telephone be, whether it rings or not. I tell you, whoever you are out there, we are all in this together.

FRED ANNESLEY

Charlie Barley

Straight, don't talk to him about straight. You don't find
straight like that every day. Allowing himself another long
look at the straightness of the draught-proof piggery door, he leant
there all on his own on the low wall of the pen at the back of his
sheds, taking in again the lovely levelness of his work. He'd like to
meet the man able to do that with nothing more than his eye.

It was the smartest-looking of his pigs that he had picked for the
test. The pig finished its business, checked one last time on the
empty trough and got on with getting back in out of the cold. It
stepped daintily to Joe McGonigle's invention at the entrance to
the concrete sheds, stopped and waved its lifted nose in search of a
message. The McGonigle Draught-proof Piggery Door, patent
pending. The door was plate iron with half-inch pipes welded to
either side. Rods on the wall ran down through the pipes and a
counterweight hung from a pulley wheel above the door. At the
bottom of the door was a wooden roller and just above the roller
was a metal flange. There was another flange just like it on the
inside of Joe's invention.

Lizzie came to her father's side just in time to see the show. She
stayed quiet by him as the white, three-quarter-grown landrace
checked the bottom of the door. The roller was settled in wet
straw. The pig put its snout under the flange and hoisted. Joe's
door weighed exactly one pound more than the counterweight
and slid easily up the greased rods when the pig marched forward,
the roller travelling up its brow, along its back and descending
gently toward the soggy groove it had been lifted from. The pig's
tail vanished in the dark of the shed.

'Draught-proof, Elizabeth,' Joe said. 'Pigs do best in a warm
shed.'

Lizzie hugged his arm. Never mind that the pigs in the modern sheds of the farms all around the McGonigles never had to worry about going out in the cold. The modern sheds had slotted floors with conveyor belts below to take away the manure.

'There's a fortune there, what do you think?' she said.

'Ah, now, Elizabeth, you're too hard on the old man.' The nights that had been spent figuring how to mould a counter-weight that would be a reasonable size, just as if the device really would be going on the market. The cost of the iron door was right out of the question. Lizzie swatted the loose backside of his corduroys.

The grass was rough and tall where they stood. It grew in big islands where the pig shit seeped from the pens into the gritty ground. Joe hugged her to him and she rubbed her cold cheeks on his rough lapel. 'We can do the letter for the patent office tonight,' Lizzie said.

'Sometimes, Elizabeth, I think you're as bad as me.'

Frankie Taggart, the calf smuggler, had his palms squeezed into a vacuum and stuck between the tweed of his thighs where by now it was only the hands that had any heat in them. The wrists were bare, the silk lining of coat sleeves like skim ice on forearms he couldn't be bothered to draw shirt linen down over back three hours when the whiskey was putting him out. The cold up at the outside of his shoulders made him shrug and he opened an eye to the stitching in the navy-blue leather of the passenger seat. The hump of the driveshaft had been digging into his side in the sleep and now the soreness was full, got him angry enough to reach for the steering wheel and pull himself up into the driver seat.

The van was sitting by an island of three stout beech trees in the middle of a misted meadow. Pink cracks were showing in the sky and crow streaks on the glass had started giving way to the dew. He started the van and it ran for a minute and quit. Then he got out to empty his bladder while the engine warmth chased the damp. No nonsense from the van this time, and when it started it was sent skittering out of that meadow with no chance given for loss of compression. Out on the narrow tar he drove like a man who was chancing all, the way he tore into corners and sailed over brows with no room left for anything that might be coming other than a careful bicycle. But he was no chancer, not on the road. And the drink still far from out of him did no harm to and maybe even sharpened the primeness of Frankie Taggart's radar, definitely a young fellow in his prime, as the police sergeant who headed the hunts for him had many a time been heard to say. For Frankie's senses were such that he could pick up trembles in the hedges and tyre-warmth from the road and his nose said when a muck spreader or a flatbed full of chicken crates was near or had been near, how long diesel grease had been on the wind and how far cows might have travelled since their bowels last cleared some room.

He lifted a yellow drover's boot well splashed in green away from the accelerator and whirled the van at a high bramble hedge. Brier hoops jiggled and swung up and away nearly before the snout of the van touched them and Taggart flogged into Clements' lane. In the din of scraping branches he rocked down the lane, feeling better all the time. The boot came quick off the pedal when Taggart caught sight of a Land Rover roof peeping above the wall of the Clements' farmyard. He had still a hundred yards to go to the gate but the boot stayed away from the brake and then went down hard on the juice. Only inside the gate did he tramp on the brake and the tyres grabbed at what gravel they could get. The whole rattling show nearly went in the kitchen door. Off to one side at the bottom of the sloped yard three RUC men were being careful of their uniforms during the business of lifting calves over the tailgate of the Land Rover. One policeman, skinny with a white face, turned and stood looking up in the direction of the kitchen. He had his cap in one hand and a handkerchief in the other and he'd stroke at his tunic with it.

'We might have you near broke now,' he shouted. Taggart did look directly at the constable but it wouldn't have amounted to a second. He touched finger to eyebrow before going on in the kitchen.

Charlie Clements, young but not far from where he'd be more fat than hearty, sat at a hinged-down dining-room table hard by the kitchen window and its drawn dirty curtains. He was shovelling bacon and potatoes and curly cabbage into himself and crying at the same time. Taggart took a seat at the other side of the shortened table.

Charlie got his voice after a slug of milk. 'They won't stop,' he said, the crying finished with but nothing near him for wiping tears off his cheeks, 'until there's not a Catholic farmer left in the county.'

Taggart moved a curtain enough to get a peep at the policemen pulling the last of his calves out of the pen Charlie had made from the roof frame of an army surplus transport. 'Those boys don't care what you are.' He took a big linen handkerchief out of his jacket and pushed it in a bunch at Charlie's chest where he had to grab at it.

Charlie gave his face a good rub and then folded the handkerchief before handing it back.

'You're beyond me, Taggart, I'll tell you that. What the hell do you mean they don't care? Ever since the old people died they've been coming here, looking for beasts, seizing beasts.'

'My beasts,' Taggart said, and he got up and stood by the dopey fire. 'You're hardly going to go broke for lack of the bit of board I paid you.'

'Paid is right, for that's the last of them.'

Taggart turned to the fire and kicked up a few sparks. The Land Rover snorted out of the yard. No contest. Those calves would be forfeited to the Crown, fake markings too fresh on them for his lawyer to waste time on a bluff.

'Charlie,' Taggart said, 'work the place, will you? I don't know when I've seen a man with as many stories for doing nothing.'

Charlie studied the table for something clean to give Taggart tea in. 'Pass me down that box there,' he said and Taggart got him the crate of china off a high shelf. Charlie unwrapped a cup from the wedding gift his mother had never done anything with. He poured tea, milk and sugar already in it, for the smuggler.

'You're some boy, you are, telling me what I should be doing on this place. I'd like your father and mother to hear you saying something like that to me. Your sisters and your brothers that do the best part of the work about the Taggart place would love to hear you saying something like that to me. The sergeant at the station would get a boot out of hearing you say that, him going mad at the very idea of a Protestant boy from one of the biggest Orange farms in Fermanagh smuggling calves for a living.'

Taggart had taken himself back to the fire. 'Orange is all in your head, Charlie boy,' he said. 'Put a bit of butter on that end of bread there for me.' Charlie did it and folded the heel before tossing it to Taggart.

'What sort of talk is that?' the smuggler said, sounding angry now that he had thought about it.

Charlie was embarrassed. He lowered his head and shook it. He looked up at Taggart, who was getting the bread into him. 'The farm,' he said. 'I didn't say you.'

'The Orangemen have had no luck signing up any of us since my grandfather's time,' Taggart said and he swallowed down the rest of his tea. When the mug came away from his face, no sign of annoyance was there. 'You need to get out for a run, Charlie. Thinking up politics in here is doing you no good.'

Charlie got up and brushed at bits of potato skin sticking to the front of his trousers. 'I tell you what I need to do, Taggart. I need to join the fucking IRA.'

'What's amazing to me is that they haven't recruited you long ago,' Taggart said, standing with the kitchen door open. 'Come on for a run before you go mad altogether.'

McGonigle children were hopping around their big red-tile kitchen with saucers while Lena McGonigle browned potato slices for them in a skillet of bacon grease, the children putting on a show as if they were Fagin's waifs. The McGonigle pantry could feed an army. Lena's ears had the van before any of her youngsters, even Lizzie, who was being the adult at fourteen, sitting on a leather sofa in the shadow of a window curtained against the dullness of the day. Joe didn't hear the van but Joe could sit there by the grate and not hear the children either.

'There's the wild colonial boy now,' Lena stated, slicing on.

Taggart's van rolled into the yard in a big cloud of steam from the muck on its underside. The white-faced smuggler stepped clear of the vapour and stood for a minute like a tired ghost. Lizzie was up on her knees on the couch with her face through the curtains. She was springing her knees to jump down and run to meet Taggart when she saw a pair of boots come down in a puddle at the far side of the van. She stayed where she was and watched Charlie Clements step his way to Taggart's side. She let her father go to the door.

'I would like you to tell me,' Joe McGonigle said to Frankie Taggart, 'how a body is expected to get anything done in this shape of weather.' He held the door wide waving them in, but kept his eyes from Charlie's although he did know Charlie. Joe knew that Charlie's parents had died close together not long before, but without time to think it out he thought he might be able to give the appearance that he didn't know and get away from having to mention it.

'This man,' Taggart said to Joe, sitting down on a kitchen chair, 'has been doping around the house since his mother and father died and I thought he needed to be where there's some noise.'

'I was just going to say about that,' Joe said. 'Very sorry indeed to hear it.' He got a chair for Charlie. 'There's enough noise here anyway.'

Lizzie was working at getting around her mother to reach the teapot at the back of the stove. She had to duck when Lena swung to face the visitors.

'Would you have any idea,' she said to Frankie Taggart, 'how that man Dunion got a certificate to teach?' She looked to Lizzie who was stretching for cups on the mantel. 'Tell Taggart the kind of questions Dunion was asking in your class yesterday.'

'Ah,' Taggart said, 'they're not normal people anyway.'

Lena McGonigle squinted at Taggart as she held out a saucer of black-trimmed chips to him. 'Indeed it would be nice not to have to pay any mind to them,' she said.

'It's too bad,' Joe said to Taggart, 'Taggarts don't have any pigs.'

'Is it?' Frankie Taggart said, giving a smile to Lizzie pouring the tea.

'Ask him about the draught-proof piggery door,' she advised.

'That's some teapot for a woman the size of you,' Charlie said, looking at the lightness of the wrist swinging the gallon of tea about without a quiver. Lizzie gave no sign she heard him.

'You bought some sort of door?' Taggart asked Joe.

Lena came to Lizzie with a cup and got it filled. 'The children won't pass exams if they have to depend on that Dunion for lessons,' she said.

'Dunion knows well enough about what the children need to know for the exams, never you worry about it,' Taggart told Lena. 'What is this about a door?'

'Some thing of Joe's,' she said. 'You know I know for a fact that school of Father Logue's has far better teachers.'

'Dear me, Mrs McGonigle,' chipped in Charlie, 'I don't know where you got that.'

Lena was embarrassed at forgetting about Charlie. Her voice went down soft like a woman's. 'It agitates me, you know,' she said, looking to Charlie to forgive her in case he surmised it was just one more charge of conspiracy against the Vatican, 'the sort of people the government will employ.'

'It's easy enough taken care of anyway, Lena,' said Taggart, easily the youngest person alive able to call her Lena. 'Join up with Logue. You still won't know how to pass government exams, that's the thing.'

'Here come the cowboys,' said Lena, and the clank of the plated Land Rover came through to the rest of them.

'Those boys are suffering from too much excitement,' Taggart said, turning for the door. 'I'll just see.' He went out.

'Are you not going out?' Lena said to Joe.

'Give them time. They hardly came to see us.'

Both Lena and Lizzie knew why the dropping tone of shame. If it wasn't for the idea that going against the police was some way disloyal, he'd be taking a crack at the smuggling himself just to join in Taggart's fun, was what Lizzie thought. Lena knew that Joe wanted to play bandit too but then that was men all over, and she was certain he lacked the nerve. Joe blamed his granny, who would have had no views on police because they were all helpful bobbies in helmets in London newspapers to her, for making him nearly as Christian in his ways as she was and him not convinced at all the Christians were on to anything. If Lizzie could ever have come out and said to her father that he might be well out of touch matching loyalism and government cheques he would have been pleased with it as an idea to play with. Lizzie, who knew plenty, didn't know that.

She went and stood on the couch and looked through the thin gap in the curtains. She saw Taggart standing with one boot propped on the lip of the galvanized water tank that sat just to the front of the Land Rover. The tank was full, the edge nearest Taggart banked by the wind with apple-blossom petals and bobbing at his sole. The wind snatched cigarette smoke from the Land Rover's openings.

'What are they at?' Lena asked.

'The weather is what they're at,' said Lizzie. 'The police are staying in where they are. They know very well they have no business here.'

Charlie Clements creaked back in his chair. 'There's nothing in the van,' he said. 'Not a thing those gulpins can do.'

'They have that van on the brain,' Lizzie said, cleaving the curtains and letting them drape her shoulders. 'They don't have the first idea what to do now that they're in here.'

Joe, who was reaching for the door, paused. 'They might give it the test. That machine would never pass a test.'

'Oh, Mr McGonigle,' said Charlie, 'I'd venture to say Elizabeth has the way of it. They have no interest in testing anything.'

Mrs McGonigle got to gathering up saucers from the children, all of them gone quiet. 'They would do well to test it. Taggart likes to think he can get away with anything but the fact is the vehicle is not safe and he could hurt somebody.'

'It's true enough,' Charlie said. 'He can get away with anything.'

Lena chuckled coldly at Charlie's nerve.

Joe looked right at Charlie and then his gaze wandered on along the far wall as if checking through picture glass that never knew more than a feather duster in all its years of the

highland cattle painted there. Charlie didn't miss what he was
being told because it was what he knew but had got careless
about: forget, Fenian lad, about trying to get near Lizzie by way
of the Mrs.

Lizzie waited no more for her father to open the door and
marched out herself.

'It wouldn't be the first time,' Taggart was saying to the Land
Rover, 'that we might have to buy hay,' answering the police in
kind because they, just the same as Joe McGonigle, could not
address Taggart as a smuggler, certainly not in this case where
only nosiness had brought them into the yard.

The same starved-looking constable was at the wheel of the
Land Rover, easy enough to tell even with the window nearly
shut. A man not even from Fermanagh, for the RUC was careful
never to station anybody in home territory, he could be heard
grinding on about the wonder anybody ever got hay saved in
Fermanagh at the rate the sun showed itself.

The voice of the policeman, so sure about farming as long as he
didn't have to work at it, and the idea that the smuggler was
putting up with this talk made Lizzie wriggly and she twisted
inside her folded arms and bumped Taggart's stretched hip,
sending his boot plunging down into the tank.

Taggart had to put his leg all the way in to get it out again and
pink and white petals stuck to him from thigh to boot. The police
weren't shy about laughing. They roared, more of them in the
back behind the plastic from the sound of it.

Taggart kicked at the Land Rover with his wet leg and the boot
bounced off the bumper and the sodden tweed slung petals at the
flat snout. 'Get the hell's gate back to your proper work,' he
shouted, his colour risen from white to tan. 'Go on back to the
guardhouse fire and tell that thick sergeant of yours livestock is
not what he was sent down here for.'

The laughing kept up in the Land Rover but not as loud, the
men in the back making sure the lead constable was still going
before they kept on.

Lizzie grabbed on to Taggart's arm with her two hands and
then she felt her father coming up behind her and she took her

hands away. Noise from inside the Land Rover stopped. Joe wasn't able to say anything and just stood at the back of his daughter.

The white-faced policeman let the door of the Land Rover fall open, showing himself but not moving to get out.

'What were any of us sent down here for?' he said, and it seemed he was talking more to Lizzie if he was talking to anybody. Nearly thirty, the senior constable had very dry skin and he was called 'Scaley' at the RUC station. His always sleepy wife was never heard to call him anything and the sergeant called him Constable. Farmers when they spoke of him said 'Scaley' and 'Scaley' was what children hooted at him from the playground wall. Taggart knew well from court documents that his name was Hewitt.

Charlie Clements's voice, changed to nearly soprano, came from the kitchen door. 'A man in Dungannon is why you're here anyway,' Charlie said. 'Big fellow with the party thought he could drive a car any time he liked.'

'I showed him, Charlie. Isn't that what anybody'll tell you? I showed him, Charlie, and here I am.' Hewitt took off his cap and set it on his knee.

Taggart, nearly pale again, raised his chin. 'Down here,' he said. 'With the rest of them.'

'No way out,' Hewitt said.

'Except the one,' Taggart said. 'I don't know why that sergeant can't leave Customs men to their work.'

'The sergeant likes to see respect for the law. So do I,' Hewitt said.

'And how did the sergeant come to get sent down here then?' Taggart asked him. 'You got sent down here for acting stupid. How did he get sent down here if he's so keen on the law?'

Joe helped Hewitt out. 'The sergeant was sent here well before the bombs started,' Joe said. 'Big country fellow just right for the farmers. It worked rightly for long enough, although he never came around this place.'

'That's right,' Lizzie said very proudly, catching onto Taggart's sleeve again. 'The sergeant has never set foot in this yard, has he, Da?'

Lena gave Charlie a bump so she could have the kitchen doorway to herself. 'That's Elizabeth,' she announced to Hewitt. Lizzie jumped and got her hands tucked quick to herself.

Hewitt rotated his backside on the seat and sat facing Lena with the heels of his boots hiked up on the edge of the Land Rover door frame. He gave Lena a full smile and long enough that she had to give her head a tiny bit of a toss.

'Maeve,' he said. 'That is what my wife's mother and father called her.'

'Progressive enough, no doubt,' said Charlie Clements.

'To get shot at,' Lena said. 'What are you asking us for?' She glared at Hewitt to let him know how stupid she thought he was.

Hewitt swung his legs back up inside the Land Rover and smacked the door shut, but he did roll the window all the way down right away.

'Ah, now,' said Joe McGonigle.

Taggart was standing up very straight now, mostly to keep the sopping tweed out from his leg. 'What else do you have in there in that wagon?' he asked Hewitt, Taggart all tense and his tone very flat. 'Fuckup recruits and Orangemen.'

'And you don't need any of it,' Hewitt said. 'Isn't that it? We're not all from big farmers and can afford to play about like you.'

'Not everybody can play about like Taggart,' Joe McGonigle felt brave enough to say. 'Whether they're Taggarts or not.'

'Joe,' Lena said in an urgent way and when he turned his head to her she hoisted her chin for him to come back to the kitchen door. Joe went back to looking at Frankie Taggart who had never taken his eyes off Hewitt.

'There's only one way out of here for you, Scaley,' Taggart said. 'And anybody knows it too. Putting me broke, or better still catching me at whatever it is you say I do. The sergeant will make sure the man that does that gets his transfer application signed.'

The Land Rover changed into reverse and Hewitt's window went up. The Land Rover made a hard, fast arc and the back end of it piled into the wall of Joe's pig pens. The four pigs that were out in the test pen forgot all they had ever learned about the working of the iron door and ran squealing mad in circles.

The Land Rover went on out of the yard and the sound of it was swallowed quickly by the wet orchards that lined the road. Joe stepped over to scowl at his pigs. The pigs could be seen forgetting about the commotion as they stopped quiet and watched Joe. Joe, not showing any signs of doing them any good or doing them any harm, had the pigs bored in a very short time and one of them broke from its sideways stance and went and hoisted the piggery door, and the three others followed so close that the roller was passed nearly straight from rump to snout.

Joe, set right again, turned and dawdled up to Taggart's van where he stood looking at the speed-wrinkled clabber on the side of it down near the bottom. Lena and Charlie Clements were getting themselves back into the kitchen. Lizzie stood looking at her father looking at the side of Taggart's van. Taggart was watching Joe too. A black hen, confused by the silence, stopped picking at yard gravel. Taggart, deciding it was too late to step over and distract Joe, walked to the wall of the pig pens. Taggart's walk was casual, paying no heed to the soaking tweed and squirting boot. He watched the piggery door although there was no movement there now. What he was really looking at was the black, sander-sculpted core sample that was Joe's counterweight, an iron-loaded rock Joe could only have found at the quarry in the mountainside overlooking the Cavan border. It was clear Joe had put a lot of work into the creation of his counterweight, suspended so straight on its cable, and it was safe to say he had drilled his samples at the old quarry long before Taggart had penned his calves there.

Joe took one step closer to the van and decided he was right about what he had been thinking. 'That muck would put a fair drag on her,' he declared, knowing Taggart was standing somewhere behind him. 'You have nearly an armoured vehicle here, Taggart, for that muck is loaded with iron. We know where that came from, do we not, Elizabeth?'

Lizzie rolled her eyes up at her father and held them there while he wondered why she was doing it, and when it came to him she turned and went back to the house. Joe tugged at his nose for a minute and then, instead of turning to Taggart as he wanted to, he said, 'Let the fire at you before you freeze,' and marched at the kitchen door.

Taggart did not move from the wall. He knew very well that Joe would tell Lena that the last of Taggart's calves were hidden in the quarry. Joe would not burst into the kitchen and announce this. Joe would go into the kitchen and not be able to look at Lena who would just be getting down from her lookout perch on the couch by the window. She would take Joe by the arm and stand them near the wall with no window in it as if they were in private. Then Joe would tell her.

Frankie Taggart stood at the rough concrete wall rubbing his palms hard on the edge of the badly made blocks that would have been mixed well before Joe's time. He rubbed the palms forward and back until there was such heat in them they could have been bleeding and he wouldn't have known. The telephone wire was not far above his head and he knew it and let the thought tingle in him that it might even be busy already. He spun and ran for the van, his boots digging so hard the gravel couldn't hold and had him stumbling so that he hit the door with a boom. The back doors shuddered from the pull as he cut a fierce circle and shot out of the yard.

Taggart headed for the dung heap where Martin Kinnersly lived, a distance of only half a mile. The pile of manure was bigger than Martin's cottage and the way it sloped up the gable in danger of snuffing out the chimney, the house was more like a lean-to at the end of a midden.

Martin suited the place. He was well aged and his black suit and lace-up shoes were well softened by the strong air. The man just about lived on field mushrooms. Fungi, Martin liked to say, his rusted grin meant to pretend learning when the only time he had seen the word was on an illustrated poison warning in the Post Office. 'The stove is perfect for a bit of fungi,' he said to Taggart, pulling the smuggler inside.

'I needed you to give me a hand,' Taggart said, doubtful even in his panic that he could sway Martin from the mushroom presentation.

'I thought that,' Martin said, peeling at the ragged edges of flat big mushrooms with his black nails. 'The sergeant left the bog in a big hurry there.'

'What is that?' Taggart nearly shouted.

'One minute he was standing watching the two white dogs play about and the next he was on that microphone he has in his car. He ran and caught one of the dogs by the collar and the other one followed him back to the car. And the sergeant was gone. Quickest visit he ever made to the bog.'

'Martin, Martin, never mind about the mushrooms,' Taggart said, frustrated at the way Martin was concentrating on dropping big grains of salt into the rills of the scorching mushrooms.

'It could be IRA business,' Martin said. 'Did you ever think of that?'

'No I didn't, Martin, and neither did you. You just said yourself you knew.'

'Well, you could lose the van if you move too quick,' Martin said, studying the cooking on the stove. When he saw the salt change to water balls on the first of his mushrooms he grew more intent, claw ready over the stalk. The first ball to make a run for the surface of the stove was his signal and he lifted the mushroom to a plate and then hurried to pick up the others, salt beads too quick for him skiteing over hot iron. 'If that's what you're sure it is.'

Taggart took the inky plate from Martin and sat down at the table to cut himself chunks of mushroom with a teaspoon. He had his head tilted back trying to keep the roof of his mouth from getting burned, when he heard a handlebar scrape on the pebbledash outside. 'There you are now,' he said to Martin and got up to open the door for Lizzie.

Lizzie stood in the doorway quiet, doing a strong job of making it appear she was not out of breath. When Taggart tried to look into her eyes she looked away and when Martin called out she jumped. 'Bring her in here for a mushroom and shut that door,' he said and then she looked up at Taggart and showed the fright with her round eyes.

'Never fear,' Taggart said to her. 'Come on inside and have a mushroom.'

Lizzie had come to say something. Taggart was sure he knew what it was. She was scared of the dark house and, maybe outside of her mother, was the least timid of the whole McGonigle bunch. There was less light in the Kinnersly kitchen than was in her own kitchen. It was nearly like night and the lines that could be made out in the wallpaper patterns were like tombstone script. Taggart's hand was light on the sleeve of her cardigan as he drew her into the room. Lizzie was trying to see if the fingers Martin was using to peel mushrooms really did have black tips or were just in shadow.

'The police,' Lizzie whispered.

'Watch now,' Martin said, grinning at her. 'They might hear you.'

Lizzie stared at Martin and then she gave him a little smile. She got her voice. 'The police know there are calves at the quarry.'

Taggart steered Lizzie to a chair and brought steaming mushrooms to her. She sat holding the plate on her lap but didn't touch a mushroom. 'Your mother,' Taggart said to her, 'was sure to do this. It's not as if it never occurred to me she would do something like this.'

'My mother?'

Taggart took a mushroom off Lizzie's plate. 'She can't bear my way of working. She's hardly on her own in that.'

'My mother would never do that, much as she thinks you of all people could behave himself. Frankie Taggart, I never thought you would speak like that about my mother.'

'Somebody telephoned the station, Lizzie. I'd like to know who else would have done it and I'll guarantee right here that it was not your father. There's no doubt at all, and I'm sorry to have to say it to you, Lizzie, that it was your mother.'

'It was Charlie Clements,' Lizzie said, taking the plate off her lap and setting it on the table and brushing one palm off with the other.

'So it was,' Taggart said, looking up at the ceiling that wasn't far from his head. 'How is it you didn't think of that, Martin?'

'We should leave them,' Martin said. 'What's a vanload of calves anyway?'

Taggart was standing at the table feeding himself mushrooms off Lizzie's plate, dropping them by the stalk into his jumping jaws, his eyes wide and looking to the ceiling. 'There's just the seven,' he said. 'They would all go in one load right enough.' He turned to the stove where Martin crouched, very unhappy about the way Taggart was sounding. 'That's what I'm looking for, Martin, to have not a beast there for them to find. That Land Rover, Martin, is nothing but a load of batteries and iron plate. We'll be there before it.'

'It might be there now,' Martin said, but he adjusted the damper on his stove. Lizzie was the first out the door.

Taggart was spinning at the steering wheel and trying to move himself a bit so that Lizzie, squeezed in between him and Martin, could shift her legs.

'How did you catch him?' he shouted as they walloped through the holes in Martin's lane.

'He never thought any of us were fly to him. When he heard what the whispering was he just asked to use the phone in the hall without as much as making an excuse. I was fly to him. I wouldn't have needed to go near the hall door to know what he was up to. But I was near enough to hear him end up without any goodbye. I headed out the back for the bicycle.'

'No surprise there,' Taggart said, double-clutching to get into first for the pull out of the slope at the road. 'Charlie, Charlie.'

Lizzie and Martin looked straight ahead, Martin trying to hold an elbow from touching Lizzie's cardigan. Taggart leaned at the wheel like a jockey in the final furlong, stroking into top gear at the very point where one more rev in third gear would have been a rev working against the bounding van.

With no churches in that part of Fermanagh, the nearest ones in Enniskillen and in County Cavan being too far, a clean car is hardly ever seen. Even with the light poor and fading to none, the chrome the sergeant's wife madly polished gave itself away in among the yellow of the whin bushes on the hill that for want of a challenge is called a mountain. Taggart had the van grinding up the grade in second when he saw it. He threw the knob to neutral and stood on the middle pedal.

'Do you think he's in it?' Lizzie whispered.

'It hardly makes a difference,' said Taggart. 'He can do nothing with an empty van. But I would say he's just done a bad job of hiding the car here and gone on up.'

Martin was twitching his chin right and left. 'The jeep was never here,' he said.

'Soon enough,' said Taggart and drove on.

Going past the place where the sergeant's car sat, there was no sign of life, the windows shut and clear.

Lizzie hugged her knees and rocked. 'You definitely should listen to Martin,' she said. 'What is seven calves to you?'

'What?' Taggart nearly lost the van in a culvert. 'Elizabeth, what has got into you?'

'They have guns.'

'Ah, don't.'

'That'd be just like you,' said Lizzie. 'I suppose you think they're toys.'

Taggart came to the mouth of the level pebble lane that led into the quarry. He stopped and let his hands fall from the sweat-dulled wheel. The smell of calf spittle was rising with the warmth in the van. 'What would be just like me?'

She turned her face to him, chin up and snippy. 'I'm going on to be a nurse.' That was news to Taggart but he could see that she was. 'And here I am with the two of you.' She had put on about four years. 'Helping you against the police. And if that isn't bad enough,' she said, chin moving up near Taggart's huffy face, 'you do not even have the sense to be scared.'

'Get the calves if we're going to get the calves,' Martin said.

Taggart's annoyance showed in the shaky way he moved the van forward.

The pen for the calves was at a weak waterfall that had weed trees reaching up either side shaping a green grotto. Martin was out of the van and twisting at the wire keeping the gate on before Taggart was finished backing up. There was very little light left but any light was enough for Lizzie, the way she sat at the open door with her eyes at full bore. 'This is madness when you know he's here,' she said in a voice that had shed all strain.

'But you don't see him,' Taggart said. 'He's stumbling about lost somewhere, Lizzie. Come on, Lizzie,' he said, throwing his own door open, 'this is the only chance there is.'

Taggart trotted toward the pen and was nearly knocked over by Martin who was quick-marching a red calf by its doubled-up tail. Lizzie sat where she was and then she jumped down and raced into the grotto, getting to a calf before Taggart, knocking it over and gripping a front leg and the opposite hind leg and skidding away with it. Taggart took one in a neck lock and stumbled after her. Martin was right at Taggart's heels with another by the time Taggart and Lizzie had between them got theirs in the van. There was a black one that Taggart had trouble catching and he got to the narrow gateway with it in time to bump into Lizzie who was hugging at the head of a blunty blue one. Lizzie looked up at him in the beginning of the shine of night and there was a welt made from a weed tree high on her cheek, and the colour of her wide eyes, a mixture of heather and rain, was nearly a match for the hide of her calf.

'McGonigles,' was all Taggart said.

'Who's like us?' said Lizzie, ducking for a better hold and then rising, the head of the calf locked tight to her and its front feet lifted off the ground. 'Not Taggarts anyway.'

'Shows you what our Charlie knows.'

Taggart hoisted his calf in his arms, the weight making him sway and spin as he waited for Lizzie to bundle hers into the van. As he swung, Taggart saw two close white dots sliding down the slope above the lip of the quarry. The Land Rover would have had to go into Cavan to come at the quarry from the top but there was no doubt about the narrow-set headlights of the RUC vehicle. The headlights stopped moving and went out. A big voice came from the other direction. 'Just stay there, Mr Taggart,' the sergeant called in his senior tone. Lizzie squatted. Taggart chested his calf into the van and closed both doors. He walked the length of the van, watching the flashlight that sat steady maybe thirty yards back up the lane. Taggart reached in and pulled the headlights on. The sergeant couldn't be seen and his light vanished.

Taggart turned his head back to the dark. 'Forget about the beast,' he said in Lizzie's direction. 'Tell Martin, forget about it.'

'I'm getting tramped on here by the bloody thing,' Lizzie said. 'Come here and open a door.'

Taggart skipped back and the two of them rammed the lonely calf in, drumming on its bones with the door.

'Stop,' said the sergeant, still out a bit but more to one side.

'Martin's hiding somewhere,' Lizzie said. 'He'll never find him.'

'Those other boys are up at the top,' Taggart said. 'They'll be on their way down. Start the van. Do you know how? That'll send them back up for their wagon and maybe draw Martin here. I'll watch for him.'

'They have guns, Taggart. Didn't I tell you?' She stepped to the side of the van away from where the sergeant's voice had been. 'Come here, will you, standing there in the tail lights.'

Taggart had no sooner left the ruby haze than the sergeant walked into it, a tall man with a pile of grey curls, no cap, tunic half-unbuttoned and no gunbelt. Lizzie had never seen him before and Taggart had never looked directly at him before. The only place Taggart had ever been near Sergeant Farrel was the guardroom of the RUC station, and there the sergeant would stand off to the side, quiet while the other uniforms wrote up details on Taggart. Here Sergeant Farrel was alone, and his grin made the balls of his cheeks glow in the electric light.

'Aren't you two the pair,' he said and he might as well have been addressing his own children, had he any.

Taggart and Lizzie both moved toward him and more into the glow.

'Charlie Clements isn't getting paid by you fellows, is he?' Taggart asked him, very businesslike, not going along with any talking down the sergeant was trying to do.

'Charlie?' said the sergeant. 'No call to pay Charlie anything, Frankie.' The sergeant looked as if he would have sat down if there had been something to sit on. Instead he shoved his hands down into the pockets of his trousers and swayed back. 'Charlie Barley won't miss a chance.'

'Tell me this, Sergeant Farrel,' said Lizzie. 'What would he have against Martin Kinnersly? For he has Martin Kinnersly hiding out in the dark there scared to death.'

Sergeant Farrel stepped through the two of them so he could get himself turned to the quarry and lean his back on the van's rear doors.

'Martin's a rare bird,' he said as if he had the whole night to talk. 'I heard that him and a brother lived in that old cottage well before I came here. And I heard too that the two boys were left there by their mother and you'll hear some say she was not even from this country but I don't know. The brother is long dead.'

'Those policemen,' said Lizzie, all of a sudden setting the sergeant apart from what she saw as police, 'have got guns. How many times do I have to say it?'

'Indeed I know they have guns, Miss McGonigle,' the sergeant said. 'I know that very well.'

'They're hardly carrying guns about for chasing me,' Taggart said.

'It's the fact that they're carrying guns at all that they're chasing you, Frankie,' the sergeant said and he slid down the dirty back of the van until he was sitting on his boot heels. 'You see, those boys are dangerous when they're bored. The young ones in particular think up some terrible badness when they're bored and there they are with those guns that have only to do with politics. A good many of them are very Orange, Frankie. They have nothing to do, these boys, don't you see. Undercover boys do any of that other work, anybody knows that. So I'll tell you, your friend Charlie is not so far off the mark.'

'He hates us wholesale,' said Lizzie.

'He does. And those bored young buggers at the station would give him and others like him a good deal more reason to cry if I didn't watch them.'

'I hardly see what that has to do with me,' Taggart said.

'You're the boy,' Sergeant Farrel said. 'I have them chasing you for you're the very boy for keeping them out of worse things, Frankie. I have no trouble getting them to chase the smuggler who won't back his own side.'

Lizzie stepped right up to him so that he had to get to his feet or

sit with his face at the front of her skirt. 'Do something about
Martin,' she said. 'Hurry up.'

The sergeant stepped round her and lifted his head at the dark.
'Come on down here,' he roared.

Tumbling dirt and rock made a light rattle and then there was a
loud pop. There was a great swishing of the weed trees and a
thump.

'That's Martin,' said Taggart, looking out at the shades of
darkness. 'Get your light and find him,' he told Sergeant Farrel.

The sergeant walked at the grotto with the flashlight at belly
level. Lizzie and Taggart came behind him through the gap.
Martin was on his back on the flattened ground the calves had
made their bed. The flashlight showed him raspberry and grey
from one side of his belt buckle on up to near the nipple on the
same side. The tear in him was a triangle with the point down at
the belt. It was moving. It wasn't at all what a bullet might be
expected to do, but whatever way it hit Martin or whether the
bullet was an exploding kind it was what a bullet had done. While
the sergeant and Lizzie and Taggart stood there the raspberry and
grey stopped moving.

Constable Hewitt stumbled down into the grotto, his revolver
hanging bare from its lanyard. He stared only at Martin's face,
which was perfectly dead.

Taggart sniffed so that Hewitt would look at him. 'That's a
transfer too,' he said, so quiet.

Hewitt sank down and Lizzie stepped straight to where he knelt
and toppled him. She stood in the gap of his legs. 'Tell us who you
have shot here,' she said. 'Tell us.'

Hewitt tried to see where the sergeant was. 'I thought it was
Taggart being shouted at,' he said.

'And who is this?' Lizzie demanded.

'I know who it is,' Hewitt said.

'No, you do not,' Lizzie said. She spun to the sergeant. 'Are you
taking this man's van or not?'

'Not this day,' Sergeant Farrel said.

Lizzie went to Taggart and turned him about. 'Get in there,' she
said. 'You're the big driver.'

PATRICIA HICKEY

Mother's Day

Her mother had always resented her entry into the world of books.

'Oh, I see Anne is reading again,' she was given to observe in a distant voice on entering a room and finding her daughter engrossed and alone. Talking about her daughter in the third person in this way offered her the opportunity to examine her, make observations, almost as if she were talking to herself. It placed her daughter in a different order of things, some inferior place, another world into which she could never enter.

'I mean to say, Anne, all those books, dear. They're such dust collectors don't you think?'

'Umm, I suppose you're right, Mother.'

Distancing had made colluders of them both.

But today was different. Mother's Day. It dawned harsh and raw, a yellow streak in a betrayed sky that lingered briefly as Anne prepared the breakfast, and then was suddenly gone amid the wet, ragged clouds of a March morning.

She moved slowly around the kitchen, filling the small space with plopping, watery noises and sharp metallic rattles. Early morning sluggishness had not left her body and she bent slightly in the effort to keep moving, her slim shape tautly wrapped in a threadbare dressing gown. She blended well into the tired kitchen and the plain delft on the tray, her life a melding of routine and duty.

'I'll always do my duty by you, dear,' her mother was fond of saying, 'come what may.'

Duty, Anne mused, as if discovering a quaintness there. The selfish virtue. Do unto others whether they want it done unto them or not.

She pulled her gown tightly about her, a shadow of the spinsterhood feared by her mother flickering in the brusque, obliterating gesture. Anne did not consider her future in these terms. It was just that she had no sense of time passing. Time was there at her disposal, for reveries and books, for stepping into her other world where her mother's time, with its routines and expectations, could not wash over her.

She sighed. She had prepared the breakfast tray in the routine way of her mother, so that it appeared thoughtless, as if it had required no effort on her part. She left it on the table and walked out of the kitchen into the garden. Frost-rimed leaves of blackened geraniums shuddered in pots at her feet as she moved along the path. An eerie light rose from the silvered grass and for a moment she sensed she was floating in a metallic dish, like a candle in water on a pale dinner table. Storm-tossed shrubs crouched hump-backed around her as her eyes sought beneath them for a flash of colour. Bending, she gathered the tiny purple primulas and buttermilk primroses and ran to the kitchen, clutching them in a whitened fist, dropping them quickly into a small bowl of water and placing them on the tray.

'Happy Mother's Day,' she called cheerfully as she kicked open the bedroom door. The cloying smell of another's intimacy greeted her like a pink, woolly wall, its overheated stuffiness leaving her briefly nauseous.

'Oh, but you shouldn't have, dear. You look so tired. I should be doing it for you.'

'I'm not tired, Mother,' Anne replied. She smiled quickly to hide her impatient tone, a pinched tautness visible at the edges of her mouth so that the smile became a measured gesture, something half-given. She stood patiently holding the tray as her mother heaved her body up against the pillows in a half-hearted attempt at making herself comfortable.

'Of course I've never been a great one for breakfast in bed. I never seemed to have the time, what with getting the rest of the family fed and ready for work and school.'

Her mother patted her woollen bed jacket into place as if to punctuate the hidden remonstration in her words.

'When you're a mother yourself . . .'

Her voice faded in the customary way it did when repeating one of her aspirations for her daughter. The wish and the futility of the wish were symbiotically bound together in the utterance. She raised her hands for the tray, something childishly insolent in her appraisal of her daughter's face, as if daring her to respond. Anne ignored the outstretched hands and abruptly placed the tray down on the bed beside her mother's legs.

'I'll get you the paper,' she said, grasping the skirt of her dressing gown in her hands, clutching the worn material before her as she left the room, as if she had plucked something away from her, and sought to discard it in haste. Anne returned to the kitchen and reached for the coffee pot, dragging it across the electric ring. Sparks hopped and sizzled in the spilled liquid. She poured strong, black coffee into a blue mug and stood gazing into the rising steam, her glance sinking lower into the seductive darkness shimmering beneath.

'The higher the mountain, the sweeter the coffee, the greater the exploitation,' she said suddenly aloud, recalling the vividness of a poster on worker exploitation in distant coffee fields. Massed jungle plants – the *monstera deliciosa* and sweetheart vine of her sitting room – tumbled in the background. The palpitating weeds of a tropical valley were the backdrop to the rural romance of coffee-workers harvesting the enigmatic bean. How easy it was, she thought, to appropriate another's reality and re-present it to the world for its delectation.

She shuddered as the bitterness of the coffee broke through, but continued to sip her unsweetened drink in her mother's plain blue and white kitchen. Tiny blue tiles of tilting windmills and billow-sailed schooners intruded here and there into the clinical coldness of the walls. Cobalt coldness. It seeped forth and tinted the air with its hue. The grey March morning drifted furtively in and set its uncertain light in pools on table and worktop, leaving Anne isolated, like floating driftwood, directionless.

'Well, that was very refreshing.'

Her mother breezed into the kitchen and noisily deposited the tray.

'Oh dear. I completely forgot to bring you the paper,' said Anne.

'Never mind that. You know I'm not one for lying in bed. Now, which Mass shall we go to today?'

Her mother moved brusquely through the kitchen, reclaiming her territory in hurried movements around her daughter. She dropped her expectations one by one into place, until Anne felt pinned down, her confinement masked by the soft petals of her mother's words. The reality of her day was in place.

'Yes, maybe we'll go to the twelve o'clock today. It'll be that nice Father Burns. He always gives such hopeful sermons. Probably because he is so much at ease with himself. It's so comforting to see.'

Anne lowered her head as she thought of the priest with his drink problem and his personal tensions in a job that everyone expected him to do well because once, a long time ago, that was what he believed he wanted to do. And now that view of his reality was no longer apt. She wondered if he sensed this appropriation of his world by people like her mother, pedestal people. They raised the ground on which individuals tried to centre themselves until suddenly it was on a different plane, slowly converting it to an edifice of praise and worthiness. And all the while they plugged the gaps in their own certitudes and doubts so that any stepping down from the pedestal was resisted, as the drawing back of the veil on their own disbeliefs was resisted.

'That's fine. Twelve o'clock it is then.'

Anne acknowledged the decision in the tight little way she had developed of late in dealing with her mother. And the day drifted dreamily down around them in a haze of church yellows and golds, dust motes floating on stained-glass light, disharmonious voices responding to the priest and politely calling pleasantries to each other above the cold March wind in the church grounds.

After lunch Anne and her mother sat reading the Sunday papers. The capricious wind had moved into the north-east, thumping its icy syncopation against the gable end of the house. Inside the room the turning of newspapers rustled occasionally across the space between mother and daughter. Anne's eyes remained fixed steadily on the top of each page, on the slim, blank border above the print.

After some time she left the room, returning quickly with a book in her hand, and resumed her seat in the armchair. She opened the book and began to read, sinking back into the cushions, her breathing becoming slower and shallower as she read. Her mother looked over her glasses, watching her steadily for several moments, then noisily closed and folded her newspaper and placed it on the table in front of her.

'I think it's time we had a cup of tea, dear,' she said brightly.

Anne did not answer, appearing not to hear her mother as she left the room. She returned a short time later with a tray laden with tea and cake. As her mother rattled the cups and saucers, placing them with abrupt sounds on the coffee table in front of them, Anne sighed inaudibly and put down her book.

'Another new book, dear? You really keep those publishers in business, don't you? These things are so expensive these days, I always think. What's in them that you can't get from the newspapers, anyway? They only cause you to think too deeply about things, you know, and that's not good for anyone, now is it, dear?'

Anne inclined her head imperceptibly. She filled the pause with the passing of tea and the cutting of cake, symbols of a sharing ritual that extended beyond their personal history. They sat and drank and talked of items of news in the papers. And when they had finished her mother announced that she would have a little nap.

'Just a few minutes, mind you.'

She placed a cushion behind her head on the high-backed sofa, folded her hands across her lap and closed her eyes. Anne reached quietly for her book and sat holding it in her hands, unopened. She remained still for some time, then quickly placed the book on the table and left the room, entering her study and noiselessly closing the door.

She stood there, eyes ranging along the shelves, slowly and deliberately seeking out each book as if trying to memorize every detail of colour and size, title and position on the shelf. Then, having dwelt on one her eyes moved to the next one and performed the same exercise, arms hanging limply, hands half-closed, as if ready to seize something, awaiting a signal.

She moved to the bookcase and crouched at the lowest shelf, taking book after book from it, stacking them high on her arm until her chin rested on the topmost one. Then rising unsteadily to her feet she made her way out of the room. Returning some moments later she repeated the removal of books, as if in a deliberate thought-out performance, choreographed by some hidden watcher. Her face was composed, a slight dream-like air about her as she worked, moving stealthily on slippered feet. Her eyes never wavered, as if fearful that her gaze might light on something which would arrest her, detain her from her vital task.

At last the shelves lay bare, dust marks the only delineators of the world of ideas that had recently lain there. The room remained still in the gathering gloom of the March evening, stirred now and then by the movement of shadowy limbs on the walls as the bare trees in the garden bent to the wind. The shadows began to change, the light that surrounded them altering from murky grey to a warmer tone until the shadows grew grotesque and deformed against the rosy hue.

Anne stood leaning against the door to the garden, her eyes closed, palms flattened against the timber, the better to keep some terror behind her. She remained still for several moments, then moved to the window and looked into the garden. Behind her the tree-shapes leaped frantically on the wall, enormous now, as if seeking to free themselves from their plaster prison. In the garden a glow was spreading and the sounds of occasional crackling could be heard and the piteous breaking of leather spines. Anne watched until the books settled into a luminous ash, charred pages like shrivened souls, adrift on the wind. She turned from the window and re-entered the sitting-room where her mother was stirring on the sofa.

'My goodness, I really didn't intend to sleep for so long. What time is it? It's so dark. And what's that strange glow? It must be my eyes. They haven't adjusted to the light. I do hate sleeping in the daytime. You know that, dear.'

'It will do you a world of good.'

Anne's face shimmered with a purged pallor. Her body was taut with energy as she drew a large notebook towards her and, opening it at the first blank page, began to write in an urgent scrawl.

'After all,' she said, her mouth lifting at the corners as she looked towards the window, 'it's Mother's Day.'

FRED JOHNSTON

The Ghosts

'Here with her face doth memory sit
Meanwhile, and wait the day's decline, . . .'
Dante Gabriel Rossetti – *The Portrait*

The knowledge that Henry's wife sat in the other room always
made Alison uncomfortable. It didn't matter what he said, or
how he reassured her. Henry's wife could not be ignored. Sitting
all day at that small bedroom window. Staring into nothing.

May was completely paralysed, unable to speak, barely able to
hear. While Henry brought his wife tea, sat on the side of the bed
tending to her, wiping the dribbles of tea, milk, the crumbs of
food from her quivering lips and chin, Alison sat patiently in a
venerable, generous armchair and waited. It had become a
ritual.

He had introduced Alison to his wife on her first visit to the
cottage. Only with her eyes did the skeletal, grey woman under
the heavy-looking, decorated quilt make any sign of recognition.
She blinked. She could not move her head. Embarrassed and
desperate, Alison had smiled and withdrawn walking backwards,
like a nervous courtier, from the hot little room. She had taken up
a position in front of the gaping black mouth of the enormous
fireplace and smoked a cigarette. Henry had emerged from the
bedroom with a benevolent, indulging smile.

'Please don't smoke,' he'd said. 'May can't stand it.'

But she could not come here any more. It wasn't right. She
didn't feel right. She made one lap of the cluttered, Edwardian-
feeling room with its bric-à-brac and heavy furnishings, its
glaring trumpeting brasses and tiny framed photos of men in

moustaches and women, seated, in voluminous dresses; each time she felt the room for change, for something new, but it was not a room in which anything ever happened. The TV and video player were new-looking and incongruous; there was an ancient blue boxy record player and a tidy pile of ancient records, Handel, Bach, Albinoni, the usual Baroque heroes, mostly. There was a radio. Henry said he always kept it tuned to BBC Radio 4. The best for news and sport, he said. The cricket, *The Archers*.

'The reception is not good here, because of the mountains, I suppose,' Henry had explained. But he listened a good deal to the radio. 'Every chance I can get. And May likes it, too. Brings her back.'

They'd met at a local writers' group. Someone had pinned a badly copied notice up on the green baize board at the supermarket. *Writers' Wanted!* It had just enough brash schoolyard enthusiasm to appeal to her. She had written poems when younger, published one or two, before marriage and family had intervened. Someone had remarked in a college magazine that her work showed promise. Her life had not, but her poems had.

Too often these days she found herself thinking about the past. It was, she knew, a useless and self-indulgent exercise which led nowhere. Nothing new could be proved, decided, discovered. She saw herself as having been a frightened, unacademic type with no desire to chase young men who had money, flash cars, or anything like that. She'd found herself married to a very ordinary and very nice man whom cancer had devoured rapidly and painfully in his early fifties, when he had begun to talk to her about early retirement and Ireland. Her two sons had dissolved into advertising and the software industry and disappeared. She rarely heard from them even now. A card now and then, a Polaroid snapshot of her grandchildren.

But her life had always been like that, a photograph, an image of the substantial made insubstantial. Someone else, she often thought, had lived her life in tandem with but never touching hers. She had found herself looking longingly at those tattery college magazines – those photos of women who had married, died, one had been murdered – and her half dozen poems of old promise. And then she'd seen that notice in the supermarket. At the group, she'd met Henry.

Tall, early sixties, grey-haired, wide-shouldered; a Hemingway figure, Alison had thought, with an English public-school accent. When he'd stood up that first time to read his poem, she'd been unable to suppress a giggle. But he was undeniably attractive. An old-style hero. When he read a poem to his ailing wife she'd felt jealous, and carried home a little belly-deep burden of guilt for feeling so.

The group hummed and fidgeted around a slight, fragile-looking Dutchwoman whose Amsterdamer husband sulked from pub to pub in the village and sketched, when the weather was good, down on the harbour. Here was a poem about a lost child; here, the beginnings of a short story, naïve and maudlin, about a mother who had never shown love; here, a group of poems about someone's children. Scribbled, typed revelations too personal to entertain anyone but their authors. Private items of hidden sorrow and regret and smugness, paraded on paper in a small back room, ill-lit and smoky, attached to the community hall. The room smelled of sweat and things unfinished, and plaster peeled depressingly from the walls. It might have been a store-room in a hospital or a waiting-room in a prison. The one uncurtained window was cemented shut with rust and looked out over a wide expanse of dull brown bog and grey fat rocks. Through this window, the sky was always low and grey and watery. As winter came on, the yellow strip-light had made them all appear sickly and jaundiced.

Alison had begun with the poems from her college days. There had been polite applause and a grunt or two. It had taken Henry several meetings to say hello. She knew nothing about him, had heard nothing. She noticed the wide gold band on his wedding-finger and felt ashamed of herself that she had let her eyes stray so readily in search of it.

'Poems are good for the soul,' he had said as they sipped tasteless instant coffee out of plastic cups. 'I always read, when a boy. Very necessary. No one writes poetry nowadays. Not really.'

It had seemed like an invitation to polite argument. Alison had found herself walking away from the cream-painted, corrugated-iron-roofed hall with Henry at her side. The others, including the fragile Dutchwoman, went yabbering off in the gathering dusk towards the nearest pub. Their animated conversation echoed over the lonely, empty road.

Henry had looked after them.

'You're not a pub person, then.'

'Not particularly.'

'Nor I. Boring sort, I am, really.'

Alison had smiled shyly. They were walking alongside ancient stone walls that kept nothing in or out. Gaunt, terrible trees gloomed over them and raucous crows cawed loudly and peevishly in their black branches. The trees leaned away from the mile-off sea, whipped to bent subservience by winter gales and spring storms. Stone was everywhere; in the sloping, hopeless acres, in the sky. Ragged sheep, their coats scruffy and untidy and their legs impossibly thin, wandered awkwardly, as if in a trance, from one mean tuft of grass to another. Shivering a little, Alison felt a need to explain to herself her presence in this burdened place.

'My husband and I came here on our honeymoon,' she said. Henry had put on a hat, a sort of battered Panama, but made of cloth. It gave him a rakish, colonial air. Alison found herself comforted by his accent. Like old Sunday movies, Rex Harrison, Trevor Howard. More like Trevor Howard.

'Ah! But Americans love Ireland, so many of you come here every summer. Looking for your *roots*!'

There was – it was undeniable – something mocking in his tone. Alison looked quickly at him. The sharp grey eyes, the lines of age that modelled him into a no doubt false ruggedness, lent him character, hinted at mischievous backgrounds. He was smiling at her, so she smiled back.

'Well, no,' she said, watching the ground disappear beneath her feet. 'My husband was of Russian peasant descent. Not a drop of Irish in him.'

His grandfather's name, her husband had once said, had been unpronounceable by the Ellis Island officials, themselves sons of immigrants. They had written down Selinsky and left it at that. Alison Selinsky.

'Never here in my life before,' Henry told her quietly. 'But here I am.'

They'd parted, significantly, at a crossroads. The village smoked and whispered half a mile off towards the harbour and the rocking fishing boats. Alison's rented bungalow was a black square on top of a hill in the opposite direction. It was almost summer. The sun was down but the air was luminous and lights in the village came on reluctantly. Water chattered in a stream under the crossroads. Water, the locals said, that was clear enough to drink.

'Thank you for walking me,' said Alison.

'Thank *you*,' said Henry, doffing his would-be Panama. It was a game of coquettishness and gallantry, innocent, signifying nothing. He hadn't mentioned a wife or family. The ring kept its mystery. 'We'll meet again around the village, I'm sure,' he concluded. Shying from any possibility of subtle insinuation in his words, Alison had smiled a goodbye and walked on, quickly, up the hill. She heard his shoes on the gravel of the road behind her. Once she'd turned to look back, but he'd disappeared.

It seemed all a very long time ago, but it could only have been a matter of months. Having introduced her to his wife, Henry had thought it within the limits of propriety that they should occasionally meet up in the village, at the Post Office, at the supermarket, and chat about this and that and walk a little. At first the meetings had been accidental. Then they had appeared to take on the nature of something planned and arranged. Alison surprised and shocked herself to realize that she loitered too often in the vicinity of places where she knew Henry might appear. And she knew that Henry loitered too, waiting for her. They were friends, of course, so they could do this sort of thing without feeling too much guilt. Alison reassured herself that friendship would prevent them from ever falling in love.

But something else had happened. A pattern had been established between them, cementing them into routine and habit. Pleasant enough, but remorseless. There was a metallic dullness to their weekly writers' group arrangements. Something safe and rather *domestic* had fallen over them. Alison would stroll down to Henry's cottage – it had real thatch – and sit in that cluttered room waiting for him to tend to May. She'd go in and offer the paralysed woman a smiling hello, retreating to wait to go out with her husband for the evening. Alison could not avoid, more than once, feeling wrong and slightly sick about the whole thing. I'm overweight and I've got more grey than black, she told herself loudly one evening in front of her bedroom mirror; but I can walk about and talk. She must notice this. She must hate me. She probably thinks we're sleeping together. Of course she does.

A very rare postcard came from her eldest son. Well, the way things were with work and all, he wasn't going to get over to see her this Fall, but maybe she'd come home for Christmas? Alison tore the card up, angry at him. At Christmas, at home, she'd be in their care, doing what she was told, fitting in with their arrangements. It had been like that with Arthur. It would never be like that again if she could help it. Arthur was gone and she was here, with a lot of other outsiders, and she'd make the best of it.

But she'd wanted this place, after all. She'd spoken of coming here and a sort of vague reverence would enter her voice. A promised land, a sea-blown God's acre at the end of a rainbow. Being here defied something, the onset of age, she didn't know what, exactly. Her sons would not understand that. It frightened her to be here. It elated her. She'd been here with Arthur.

Made restless and angry, she'd put aside thinking about her sons and strolled stiffly down to Henry's place. Henry *and May's* place.

Now she sat waiting in the familiar room, fixing her eyes on Henry's books, his carelessly flung newspapers, repeating to herself the words and phrases she would use to tell him that she did not feel comfortable coming here. Your wife, she rehearsed; what must she think, Henry? *I* know what we do, and *you* know what we do, but May doesn't, May can only guess and it's not fair. The whole village must be talking about us, we're seen about together so much.

Her arguments were rooted in reasonable notions of decorum

and public good taste, but failed to sound convincing to her. She thought of how angry she'd been tearing up her son's postcard and this made her remember her loneliness. Next stop sixty, a bulking American woman by herself on the rocky ledge of Ireland, the world, where everyone except other exiles spoke Gaelic – or was the proper term *Irish?* – and everyone could be talking about her to her face, for all she'd know.

Lonely here or lonely among grandchildren; what did it matter? The Dutchwoman who chaired the writers' group was taking Irish (Gaelic?) lessons once a week and could say hello and good evening and goodbye. They all, it seemed, took classes or courses, tried desperately to fit in, blend, be at home. Be here what they could not be where they'd been born and raised.

I'm one of them, Alison thought. I'm in exile, scared, getting old. This is the place I've retreated to. This is where I make my last stand, with the others. Let whoever wants to fly our corpses home.

Above the gaping fireplace rested coloured photos of Henry and May's children, grown now like her own, with children at their feet. Respectability shone from them like light from the faces of the Righteous. Alison looked up at the photos and felt vaguely sad. A life could be compressed into a photo frame. Images of the real, yet eloquent, noisy. She had never been real. Arthur had told her once that, so silent was she in a room, often he had believed her to possess the power to make herself invisible. The Russian myth-loving blood stirring in him. But was it true? Was invisibility her one true virtue?

Well, I'm sure I'm not invisible to May in there, Alison thought. I'm sure that poor woman can see me well enough.

She listened to Henry's attentive potterings, his low-voiced reassurances; she pictured the woman as she had become of late, a wisp of a figure fading into propped pillows, only the eyes moving. There were photographs of May around the room, affectionately placed, obvious; a bright-eyed, smiling woman, slim even into middle age. The sort of woman a man would describe, with a dry crackle of lust, as *mature*. She thought of the feel of Arthur's arms around her; she could feel them still, if she tried hard enough. She saw again the arch of his back and felt his warm, wet, hungry pummelling against her groin. She felt blood quicken in her cheeks. Ridiculous, she told herself. To be thinking of you now and here. Out of place. Inappropriate. *Mrs Arthur Selinsky.* Her mother had wept. He looks so . . . *foreign!*

She listened and heard May moan softly, like a woman in a spasm of love-making. Alison looked into the mouth of the fireplace, dark and humming with chimney breezes. It would not be easy to tell Henry she couldn't come here any more. Coming here was something, a point of reference, a pivot around which other routines could be measured and given their significance. Perhaps her feeling uneasy was silly, after all; perhaps she should postpone saying anything. But she heard May moan again, and the weight of being in the stifling, overloaded room took hold. She was not a guest here, could never be; she trespassed on ground made private by May's suffering. A ritual was needed to clean the air, to remove all trace of her, to restore the space to its rightful owners.

She felt absurdly clumsy. Henry was emerging from the bedroom, closing the door behind him with terrible care. He smiled at her, straightened himself to his full height.

'You look very smart,' he said.

'Thank you,' was all she could reply. All those other things to say, crowding in, pressing her, decisions made. But she couldn't manage them. Henry looked at her and her resolve evaporated. In such moments, she thought idly, has sin its beginnings. There is no morality here, she thought, just loneliness.

'I do hope we get enough people,' he said, helping her on with a knitted, cottage-industry-style cloak. 'Can't dance properly if there aren't enough to make up the sets.'

This was a new thing, set-dancing. Henry had introduced her to it. She saw her Friday evenings blacken under their weight. She'd been on two occasions already and each time old men in cloth caps eyed her from the bar, eyed Henry, slopped back their pints of Guinness and made remarks in their own language. They may have been talking listlessly about the weather; it made no difference to her. The impact of their voices was sufficient to fill

her with guilt. Others, too, looked at her differently. At least she
imagined they did. And at Henry, also. Exiles like themselves, and
that was particularly damning. Cut off by them, there would be
no question of surviving here. The locals were socially removed
from her; she hadn't worked at it, but it was a fact of being there.
One thing to talk to them, smile at them from time to time; it
didn't, in the end, count for anything.

Alison thought of these things as she walked with Henry down
towards the pub with its too-yellow thatch and its pink walls and
its green sign, *An Feadóg*. On the sign a little fat man in a green
pointed hat played a tin whistle. The pub was an oasis for tourist
buses. The owner, she'd been told, had made his money in
America and come home to show it off.

Inside, the pub was dark, one enormous beamed room, a
stained wooden bar with dozens of American university pennants
tacked to its wide mirrors and a yard-high model of the Statue of
Liberty on the counter. The statue was actually a computerized
cash-register. A light came on in Liberty's torch when a transac-
tion was made. High behind the bar was a smiling photo in colour
of President John F. Kennedy. There was a rainbow-lit jukebox in
a corner of the room near the Gents. It was silent now and dark.
The predictable clutch of old men squatted and perched like
wrecked birds on the spindly-legged wooden stools.

Henry seated her near the piano. In time the others came in,
cautiously looking about the room as if this was their first visit.
Immediately, ancient cackling began at the bar and odd, cracked
laughter. Alison looked up sharply. The frail-looking Dutchwoman had arrived, her husband, several others, including a
very fat Scottish woman who knitted her own hats and was
boisterous and loud. Her skirling accents whacked around the
dark, wide room and the jibing at the bar ceased.

The Scottish woman seated herself at the piano. She would
provide the music, but a tall, completely bald Frenchman who
did something with fish and lived by himself would direct the
dancing. Drinks were purchased, greetings of sort exchanged.
Nothing knits us together, Alison observed sadly. We are not
united in anything, even in our exile here. We orbit about one

another. Alison thought she would have her astrological chart done at some stage. The Dutchwoman did charts, it appeared.

She relaxed under the drinks. The room was hot and smoky when the Scottish woman thumped at last on the cracked, orangey piano keys and the music, slightly out of tune, reached out over the room. Alison viewed the other women who had drifted in; their faces were no longer pretty, age and life had rutted and terraced them, their eyes had gone out. The exiled women carried their lives in their faces. As, no doubt, I carry mine, she thought.

The Frenchman, in heavily accented English, called out steps into a harsh and treacherous hand-held microphone. His voice was louder than the piano. It sounded hysterical and frightened. Henry waited, tapping his fingers on the formica-topped table. Alison imagined May propped up in her bed, dozing, admitting God only knew what dreams and terrors. We betray her, her husband and I.

Henry waited, and when the Frenchman called out *The Clare Set*, he stood up, leaned over the table and the glasses, and took her hand. She dreaded this moment, this act of finger-touch which was witnessed by the entire room and most hurtingly by herself. She felt imposed upon, almost violated. It was a momentary feeling and it passed quickly. But it existed none the less.

She stood up and walked with Henry to the middle of the room and lined up facing the other dancers. Everyone looked serious and schoolkiddish at the same time. The piano exploded and the stiff, foot-working dancing began, back and forth, around, in and out. As other dancers passed close to her she inhaled their odour of sweat, of age, of menstruation, of hair tonic, of cheap after-shave, of too much elderly talc. And they inhaled her. This evening she'd applied a light touch of face make-up and a daub of a perfume called *Classique*.

The dance ended and they applauded each other, smiling with relief.

'Ho-Kay! Ho-Kay!' exclaimed the Frenchman. 'Get ready the next set, everybody!' At the bar, a capped, shrunken man sniggered loudly.

'I think I'll sit this one out,' Alison said, sitting down very deliberately.

Henry huffed and sighed his way into his seat. He was winded, out of breath, a man after love-making or a long run. Alison looked at him, saw the little breathless boy there, the man struggling to get out. If I reached over now and touched your face, she thought, you'd misconstrue. But there is a moment in such alliances as ours when the line is crossed, the thin invisible line that protects us. When everything we resolve, everything we promise ourselves in the smothering darkness of our privacies and in our heart, is thrown out, dismissed.

Alison looked around the room, making a point of taking her eyes off Henry's face. They danced again and fell into silly conversation with the Dutchwoman and her husband. Henry spoke of painting.

'Europe never discovered Ireland as a place to paint in,' he said. 'That has often puzzled me. Europe came here, but looked for something else, the literature, the folklore perhaps. But never to paint. Not to my knowledge.'

'Maybe less now,' sulked the man. He looked up at Henry from beneath hedge-like eyebrows. 'For example, *I* am here!'

The Dutchman crashed into a huge laugh and tried to pat Henry on the shoulder. His wife tittered like a terrified bird.

'A joke!' he cried.

Everyone was saying goodbye now, standing about fretfully in the pub doorway, smoky light lying softly over them. Alison felt the cold black air strike her face. *Slán! Slán!* muttered the old men to each other. *Slán!* said the Dutchwoman timidly, to no one in particular. Alison suddenly felt very old.

Henry was quite drunk.

'Silly of me to get into conversations with people who are drunk,' he said.

'He is an artist,' Alison heard herself say.

'That remains to be seen,' said Henry. 'I have a poem for you, by the way. Meant to give it to you earlier.'

He stopped in the middle of the empty road and fumbled in his pockets. At last paper was dragged out. Alison imagined it struggling to stay where it was. She giggled tipsily. Henry opened the sheet of paper, looked at her, held it out to her.

'No,' said Alison. 'I want you to read it to me, please.'

'I'll be dreadfully embarrassed.'

'We are long past the point of embarrassment,' Alison replied and immediately regretted she'd said it. Henry seemed to hesitate. The silence between them grew.

'Well, right then,' Henry said. 'With your permission.'

Alison stood a little way off. Drunk enough, she listened to the suave, languorous sound of the salted wind strumming the thin branches of the trees. Natural music, she thought. The sound was sad and yet terribly attractive. You wanted to reach up and drink it in, cup the sound in your hands, drown in it. And behind her, Henry started to recite his poem:

> *'We two, sheltered by a sort of love,*
> *Number ourselves among the lucky ones:*
> *We reach out from our hidden hearts*
> *And blaze in secret, like forgotten suns.'*

'I call it "Hidden Hearts",' said Henry. His voice was dry, full of unspecific emotion. Alison heard his foot turn on the gravel. No, she thought; do not do this, Henry. But when she turned round defensively, he was still a number of feet away, he hadn't moved. The ghost of his desire, perhaps, had moved. That was all. She heard the music chording from tree to tree, each tree a new and differently tuned instrument. Above it, in the distance, a motorcycle yacked and barked and faded out. The world was still there. The music went on regardless of the world. Regardless of herself and Henry, and regardless of May, who could not hear it.

'I think it's ridiculous, Henry,' Alison said. She looked at him, saw his handsome lined face break up in the shadowy half-dark. 'It is mawkish, to say the least, and it's the sort of thing a love-smitten adolescent would write and try to slip in your schoolbag at break-time.'

Henry did not move. He was standing there, paralysed by her words, her unconcern. Alison felt a great pain move into the bottom of her throat, cover her chest. She could barely breathe. All the same, the words came out, one after the other, unhindered, remorseless and cruel.

'We are not *sheltered* by a sort of *anything*, Henry. We should be ashamed of ourselves. We do not have a *sort* of *anything.*'

The wind rose. She was shouting now. She hadn't meant to raise her voice. Henry was trying to say something. She heard the beginning of it.

'Look, Alison . . .'

'Our *hearts* are not *hidden*, Henry. The whole bloody world can see them.'

'Metaphor,' said Henry. 'I'm using allegory, that's . . .'

'No you are not!' Alison shouted over the music in the trees. 'And, if so, what are *we* a metaphor for, Henry? What allegory are *we* supposed to be, you and me!'

She stared at him. Her heart banged loudly, she wondered if he could hear it. She was in pain, but it was not like anything she'd ever experienced. A world was disintegrating.

She saw that Henry was moving away from her, he'd gathered himself together, put himself together, sobering; was moving away up the road and into the consuming silence and darkness. His hands dangled by his sides and in the fingers of one of them he held, still, stupidly, his failed poem.

Alison ran after him. She saw herself, an overweight, over-middle-aged woman running on a gravel road on the west coast of Ireland. She saw herself as if from a great and terrible height. The tree music had stopped; nothing now but the panicky drumbeat of her shoes on the gravel. Henry turned round.

'Let us for God's sake be civilized!'

'I don't know where all of that came from,' Alison said.

'It doesn't matter.' He handed her the crumpled page. 'Damned silly of me,' he said. 'You're quite right, of course. Damned silly.'

'I'm confused, Henry,' Alison said. Henry brought back his hand, still clutching the page.

'Nothing to be confused about,' he said. 'Go home. *I'll* go home. You do the same. Good night's sleep.'

Alison felt something fall away from her, fall irretrievably into a hideous and unfathomable well that was somewhere in the sky, somewhere under the earth. Absurdly, she fixed her eyes on two winking distant harbour lights just over Henry's shoulder. I have condemned myself, she thought. I could have said nothing and none of this would be happening. And now that it's all said, how exactly do I feel?

'Clash of cultures,' Henry said, smiling, trying to make light of it.

'I imagine you're right,' Alison agreed. Whatever was gone was gone, and in its place a cold reasonable hunger settled down. 'Perhaps we should shake hands.'

Henry held out his hand. Alison took it. They shook hands with exaggerated formality.

'I do love my wife, you know,' said Henry.

'I know. I respect that.'

'I feel somewhat better now,' Henry said. 'But it's late.'

'I want to walk a little by myself,' Alison told him. 'I feel suddenly wide awake.'

Henry turned and walked away. Alison leaned back against the cold stone of the wall beside the road and watched him march awkwardly into the darkness.

A limp pale sheet of mist rolled over the fields. The vibrating pillars and waving slivers of mist looked alive and curiously human. But it was not true that ghosts lived in darkness, she thought.

Ghosts lived in the light. They rejoiced in the heat and light of noon. They passed through each other, formless, curiously happy.

CÓILÍN O hAODHA

Her Blood Dripped into Grass

When she was certain he was dead, she hung him on the wall. Only when she was certain. And hanging him, his picture, made it seem more so. It struck her fully for the first time when she bent with a back-stabbing pain to return the hammer to its hiding place of three years. Three years of dust motes parachuting safely onto the scuffed carpet and how many generations of spiders spinning in the cupboard under the stairs, where noises meant rainy Saturday mornings, the time he used to spend doing small household repairs. If he really had to be remembered she would remember him like that: bruised thumbs and tired arms and a soft sweat.

What a place to hang your memory, just over the mantelpiece, where the smoke had left its black lick and the edge of the wallpaper was tearing free. Hours of scrubbing and the little pot of all-purpose glue, for nothing. But then she'd done things like that before. The morning he stopped breathing and everyone had arrived to tell her that they were sorry but she had to move on, though she hadn't stopped for a minute; that morning, she'd hung her heart out on the line with the washing. The wind tore through the back gate, and became entangled in the sheets, struggling like a trapped animal. It went right through her, her heart, through the gap his breath broke open on his way out. And she felt the blood drip down and soil the clothes in the expectant basket. He looked just like he was asleep. *Are you asleep? Wake up. Wake up, John. Please.* But blood is another stain that never washes out.

She bent down and sternly grasped the next wet sheet waiting to be freed, as if to warn it that it could never really be. Not it, not anyone. There were too many ties. Though she didn't wash those

very often. Today she did, but for no particular reason. They
simply had to be done. Or she simply had to be done with them.
She scolded the wrung sheet saying that there was more to the
wind than fresh air reddening your face and the smell of the sea
and the way when you held hands, then, they always felt warmer.
And fish for tea, from the small shop. No cooking. *Isn't this a fine
break for you?* The breeze stinging your eyes filled them with tears
and made it look like you'd been crying though you hadn't really
been. Not really. *I'm fine.*

There was no point crying over spilt milk. He always said she
worried too much. About what the neighbours think. But she
knew them better, the colour of their tongues and the shapes they
could make with spit. She'd spilt the milk that morning too. It
seemed as if she could get nothing to work properly for her that
day. She lost control of her hand and the jug slipped. Or maybe
her wedding ring had got caught on the sharper edge of the
handle and pinched. *I forget. Anyway, it was nothing.* The milk
slopped onto the tablecloth and quietly seeped away. Embarrassed. Embarrassing. *A little bit that's all.* And all forgotten.

But the milk settling on the top shelf, right-hand corner of the
fridge, beside the cheese cut painstakingly into perfect slices, was
another silent accuser, that said that such a small event as a wet-
stain on the floral print or a load of washed linen tossed in a wilder
wind meant things had changed for ever around here. That there
was no going back. Not to the small shop where they'd bought
freshly caught and cooked mackerel or to walking the prom on
Sunday afternoons fair or foul, fair or foul, or to smiling at the
milkman and asking how his wife is. *Mary. She's well? That's good.
Tell her I was asking for her. And the children.*

When she finished cleaning the other rooms, including his (he
could come home at any moment, couldn't he? being in semi-
retirement), she went back. All through the day she went back, to
make sure he was hanging straight with his crooked smile.
Straight back to the wall, staring out through the net curtains
on the front window, across the street. Sometimes she thought
that when she turned her back, his eyes followed and he was
making faces at her where she couldn't see. *I saw that.* He was

always doing that, just to tease her. *Little Miss Prim. I didn't know that's what you really think of me.* Prim. Another door clicked closed coldly. Cold as one milk bottle on the doorstep on a dark morning in November. One.

At one o'clock she still wasn't asleep. Watched traffic lights change in a quiet street when nobody's around. Red to green, blood dripped onto grass. *Prime housing, recently built, perfect for the newly married couple, nice neighbours, raise your children in peace.* Nice neighbours. She heard his eyes boring in through the wall, surveying the garden from over her shoulder. *I have eyes in the back of my head.* Saw the weeping willow and a few very tired roses, petals wilting. And cursing the rain. *I won't have that sort of language used in my house. The children are old enough now . . . I . . .* Sorry, said reluctantly. The sound of boring was Saturday morning all over again. Light traffic and the cracked skirting board in the hall behind the front door finally restored. Buy varnish, and more cheese.

And when she turned to put the latch on the little front gate, the shopping perched safely on the pillar, she felt him watching at the window. Waiting. *There's your change, Mrs Byrne. Terrible weather, isn't it? We'll have no summer at all if it continues like this.* Waiting. But no matter how fast she looked around or strained the corner of her eye, she never saw more than the net curtain twitching down to the sill. *I need eyes in the back of my head with you around.* Where the flowers grew. *I'm no good with the garden, the plants die on me.* And flowers rooted in him, plants living on him. No dying. Rose petals falling on the lawn and lying. And how did that work now? It didn't.

Not at all. *Honestly, I'll be fine.* No matter what way she thought of him lying in the dark place, like a hammer stored in the dusty alcove under the stairs or a black patch her memory hid on the wall in the lounge, it wouldn't work. His eyes kept opening.

Only asleep, *wake up, you were asleep,* and dreaming. *You're imagining it all.* Imagining. The net curtain was let fall back. She knew, but she wouldn't tell anyone, just in case. Just in case they thought she was going mad or still getting older. Older? with her heart beating out its last on the washing line and her memory caught smiling on the lounge wall like a hunter's prize. Older means more than rattled breath or sharp bones biting through marble skin, green-veined. But a single word about a quick shimmer in the window-mesh and it would be all rushing around with sweet words and soft hands to help. Help.

They were only trying to be helpful. *Where do you keep the sugar, love? Don't stir.* About her, cutlery clinked, delft stacked, a knife rattled over the bread-board, water scuttled down the sink, and whispers washed and pressed. About her: *she hasn't said a word.* Not even one complaint about the way they were messing up her kitchen. Not one tear that might say it all. All they wanted to hear. Instead, she obeyed orders silently and drank unstirred tea in the front room, and watched raindrops jostle wildly down the window as if they didn't know. As if they didn't know what everyone else knew; that he had been an old man who had a heart attack when she wasn't at home. A cat slinked guiltily past the window, in the dry patch under the eaves. Wreaths gathered quietly about her feet and eyed her with squinting messages. *Remembered Fondly. Remembered Always.* Remembered how the flowers, sent by Rose, wept petals for DADDY onto the green carpet near the radiator. And always would.

She hated him because he hadn't waited. Because he left right after she went out and didn't say goodbye. And now that she was certain he was gone, he lay in wait for her all the time; he hit her in the face every time she opened the front door and saw his left leg twisted on the floor at the foot of the stairs. As her eyes moved over him he beat her up: knee, waist, chest, hands, eyes. Beat her until her eyes swelled up and she couldn't see any more for blinking. She hated him because he had to be remembered, and she only felt able to put him back together in the hall where there was a bright light and the seams showed.

Worse still, there were days when she lost his face and couldn't place it: between his ears and around his head, down into his throat. And then she was frightened again and blows rained. She would run into the lounge from the front door and memorize his features, but even when she was sure that she finally had his face (and her face) firmly in her hands, it kept slipping out between her

fingers. Where is he gone? *Where is she gone? Why isn't she here?*
At his funeral she didn't sit in the first pew, but much further back
in a shadowed side-aisle, beside Veronica at the sixth Station. She
was another woman who'd wiped the face off a man and no one
thought she had loved him less. Or thought less of her for it.

And that was when she knew how it could all end: in a broken
smile. A shock that would make the neighbours swallow back
their hearts and clean their tongues, talking again over the
garden fence as they'd always done; about the weather and the
price of food and what the children were up to now. About her
too. And she knew when it would happen: the day she would go
out to gather in the washing from the rain and find that her heart
was flapping loosely on the line, completely dry.

When she could look at him again through unblurred eyes.
Then she could move on unstirred just like they said, just like the
black patch on the wall where the smoke had stayed. When she
could take him down and pick him up again and rock him to sleep
in a chair in the front room, his frame cutting into her arms, her
tired veins. Everything would be remembered as it should be in
the falling dark.

Falling on the garden and on the house, lying on the grass
under a warm breeze, slipping through net curtains and tripping
down the stairs, seeping into the carpet and curling under the
radiator like a scolded cat. Then there would be no going back.

Because there would be nothing to forget.

This Game

After a light supper of poached salmon and white wine the two men played chess. Father Feeny had refilled his curate's glass several times and matched him, glass for glass. Neither should be at a disadvantage. However, Gerry McCafferty was not giving the game his full attention. He wanted to be frivolous and the wine had made him bold enough to speak. He delivered his words with what he hoped was a roguish smile for he had no wish to offend the older man.

'Don't you sometimes wish you were a Rabbi?'

The reply was immediate.

' "Were"? or "Had been"?'

'I mean . . .'

'So that you could be married and have children? Is that what you're saying?'

'Partly. Yes. And we could have women as colleagues.'

'Ah. Women priests. That's your notion, is it?'

Father Feeny was a man of great courtesy. Sometimes, though, a little scorn would show through, and this could make Gerry stumble in choosing his words. Now the wine no longer helped but was clouding his brain and the ideas which had seemed so sparkling felt puerile. The chessmen were waiting; Father Feeny's breathing was quiet and very steady. Gerry, who was playing black, looked at the board and fingered his queen's knight which was still on the back line.

Looking straight at him, his superior said, 'We have women colleagues, have we not? I have Mrs O'Neill. We work together in this house. I read. She dusts. I write. She cooks.'

Gerry's smile broadened. 'Ach, Father John, you know what I mean.'

'Not at all. I value Kathleen O'Neill as a fellow worker.'

Father Feeny returned to a scrutiny of the board. 'And what about the risen Christ?' he said, not expecting an answer. 'Come along, Gerry, what are you moving? We're playing Touch a Piece, Move a Piece, remember?'

It was not that Gerry had fantasies about eyes meeting across the sacristy, none of that Héloïse and Abelard stuff, it was just that he longed for a companion, someone he could laugh with unchecked. And if a woman ever came as curate to Kilnalough, then she could take the Legion of Mary and he would have more time to coach the football team. It would have been nice to speculate about this even in an ironic way with Father Feeny. Now he pressed his finger into the carved black head of his knight. There was only one square free and it was covered by a white pawn, but move it he must and wait for the inevitable.

In fact it was only much later in the game that Gerry's knight joined all the other pieces taken by his opponent. The light they played in was rich and deep. Dark red curtains had been closed against the evening sun, and where these met only a blade of sunlight penetrated the room. It struck a framed print, one of a set showing the North Antrim coast. This one, glittering in the light, was well known to Gerry and always made him feel uneasy because it showed the Carrig-a-Rede Ropebridge. Without having to ask, he was sure that Father Feeny had crossed over on it and that his nerve had never failed him because he had neither looked at nor pictured the sharp rocks and swirling waters below. Gerry could see him calmly walking on the swaying footpath over and back, over and back, just as many times as he felt like it.

Outside the room, beyond the curtains was the bay, with the town of Kilnalough beside it facing seawards to England. The parochial house stood on a small headland. From the upstairs windows Father Feeny could have seen, had he wanted to, the comings and goings in the parish and, on the peninsula opposite, the new, rebuilt Imperial. Formerly a hotel, burnt during the civil war, this building was already considered as Father Feeny's monument. Here the Operatic Society held their rehearsals, the Badminton Club met each week and the Football Team kept in training during the winter. People even remembered the Golf Committee meeting there before the new clubhouse was built. Father Feeny had been generously accommodating to the local Protestants, welcoming them not only into the new Imperial, but in a few cases into the Church itself. The lichen-covered grey building belonging to the Church of Ireland held services only once a month. Father Feeny found it more than suitable for recitals by the Renaissance Music Group.

Sounds of laughter and shouting from across the bay had been muffled all evening by the heavy curtains. These noises were dwindling now and the night breeze began to nudge at the window. Suddenly a piercing scream and wild harsh laughter came from across the water. Both men looked up. Father Feeny strode over and opened the curtains. The sea, all glimmering pallor, shocked with its sudden brightness. On the shore in front of the Imperial leaping figures were either fighting or dancing; it was hard to see which. Or were they embracing? Gradually the screams died into laughter and the laughter into something like the chatter of monkeys. The priests were unable to hear the words. They stood for a while at the open window. The air lifted away the room's familiar smell of polish and carpet, and the less usual smell of fish and wine, bringing in seaweed and dead crabs and car fumes.

In the distance the water was pale pink, like the inside of a shell. Gerry could see but not share its calm. He was worried that Father Feeny would ask him about the youngsters making the noise. He recognized the girls, one of them, Marcella Devlin, taller than the rest. She had been visibly fending off the even taller figure of Aidan Ryan, captain of the football team and Gerry's friend. But Father Feeny turned back to the room and did not enquire.

'Horseplay,' he said, switching on a lamp.

Perhaps the older priest was tired or affected by the break in concentration. He won the game only with great difficulty, Gerry having sustained what seemed like losses but turned out to be inspired sacrifices.

On these evenings of recreation it was their custom not to

discuss parish matters. At ten o'clock they drank tea and ate the sandwiches left under a faded checked cloth by Mrs O'Neill. Then they watched the television news from London. Father Feeny looked to England for his news, his culture and most of his friendships. Every morning after Mass he collected his paper, the *Daily Telegraph*, from the Ryans' corner shop. It was clearly marked as his, but once, as a child, Aidan had sold it to a summer visitor. Now in his twenties, Aidan claimed still to feel the shame of this. His mother had been in a terrible state. Would Father Feeny take *The Times* or *The Irish Times?* Aidan had rushed to help, seizing a copy of *Time* magazine, but Father Feeny had recoiled from the mere glimpse of its slippery bright cover. In the end the priest had patted him on the head and walked away with the *Farmer's Weekly*.

Gerry had enjoyed that story. Gradually he came to realize how misleading the *Daily Telegraph* was. A man for whom routine was ritual, Father Feeny was flexible, even liberal, over many parish matters. In Kilnalough there were girls serving at the altar and women were encouraged to share the readings and distribute communion. He spoke to Mrs O'Neill as he did to Gerry, politely, with dry, remote kindness. He must be nearly seventy and yet there was an elegance about him, a lightness. Despite his reserve, his movements at Mass were graceful. The ceremonies liberated something in him; he might have been a dancer.

Gerry felt clumsy beside him. Since his arrival as curate in Kilnalough three years earlier he had become rounder, especially in the belly. Father Feeny might be a *bon viveur* but he was no Falstaff; Mrs O'Neill understood his tastes perfectly. Gerry, in the Curate's Residence, cared for himself. A fry, tea and bread and jam were his evening meal. His appreciation of homemade jam, carelessly uttered at a Bring and Buy sale, had resulted in so many offerings of this commodity that a press in the dining-room was bulging with jars all with handwritten labels showing the date of bottling. These dates were slipping into the past and Gerry was failing to seize the day, while the press door became more and more difficult to close. Then there were daily presents of cakes and scones. Aidan's mother was the worst. Busy in the shop, she had no time to bake but would send Aidan over with buns and apple pies from the bread van.

Gerry was the one they spoiled. To some of the women he was a pet, a darling. He was so understanding. When it came to comforting the bereaved it was Gerry they turned to, but it was Father Feeny they wanted to take the funeral. And when it came to relationships, doubts about commitments or advice needed, the young people went to Gerry, but they still expected Father Feeny to perform the marriage ceremony.

For long stretches Gerry felt idle. He did a lot of reading and meditating (staring into space) and drinking tea in the kitchen of the Curate's Residence. He also took determined exercise. In the early days he had walked on the beach between one headland and the next, but he was always aware that behind the palms which flourished there and the shrubs and wrought iron fences, curious eyes were watching his progress. So he went inland to the lough. He walked along the goat's path below the mountains, sat on the boulders and listened to the perpetual slapping of the small waves and told himself that most people were lonely in some way or another.

'Turn it off, Gerry.' This was not so much Father Feeny's comment on the TV news as an acknowledgement that Gerry would not want to know the sports results which followed. Instead he would go and watch *Match of the Day* at home. Father Feeny asked frequently to be reminded which team Gerry supported. He showed an amused interest only as long as it didn't have to extend to the names of the teams, the players, the managers or their positions in the league. He encouraged Gerry to work with the local team – 'Aidan Ryan's ruffians' he called them. Last year he had been very accommodating when it came to the Cup Final, letting Gerry off the vigil Mass on the Saturday. So it was a shock this evening when he said on the doorstep, 'I'd like you to come a little later and stay longer next week, Gerry. Something I want to talk to you about.'

Gerry walked back towards the town with the wind blowing in his face, muttering against his host in angry, unclerical language.

'The old bastard must *know* it's the Cup Final next week! Is he
teasing me or what? Is this some kind of a test?' He felt foolish as
he thought of all the plans he had been making. A few
Budweisers, frozen pizzas, a coal fire if the night got chill. Aidan
would be watching the game with some of the crowd from the
Imperial, but maybe they would feel like coming to him for the
evening. Stupid! Fancy trying to behave like a normal person.
What could the old man be wanting to talk about?

He pounded his way homeward without looking at the world
around him. The wind domed his brow. He looked so wise but he
raged inwardly at the coming deprivation. The tide was out and
the street lights glimmered on wet sand.

'Gerry?' Aidan was on the phone next morning.

'Yes! Aidan.'

'Would it be a sin to take Marcella Devlin, tie a stone round her
neck and drown her in the lough?'

'The lough, Aidan? Wouldn't the sea be handier?'

'Ah but the tides. She'd wash right in. The lough is deep, very
deep in places.'

So far there had been no laughter in Aidan's voice. Gerry tried
to coax it now, laughing himself.

'Aidan, for the love of God, what has the poor girl done?'

Aidan had a way of dramatically lowering his voice several
tones. 'She's trying to undermine the women's football team!'

'How *could* she do that?' It was Gerry's turn for mirthless
irony.

'She just told them. Don't play.' He put on a high-pitched
mincing voice. ' "Football is not lady-like." No. "Football does not
become a lady. It is *ugly* and *unfeminine*." '

'And did they listen?'

'Sure they listened. Two of them are making excuses already.
I'll kill her. And the way she looked at me! Triumphant. Lips
together, you know the sort of thing. Head in the air.'

'I thought you liked her. Could you not talk it over?'

Aidan growled. 'The only talking I'll do is, "You'd better go to
Father Gerry McCafferty and make your last confession." So be

prepared, Gerry, be prepared. Must go. Someone in the shop. See you later.'

Gerry had convinced himself that there was something seriously wrong with his priorities to have got so irrationally angry about a mere game of football. He put the matter well away from his mind as he concentrated on assisting Father Feeny at the eleven o'clock Mass. Aidan, too, looked no more murderous than usual and seemed indifferent to the presence of Marcella just a few feet away.

This week Father Feeny spoke about vocations. In the last three years no one had come forward for the priesthood. Father Feeny did not mention this. He was not concerned to reproach. Nor did he stress sacrifice or talk of the deprivations of a priest's life. He spoke of joy and of need and he reminded the people of their great happiness. He spoke in the quiet, matter-of-fact tones he always used. There were few images, few examples. Just the words themselves, joy, privilege, gift, love. Bliss became familiar, heaven ordinary. From where he sat, Gerry could see Aidan's mother gazing at the altar with shining eyes.

When it came to the prayers, Gerry's were private and unorthodox. Recently, on the subject of vocations they had always been the same, that the Pope would allow discussion on the ordination of women, that those leaving who wanted to could be laicized so that his friend Micky could marry Anne and that, 'if it be Thy will', celibacy should no longer be a condition of the priesthood. He also had a mumbled hope, though this was not worded as a prayer, that any new priests sent as his fellow labourers should be normal and human, not freaks or paedophiles or anyone badly afflicted with body odour.

That evening, quite late, Aidan rang again. Gerry could hear women's voices in the background raggedly singing 'I Will Survive' as though they were trying it out for the first time. Aidan sounded cheerful and no longer intent on murder.

'Gerry. Saturday.'

'Oh God, Aidan, I forgot to tell you – I'm tied up.'

'How's that?'

'I've to see Father Feeny that evening.'

A pause.

'Why, does he not know? Tell him. See we're having a bit of a do. Molloys are getting a big screen and some of the lads are getting together and you're invited. It'll be great crack.'

'Sorry, Aidan. Sounds good, sounds great, but . . . Do not say anything to Father Feeny.'

'So will you not see the match at all?'

Gerry allowed himself a bitter comment, pretending it would sound like a joke, 'The only field I'll be looking at will be a black and white one.'

'Why? You've colour, haven't you, or Father Feeny has. Persuade him to watch it, not get Cut Off from the People kind of thing.'

'I mean we'll most likely be playing chess. Thanks for asking me. I'll speak to you soon.'

Less than five minutes later Aidan rang again. The 'survivors' in the background now sang in unison more or less and were thumping out the rhythm on the ground. Aidan had to shout.

'Gerry! Listen. Great idea! Guess what. I'll video it for you. You can watch it whenever you like.'

'Of course! Right! Good thinking, Aidan.' Gerry was beaming now. Why had he not thought of that?

'Charlie's idea. I'll get the tape. Just leave it all to me.'

'Well that really changes things. Thank you. Now we won't have to drag the lough for Father Feeny along with Marcella!'

There was a pause. 'I Will Survive' came to an end. Gerry heard a wave breaking. Aidan said, 'I can't hear you.'

'Never mind. It was a joke.'

'Something about Marcella?'

'She's still alive is she, then?'

'Can you not hear her? That's her singing.'

Something like pride in his voice made Gerry ask, 'Is she forgiven?'

'Oh she's forgiven. She's just one crazy woman, that's all. Do you want to speak to her?'

'No. No for Heaven's sake. Good night, Aidan. Great idea about the video. See you later.'

On the morning of Cup Final day Gerry caught sight of Marcella walking past the Curate's Residence. She wore a flouncy skirt with big flowers, daisies on a red ground, and, on top, a loose jumper with a high neck. The skirt might have been something her mother discarded along with *Heidi* and *Little Women* and the top could have come from anywhere, chosen with the sole purpose of disguising her shape. What brought the ensemble together was the vivid red lipstick which, even as far away as the garden gate, could be seen to match grotesquely the colour of the skirt. She glanced towards the front door, then looked at the ground, stopped, and retraced her steps. Gerry's hands were full of old newspapers; he was laying a fire for that night's viewing. When he looked up again she was still there. She had always had a strange way of walking, alternating long strides, hips swinging, with moments when she would stand utterly still. It reminded Gerry of the children's game where you move up on someone, then freeze at the moment they turn round. There were fewer pauses today and she was starting to brush her fingers on top of the gate whenever she passed. She had the air of someone waiting for directions from above. Gerry muttered impatiently, 'Come on, Marcella. Touch a piece, move a piece, now.' He was afraid by the time he came back with the coal scuttle she'd be gone. He opened the front door at the same time as she opened the gate.

'I was coming to see you, Father.'

'Come in, Marcella. Nice to see you.'

He showed her into the sitting-room. 'Let me just go and wash *The Irish Times* from my hands. Like pitch it doth defile.'

She smiled remotely.

When he came back she seemed to fill the room. Declining to sit, she stood leaning against a table. From her clothes came strong perfume and a smell of cigarette smoke. Of course they all smoked at the Imperial. She shivered.

'Let me light the fire.' He had planned not to light it till the evening when he sat down to watch the match.

'No, no, not for me, Father.' She gazed at the Byzantine madonna on the wall above Gerry's head. He slid sideways, like someone tactfully removing himself from someone else's photograph. He tried sitting in the fireside chair but from there she seemed too tall. He settled for a leaning position of his own, against the arm of the chair. Her foot started to tap. She arrested it immediately and took a packet of cigarettes from a pocket in her skirt.

'Will you permit me to smoke?'

'Permit? Surely, Marcella.'

He scrabbled in the sideboard for an ashtray, embarrassed in case she caught sight of various unwanted treasures he had stashed away. But when he stood up, empty-handed, she was frowning at Rouault's *Head of Christ* over the mantelpiece. The intense, dark features seemed to displease her.

'I'll get an ashtray. You'll have a cup of coffee?'

'No thank you, Father. What I have to say won't take long.'

She took a cigarette from the packet, put it to her lips, then waved her lighter at the Rouault.

'Forgive me for saying so, but I could never find that picture very *devotional.*'

What had happened to the girl's vocabulary? He was waiting for a suitable moment to remind her that she, like Aidan and most of the others, now called him Gerry. But 'Forgive me for saying so' and 'Permit me to smoke'? He hadn't remembered her smoking. Nor the pondering air of near menace she was emanating as if any moment she might snatch the pictures from the walls and outlaw all such comforts as coal fires and morning coffee. She had lit her cigarette and was staring at him as if challenging him to defend the painting. The defiance in her face suddenly reminded him of her fight with Aidan.

'So what was it you wanted to talk to me about, Marcella?'

She started to do her walk. From his place near the fire he saw her loom up, shoulders back, bright skirt swinging. Then she paused, dropped her ash in the coal bucket, stared at the unlit fire and turned away again. At the other end of the room she sighed loudly and returned, keeping the same rhythm. This performance was repeated, her body's movements unvarying, only her face changing slightly, not in basic expression, which was a sort of determined blankness, but in where she bestowed her glance – on the madonna, on the fireplace and then finally on Gerry. She stood in front of him, looked down, and said in the deepened tone which immediately brought Aidan to him, 'Gerry, you must pray for me.'

He took a moment to find his voice.

'Of course, Marcella. Of course. But tell me . . .'

A terrible thought came to him. She was pregnant. Not Aidan, please God, not Aidan.

She sank into the chair opposite him and bowed her head. When she turned to him again her face was radiant, her eyes suddenly magnified with tears. She controlled her red, trembling mouth.

'Ever since last Sunday.'

'Yes?'

'Well, Saturday night really.'

'Oh.'

'There was this picture in the paper. Little black children, Gerry, crying for food, orphans, nowhere to go. It was some kind of appeal for money and I thought, right, I'll do it, I'll give up the fags and I'll send the money to Trócaire every week that I would have spent on giving myself cancer.'

Now her manner was confidential and she was smiling indulgently as at some youthful foolishness. Gerry smiled back and nodded at the cigarette.

'So. When do you start?'

'But wait. Then on Sunday, Father Feeny preached about vocations. You remember?'

'Of course.'

'It was brilliant. And I started to think, why not? Why not me? And it was as if I heard a voice saying, not from outside, but inside, deep inside, "What is giving up a few lousy cigarettes compared to giving up your life?" And the feeling has grown, it just won't go away. Father, I have a vocation.'

Now she seemed amazed, exultant. She looked for his reaction. 'Is that how it was for you, Gerry?'

Relief and disbelief and a deep suppressed laughter. He must go very carefully. He needed something. A drink, but it would seem too early to celebrate. So a cup of coffee. He would have to insist.

'This sounds serious, Marcella. But you're not just planning to announce it and leave me. I'll put the kettle on.'

By the time he got to the kitchen his laughter was so deeply buried he could scarcely manage a splutter. He was a little nervous as he filled the kettle and opened all the press doors before he remembered he was looking for an ashtray, thinking about Marcella. She was idle. She'd done nothing since leaving boarding-school three years ago. They'd put her in the Tourist Office for a while but she'd given a strange kind of welcome to the visitors. On one occasion, in an incident which produced open shock and secret admiration among the population of Kilnalough, she had responded to a request for directions to the Holy Well by making every member of the party remove socks and shoes and set out barefoot. Women in cotton dresses had been seen clutching each other and giggling, hopping from foot to foot as they unstrapped their sandals. The men looked awkward but they, too, obeyed. 'It's the custom,' she told them, so the story went, explaining to the locals that 'Customs have to start somewhere.'

When he returned with a tray, she was sitting in a chair with her eyes closed. Her cigarette end was in the hearth as were the empty packet and the cellophane wrapper of a new one. She seemed so unaware of her powerful and troubling sexuality that she might give that up without a qualm. But her smoking and her untidiness and her appetite for drama? He thought she had fallen asleep, but on hearing cup on saucer she was quickly on her feet.

'Stay where you are,' said Gerry, but she pulled out a seat and sat at the table.

Now he took her seriously. Listened to her, acted the devil's advocate, told her of the hardships of the religious life. She had been taught by nuns. Did she really see herself living among them?

'But I want to go to Africa, Father, to work in the places where all the misery is and *do* something. There'll not be time for tensions and pettiness out there.'

He knew himself well and deeply, deeply enough to recognize that he was attracted by the idea of a celibate Marcella thousands of miles away from Kilnalough. Therefore he made his arguments stronger, mocked her and teased her, spoke of her family and then, just as she was rising to go, said, 'Are you sure you're not just running away from Aidan Ryan and the Ladies' Football Team?'

She frowned and deepened her voice again. 'I'll not be sorry to say goodbye to the Imperial, no harm to Father Feeny.'

'Am I to say anything to Father about your . . . ?'

'Would you? Please. I've felt shy about speaking to him myself. But I'd like him to know. It was he who inspired me.'

He walked to the gate with her. She seemed more confident now and more natural, but she did hold out her hand and say with emphatic warmth, 'Thank you, Gerry. Thank you for listening to me. You will pray for me, won't you?'

'In the end I thought she was sincere. It's just that rather odd manner of hers . . .'

'Play-acting!'

Father Feeny was entirely dismissive of the good news Gerry had brought him. In truth neither of them really wanted to discuss it. The windows opened onto a gentle evening and the sun had yet to sink behind the mountain. Its light deepened the blue water of the bay, making it look solid enough to walk on. Molloy's Bar, 'The Water's Edge', had its window open too and every so often spilled out gasps and broken cheers like hiccups.

Mrs O'Neill had spread them a more sumptuous meal than usual. Gerry noticed an ice-bucket with a fat bottle resting in it. He also saw that the shining polished wood of the chess-board was empty and the box closed at its side. He was drawn to the dining table with its winking glasses and cutlery, and his pride at the news about Marcella was fast dissipating. He was also curious as to what Father Feeny wanted to tell him; it had better be big enough to miss the match for. But reconciled about the match, he was beginning to enjoy this evening. Only he owed it to Marcella to argue for her, to affirm her seriousness. Surely

Father Feeny would be glad to know of the effectiveness of his preaching.

'Perhaps I should suggest she speaks to you herself?'

'Yes, perhaps you should. Now. A glass before we dine?'

It really *was* champagne. Father Feeny opened it with such decorum and neatness of aim that Gerry was struck by the contrast with recent news images of sports heroes spurting triumphant froth into the crowd. What had he been brought here to celebrate? Last month for his fortieth anniversary as a priest the whole parish had made a fuss of Father Feeny and he had tolerated it with good humour, clearly glad when it was over.

They stood with their glasses at the window. Gerry wanted to say 'This is the life!' ironically but the irony would have seemed like bad manners. Outside the beach was empty and the waves too gentle to hear. An angry roar burst from 'The Water's Edge'. Maybe later he would guess from the video what that was about.

A breeze rattled the window on its catch and Father Feeny, handing his glass to Gerry, stooped to close it. His movements seemed slower and Gerry was aware of the will behind his straightening up again. He took back his glass and led the way to the fireside.

'What I have to tell you won't take long but you may want to ask me some questions and that would seem reasonable. Perhaps you'd care to replenish our glasses.'

As Gerry poured the wine he heard distant sounds of life from the beach, callings and laughter which just came through the closed windows. 'Half-time,' he said to himself and reflected that this was the second time today that someone had promised not to take too long.

Father Feeny selected a damp piece of worm-eaten driftwood from the creel and threw it in the fire where it hissed and sparked. There was something unusually offhand about his gesture. Gerry sat perched opposite, expectant, politely smiling.

'Well, Gerry, I've been at this game for over forty years now.' His voice sounded strangely rough-edged, like a hard man in the movies.

'It's a great achievement!'

'Yes, I think so. I've done some good things. And now I'm going to chuck it in.'

He looked straight at Gerry and waited.

'You're going to retire?'

'Yes, I'm going to retire.'

Gerry raised his glass uncertainly.

'Well. Congratulations.'

'I'm not sure that you understand. I'm retiring, yes. But I'm also, as we used to say, dropping out.'

'You're saying that you . . .'

He hoped that Father Feeny would complete the sentence but he just sat there, apparently relaxed, in his black suit, only betraying the slightest unease by the tightening of his fingers on the glass.

'You're retiring as a priest?'

'Yes. I shall become a lay person. I shall no longer say Mass or hear confessions, or bury people or marry people or baptize their children.'

Gerry was so unable to believe this that he again thought he was being tested.

'But surely you could retire, you've earned it I'm sure, and not do those things and still be a priest, still say Mass.'

'I knew you would be shocked, Gerry.' He gave the first smile of the whole encounter. 'I'm expecting a lot of people will.'

Gerry was more than shocked. He couldn't meet Father Feeny's look. He stared at his glass, at the fire, at Father Feeny's well-polished shoes on the rug in front of him. There was a long silence. Gerry tried to think of something to say.

'Come to the table now,' the old man said, 'and you can ask me if there's anything you don't understand.' The throwaway tone had gone now and he sounded kind and patient and a little tired. As he shared out cold roast meats and ham, pickles and salad and bread, Father Feeny outlined his plans. He would rent a house in Ballycastle where his sister and a niece were living. A house-keeper would be found for him and the proprietor of the Royal Hotel was an excellent cook. 'I think I shall be able to persuade him to do me Meals on Wheels.' He smiled. 'I shall walk on the beach, I may get a dog – I like dogs – there's a music society and it's within reach of Belfast which, as you know, I much prefer to Dublin. And, as I know you're wondering, yes, I shall go to Mass, perhaps not every day. It'll be such a relief to have someone else do the hocus pocus.'

Gerry nodded stupidly. He couldn't respond properly. It seemed he was always to feel confused here among the neatly hung prints and the chess pieces and to be clutching a wine glass, at a loss for words. He tried to warm to Father Feeny's plans but in most of his mind there was outrage. This was desertion – and with a smile! There had to be something behind it. Even so late in life it could happen. *Cherchez la femme!*

'Have you told Mrs O'Neill?'

'No. Apart from my sister you are the first. I shall miss Mrs O'Neill.'

'And she'll miss you. We all will.'

'Kind of you to say it. But I would have to be going sooner or later. I'd rather not wait for you-know-who to shuffle the cards once more.' He inclined his head towards the place where the bishop lived.

And then the jokes began. References to the bishop (You-know-who, His nibs, Himself) had been wry and allusive in the past. Now the jokes came like birds gathering in the branches. Gerry found it hard to concentrate. Somehow Marcella was back in the conversation. 'What about it then, Gerry? Twenty, thirty years' time and it's Marcella for bishop. Wouldn't she make a good one? I can see her in the vestments now.'

Gerry joined in but his laughter was shaky. This was more than he could handle. He thought of Micky Martin twenty years ago in that cold room in Portknock trying to weigh his love of God and his desire for Anne McCallion. Or was it the other way round? 'Do I know what love means?' he had asked Gerry, who sat frowning, trying to identify.

And now here was the champion, the man who took all prizes for integrity and commitment, raising his glass to 'Marcella for bishop, Marcella for Pope!'

Gerry felt ashamed that he had laughed at Marcella. He would talk to her again. But what could he advise her now?

He tried to return to stable things, asking Father Feeny some practical questions which were easily answered. He dealt so blandly with it all that Gerry realized this had been planned for a long time. Gerry lacked the courage or their friendship lacked the intimacy for him to ask Why? Only towards the end of the evening did the parish priest come close to explaining.

'I don't believe it's His will that an old man should rise early on cold mornings to perform a service for a few other freezing souls when the job can perfectly well be done by somebody else. I've played my part and played it to the best of my abilities. It's your turn now, Gerry. Or perhaps the Marcella Devlins of the world.'

Gerry walked home in a state of bitter confusion. The town was quiet now and the lights reflected on the bay came and went as breezes ruffled the water. His anger of a week ago had been specific, pure even, compared with what he felt now. It was like trying to walk on very dry sand. When Micky left it had been to get married. Others had political reasons. But Father Feeny had no need. The worst of it was the feeling that the old man's decision exposed his own conservatism. He was a plodder, worthy, unimaginative. There was something quietly, infuriatingly radical in Father Feeny's action.

The phone was ringing as he opened the front door.

'Yes, Aidan. Yes, I've just kicked against it coming in the door. No, not jogging, just coming in. No, you're right, don't tell me the score. Good, good, I'm glad you enjoyed it. No, DON'T TELL ME! I'm looking forward to it. I'll be watching it now. Enjoy your evening. Yes. Thank you, thank you. Goodbye.'

He set up the video and brought a can of Budweiser and a packet of crisps from the kitchen. The small lamp near the TV blew its bulb as he switched it on. He sat in the darkness staring at the bright screen. He had to stay. It was an act of duty, of love even. The game seemed like a good game, full of incident. He remembered the cries from the shore, the howls of near agony which had been the background to Father Feeny's untroubled revelations. Something Aidan said had led Gerry to expect a result

of one-all, but as he sat there with a headache deepening in his
skull, it gradually became clear that this was to be a goalless
draw.

JOE SHEERIN

The Whaler

A s soon as I rounded the corner I stopped in sharp disbelief. On the hill in front of me, past which the road led, a man was growing out of the field. His head and torso and waist were above ground. His long trailing coat, tent-like, obscured the spot he grew out of or was buried in. The light was behind the figure and the large hat and the profile and the trailing coat were in shadow. As I slowly neared the strange sight, screwing my eyes against the light, I recognized the shape.

It was the Whaler.

The idol of my young imagination. One from the old tribe of gods; hero, magician and priest.

He had left our town-land as a boy. Too small. Too myopic. Too trivial. (My father, his schoolmate, had stuck to the land like a badger.) He went to Liverpool. Jumped ship. Went to Marseilles. Jumped ship. Jumped ship again in Singapore. Turned up in Newfoundland on a whaling boat.

I had read books on whaling. And they froze my blood and boiled my imagination. The cold seas we knew so well off the Donegal coast, black tufts of water and the breakers like grouse. One wooden ship alone in the vast moorlands of freezing water hunting the monster of the deep ocean. Whale shark and hump-back, sperm whale and minke.

I knew the chronology of the hunt by heart. A boy frozen for hours in the crow's nest was the first to see them.

'Thar she blows.'

His unbroken voice reached the bosun on starboard.

'Thar she blows. Lower the boats, men.'

His voice is harsh and cruel.

The Whaler is the first man in the first lowered boat. His great

arms and his wide shoulders, the harpoon firm in his hands.
Lashed with wind and scourged with spray, he stands in the
gunnel while the boat like a corkshead fights through the walls of
water. The Whaler roars and the seas roar and the whale roars
when the harpoon propelled by those mighty arms digs home.
Deep into the demonic body. He stands on the prow and takes the
strain of the racing line and the rocking boat. Four watches later
they return, exhausted. The great body towed behind them is
subdued and lashed with rope. The Whaler, standing astride the
gargantuan shape, sinks his harpoon again and again into the
hillocks of blubber. Small wells of oil erupt with each thrust of the
point.

In truth I had only met the Whaler once, for he was a secretive
man and that secrecy increased his air of mystery. He lived alone
and drank alone. He doffed his hat to women but he was a man's
man in the way that a stag is a male's male, if you know what I
mean. Alone, watchful, silent, a bit disdainful. He didn't go to
Mass or stand for the Angelus or keep Lent. He had the cure for
ringworm, a disease of cattle, and that's what brought him to
our house. One of our cows had the rough scabs on her neck and
around the haunches of her shoulder. My father sent for the
Whaler. He came wearing his large dark hat and long coat. He
was a big man with the chin of authority. For a big man he
spoke with the still voice I associated with priests. I hung around
them in the kitchen longing to talk to him but far too shy to
phrase the first question. Anyway, my father guarded his company jealously and the two men sat drinking porter mostly in
silence.

'I will need to attend to her after dark and alone,' he
announced. The cow recovered and the Whaler accepted a bottle
of whiskey.

As I reached a point within some yards of him I realized to my
extreme embarrassment that he was defecating. The road led by
within a few feet from where he squatted. I developed an intense
interest in the hedge on the opposite side. The whitethorns were
in blossom and the wild strawberries opened a pale flower. A wren

scuttled from twig to twig. I might have escaped had not his soft voice called me to attention.

'What's your hurry, boy?'

I looked at him. And beyond him the May morning, the grass slightly wet, the mountains bluish in the distance.

'It's a fine day.'

He pulled some lush grass expertly and reached under his cloak. He made brushing motions upwards, threw the grass from him, stood tall in the meadow and pulled his trousers around his waist. He belted them with great care. I was too pained to watch but too embarrassed to move away.

'Sit down,' he said, 'it's a day for slacking.' He crossed the ditch and sat on the grassy bank, motioning me to sit beside him. I had been shopping for my mother and my bag of shopping rested beside me. A fresh white loaf sat on top of the week's groceries. A wasp looked interested.

'I hear you're a clever lad at school. Eileen Early tells me y'are.'

Eileen Early. It took me a minute to link the name. Mrs Early was our teacher. She married Jack Early. Jack, an old wounded soldier, always hoppity-hopping to the well, died a few years ago. They had no children but she loved us as she would have loved the fruits of her own body, nurturing the slow and priding in the fast. Once she spoke to us about the infinite mercy of God's love. When she had finished, I quite liked God. She made him seem such a soft and reasonable man.

'I like geography,' I said.

'The world is a big place. This,' and he pointed to the area where he had recently carried out the business of the morning, 'is a small field.'

'The world is a big place,' I replied, picking up on what he had said. This was my area. 'I've been reading books about the world. About the frozen North. About the Arctic.'

I looked at him with the dumb eyes of devotion. He was looking away vacantly towards the whale-shaped mountains.

'Y'know what I'm talking about, the Arctic, whaling.'

He looked at me without replying. It was one of those quiet mornings when conversations slow to a trickle. I was afraid he might retreat into silence where my small voice could not wake him.

'Y'know the life you led. The frozen north. Whaling. Man against beast.'

He looked at me in a pitying way. 'Can you keep a secret?' he asked. He spoke evenly, enunciating his words like a conspirator. I nodded, unsure of what was to follow. He got up. I followed. He towered above me. Taller and broader. I fixed a point about his Adam's apple. 'Can you keep a secret?' he asked again. I nodded. As I looked up into his grey eyes he reached out his right hand, the horrid hand that had previously plucked the grass. I took it, careful not to offend but careful not to infect. It was a softer handshake than I had imagined.

There was a silence when we reassumed our seats. I waited. The morning hung between sunrise and the decision of noon.

'I never saw a whale in my life.' He broke the silence.

Involuntarily I turned to stare at him in the shock of disbelief. I could not credit what I was hearing. Never saw a whale. The hero of my lonely stories. The harpoonist of my wild imaginings. This was not possible. My lower jaw hung on its hinge. He put his hand reassuringly on my knee. The left hand. 'I never saw a whale alive. I ran boats on the St Lawrence. That's in Canada.'

'I know,' I broke in petulantly. 'The St Lawrence and the Mackensie are the two main river systems.'

'You're a clever gosoon.' He used the old Gaelic term for boy.

Pride seeped in to fill some of the vacuum left by disillusionment.

'I was no sailor. I ran the St Lawrence seaway only. Small freight, fish and furs and grain. But they want heroes here. It's not enough to travel. You must see a unicorn as well. If they want to believe I fought whales, let them do it. But you're a young man of the new generation. You don't need this. I can tell you. Keep the secret.' And he squeezed my knee.

'You never saw a whale,' I repeated more to myself than to him.

'I saw the skeleton of one in a museum in Gander. It wasn't as big as you'd think.'

'How big?'

'Oh, about twice the size of that bush.' He pointed to a blackthorn deadly in blossom and shaped like a large mushroom. About twice as big as that? If that was the size of a whale it was minute compared to the whales of my imagination. One could lay it low with a crowbar. One could spear it with a pitchfork.

'I thought they were bigger,' I said in a numbed voice. 'About as big as that hill,' and I pointed to a curve-shaped outcrop of land in the near distance.

He laughed. He laughed quietly and his great size shook beside me until I thought he was perhaps drunk as he was rumoured to like a drop and was sometimes seen drinking alone as the evenings closed around him. But his merriment was not that of a drunk.

'You know what that hill reminds me of?' he asked, throttling his laughter.

'A whale,' I answered.

'Not a whale. A woman's tit. Do you see how it swells there and sags there and hangs out on a point like a nipple?' And he drew the shape in the air with his big hand as he spoke.

I didn't see for I was innocent of all trivial things. It looked like a whale to me.

'Ellen said you're an imaginative boy.'

We sat in silence. The drone of the morning descended. A wasp landed on my loaf and settled there, twitching his tail. I shooed him away for I feared the poison of his tongue might infect the bread.

'Do you like her?'

'Who?'

'Eileen. Mrs Early.'

'She's a good teacher. She knows a lot about the world.'

'She does that. And she has a lot of time for you. She's retiring early. Going back to Galway. Her mother is an invalid. You know that, do you?'

I knew that.

'We'll miss her.'

'So we will.' He got up again. 'Stand up,' he commanded as if he had reached a decision. 'Can you keep another secret?'

I had agreed to keep one I would have preferred not to have known. Another would not make much difference. We shook hands again. Now we stood on level ground and my eyes rested on his chin. We sat down. He dug his toe in the dirt. His right hand held his left hand in the gap between his two thighs. He slightly hunched over. Hairs like cat's whiskers grew from his ear. He struggled to tell me something.

'She's a good woman.' He finally spoke. His slow words crossing the gulf between us.

I knew she was a good woman. This was hardly a secret.

'She's a good woman. A man's woman.'

This was new territory. He looked at me. I noticed he had a sad face almost as if he were about to cry.

'She likes you. You're a boy who keeps his own company. I've known her for years.' He looked at me searchingly. I guarded the loaf where the wasp still had ambitions.

We continued in silence, both of our eyes wandering towards the tit-shaped, whale-shaped hill.

He turned sharply to me. 'Many a good ride I had from her. Even when Jack was alive.'

A thunderclap of silence stopped the morning in its tracks. His whaleless past was nothing compared to this. Goose pimples rose and died on my neck. I hunched my shoulders. I dug my toe in the earth. I stared at the ground as if I could X-ray the secret minerals underneath. I dared not look at him although I was aware that he was watching me. I would have taken my shopping and run for home or left my shopping to his mercy. But I was so deep in the conspiracy that he would never let me live to broadcast his secrets.

Well I'd be damned. And all the time she was teaching us religion.

He continued speaking.

'I rode her in the kitchen when he was lying upstairs and in the hayfield and in the byre. I never met a woman like her.'

The first shock of the news had aged my body. I felt very tired. I knitted my hands behind my neck and lay back. The sun filled the whole sky. He talked some more but I wasn't listening.

One of us got up. Then both. I stood on the incline above him and looked him in the eye.

'I'll keep your secret.'

He reached down right-handed and pulled the end off my loaf and walked down the hill eating it. At the time I didn't realize it but that was the last I was to see of him. A month later he hanged himself from the couple of a byre.

At the top I paused and looked down across several fields towards Early's cottage. As I watched, she came out of the house carrying a can, going to the spring to fetch water. As she walked and swished the can the light caught it, gleaming and ungleaming.

Thar she blows.

PAUL LENEHAN

Great Bus Journeys of Dublin

Lynch had been making notes a long time with a view to
making public his private thoughts on the Great Bus Journeys
of Dublin, for the same reason that a literary critic might publish a
slim volume of sestinas, or a mathematician might produce a
paper employing only Euclidean geometry to prove the existence
of God: to delight his contemporaries. To qualify as a Great Bus
Journey, Lynch had first decided that the candidate should
contain, within the environs which marked out its course, those
contrasts of scene and expectation which a route such as the 17
exemplified. The 17 began by the blocks of flats near Rialto but
ended in Blackrock, by the sea, by the old outdoor baths, the
middle of whose diving boards had provided him, nineteen years
before, his friends' faces bobbing in the pool below, with the first
stern test of his adolescence.

He had cycled to the sea in those days with those same friends
he saw no more, and had often walked his bike home when
sufficient air had escaped from the mysterious slow punctures
which were a feature of his youth. The 17 then was just that blur
of noise which passed him at Clonskeagh, or went sailing down
Merrion Avenue with its passengers in steerage, a full cargo of
parents either single or doubled, complete with progeny, beach-
towels, sun-block, spades and buckets, and often a perplexed nun,
who had boarded in good faith at Fosters Avenue. Now it was the
contrasts which delighted him most – the hard sharp streets at
one terminus, the houses with tennis courts at the other; the tiny
balconies fluttering with Monday's washing, and a window which
overlooked a cupola and the obedient sea.

Contrast, then, was the first criterion he had decided upon
when assessing the credentials of a route. And yet, a bus such as

the 46A, which departed early from grimy Ormond Quay and chugged brutally up the dull dual-carriageway before meandering through a succession of equally ignored housing developments, such a bus displayed to Lynch such a remorseless consistency of intention as to be considered almost heroic. And it, too, finished by the sea, in Dun Laoghaire, where the ferry waited obsequiously for emigrants, and for gleeful students of English returning to Europe, and, more than once, for Lynch himself. So it was that he concluded that the necessary condition for election to the pantheon was for the journey to contain some personal significance for the traveller – that diving-board, the gawping ferry.

And if the greatness of a bus journey was to do with its particular resonance, then Lynch knew the 75 was disqualified for sure, because he was sitting in it for the very first time. And wearing a suit, which too was rare. He was the only passenger on the upper deck, and was happy enough to accept that distinction on a February morning not yet bright enough to camouflage the cold. The bus choked its way to the top of a rise where, away in the distance, Lynch saw an industrial estate laid out below like a scale model. That was his destination, so he fixed his tie. As the bus swung through the first in a selection of roundabouts, he tied his shoes for a second time, tied the laces tight across each instep, and the pressure served to concentrate his mind.

Lynch had earned himself an interview for the position of Clerical Administrator at a firm which distributed car tyres from a warehouse in the industrial estate, and whose small office, finding itself with a pressing need for such a functionary, had advertised in all the papers for same. His initial application having met with a positive response, Lynch had investigated his slanted wardrobe, rediscovered his faithful suit, and resuscitated the cloth with a wire brush. And thus he found himself making his debut voyage on the 75, boarding the bus like a corporate raider, his cheeks chapped from too vigorous a shaving, which made him look younger – no bad thing all things considered, he considered, as the bus chugged on.

Lynch had worked before, of course, in the bright headquarters of a computer firm, but that was different. He wasn't much more than a school-leaver then, with a decent set of results, anxious for the respectability imparted once a young man has chosen his career-path for the next half-a-century. Lynch had pushed paper around his desk in an open-plan office, and, as the years passed, he had got to push more significant items, but always he was pushing. Often liking to think for himself, he surmised that there might be more to life, and hence took advantage of the opportunity to take leave-of-absence for twelve months in order to travel.

This he did, living in Durban where he worked for months off the back of a truck, and near Brisbane, where he often slept in a tepee, but eventually returning home, riddled with doubt that, after all, there might be less to life than his earlier calculations had led him to believe. Such doubts in time made him mope too much, and compelled him to negotiate a part-time contract with his employers which they eagerly agreed to, for they knew by then that the management-potential of the boy who had come to them years before with marvellous acne was minimal. Thirteen months after his return from another hemisphere, Lynch handed in his resignation, having saved enough money to live for a while; because the decision to opt out was entirely his own, his parents felt it only right that they should be disappointed in him.

There is no place bleaker than an industrial estate in February – Lynch knew this proposition would be difficult to disprove. Frozen trees lined the bare drives, and the huge warehouses, lacking windows, resembled stippled nuclear-silos. People left buses and ran from the wind, and vanished through yellow doors in the sides of buildings. Lynch decided, irrespective of personal significance, that any bus which entered an industrial estate was eliminated from contention. For how could such a bus compare with, for instance, the glorious 33 which, once it had shaken off the debilitating influence of the city, headed for the Big Tree at Swords, and then became almost silly, weaving a carefree path first to Lusk and from there hugging the coast into Rush, thence to Skerries (where his family had holidayed many years before in a hired caravan), the odyssey finishing at last in Balbriggan, where the ecstatic traveller, after compulsory debriefing, could purchase candy-floss from a booth?

The 75 slid into an oil-slick by a lump of broken pavement, braked hard, and stopped close enough for the time being to the terminus, a raw outpost where a nurse in a cardigan smoked a cigarette. Lynch found the warehouse easily enough, beside a great bank of soil, on top of which an earth-mover rested like a robot-sentry. Unseen, from behind this bank he heard a sound like a pick hitting rock, a lonely type of noise. He envisioned a muffled-up man left behind to keep up the appearance of industry, of progress, hitting out uselessly at the hard earth as per instructions. Lynch sheltered by that huge sculpted heap of soil and smoked a cigarette. Two taut birds jeered from a shivering tree. Lynch scuffed the welt of his shiny shoe against a slab, and the noise was sufficient to startle them into flight. They spun round for a time, then headed over the bank, over the earth-mover, and away. He killed the cigarette and dropped a pair of mints into his mouth.

A Mr Walsh and a Mr Higgins received him at the warehouse, and bade him seat himself in a dull little room into which daylight entered only by accident through an air vent. A sore yellow glow shone in its stead from filaments on each wall, and shone on the scarred table where Messrs Walsh and Higgins sat side-by-side, and where Lynch sat dutifully opposite. The two men began by poring with intent over his staunch c.v.

'Twenty-eight, are you?' Mr Walsh abruptly enquired, as if by accident.

Lynch agreed that he had reached that landmark, and his response tallied with the information given on his c.v.; and, although in real life he was not so very far away from his thirty-third birthday and looked it each morning just on waking, he took a nervous delight in the knowledge that there was not a lot the Messrs Higgins and Walsh could do right that minute no matter what age or nationality or gender or political persuasion he might declare himself to be.

'There are some gaps here, you know,' Mr Higgins then decided, pointing with his finger at the opened page.

'Yes, there are gaps all right,' Mr Walsh harmonized.

Lynch felt that first cold lick of fear in his throat, like the desperation felt by an examinee with two full questions to answer as the invigilator announces a mere ten minutes remaining in which to get a life.

'I wanted to experience different cultures, different ethnic traditions and social systems, to broaden my mind and to give me a more expansive world-view, do you know what I mean?'

The Messrs Higgins and Walsh stared hard at him, the former nodding minutely, the latter not. Lynch sat his ground and awaited their next move.

'Yes,' said Mr Higgins, 'there may be some value in what you say. But, you haven't worked much, have you, in the last good while?'

'I've been unlucky,' Lynch revealed. 'I know the economy has picked up, and that's good news for us all, but, to be frank, vacancies in my area have been few and far between. Believe me, I've tried, I've tried hard.'

This last assertion was patently untrue, Lynch knew it as he watched his interviewers turn to the next page of his hardy c.v. For a number of years now he had been content just to survive, and to claim all time as his own. If he fancied a coffee he drank a coffee on the mezzanine level of malls, or read a book on a bench, or just stretched out on the floor of his room and listened for tremors. He lived life just like the rich man, but without the hard currency, which is where his system let him down.

In what seemed like no time at all the compulsory winding-down of the interview was reached, and Mr Higgins asked: 'But why do you think you might be suitable for this job?' Lynch, having worked all those years in Admin. for the computer firm, knew that a highly motivated nine-year-old could be trained in less than a month to carry out the duties of a Clerical Administrator. Instead, he talked about the importance of his experience in a similar position some years before, about his determination to resume his rightful place in the workforce, and about the commitment he already felt to the Messrs Higgins and Walsh and their warehouse of tyres.

Why he wanted the job, of course, was because the starting rate which it offered would provide him, even after tax, with almost twice the money the dole offered, and now he needed money more; to save for the course on hypnotherapy which he coveted, to replace his ill-fitting collection of garments, and to finance his rediscovered sex drive, which had absented itself during his darkest days, but now, again fit and firm, had directed itself at the woman with red hair who supervised the launderette, and who handled his basket of briefs with a gentle eroticism which staggered him sideways.

He was allowed to expound upon the importance of staff loyalty for just a little longer before papers were shuffled, glances exchanged, and Mr Higgins, in time-honoured fashion, applied the finishing touch.

'Is there anything you'd like to . . . eh, ask us at all?'

'The bus, the 75,' Lynch enquired, having prepared his question earlier that morning, 'is that the only service into the estate?'

This practical enquiry seemed to baffle his interlocutors, for they ceased shuffling paper and sat quite still.

'Is there a more interesting route, I'm just wondering?' Lynch continued, in their silence.

Mr Higgins took a fountain pen from his breast-pocket, unscrewed the cap to no avail, replaced it, returned the pen to his pocket, and nodded, while Mr Walsh watched intently as his colleague performed his manoeuvre.

'I'm not quite sure what . . . ?' offered Mr Higgins.

'Don't you like it?' Mr Walsh enquired.

'Well, frankly, no,' Lynch decided, offering a smile to show his possession of a vibrant sense of humour, so necessary if everyone in the work-place was to pull together for the greater good. 'I mean, it's hardly one of the Great Bus Journeys of Dublin, am I right?'

'I drive, myself,' Mr Higgins was moved enough eventually to reveal.

'We both do,' Mr Walsh added. 'Why don't you ask at a depot?'

This good advice concluded the interview. Lynch shook hands

with both men, who both wished him all the best in the future irrespective of what might happen there, which was more than kind.

Outside, at reception, two gangling youths waited in grey suits, and their eyes searched Lynch for clues as he passed. 'See you next Monday,' he called to the receptionist, and strode away. At the bus shelter he lit a cigarette, less in celebration than to salute the possible – it was still possible that no eighteen-year-old with a stutter would apply for a job for which he or she was vastly overqualified; it was still possible that those ample gaps in his c.v. would be viewed as signifying an enviable flexibility of approach rather than proof that the perpetrator was guilty of treason against the institutions of the state. The more he thought about his interview, the less distressed he felt – even when the 75 arrived, and he faced the prospect of that dull journey back. He took the top deck again, and the bus lurched away, and rain began to fall on the corrugated roofs, and men in dungarees huddled beneath awnings.

Because it was still early, and the rain looked like easing, he decided to return home, collect the wedge and putter, and connect up with the 44B to Glencullen, where a golf ball could be hacked around a windy pitch 'n' putt course on top of the mountain. Due to sharing much of its route with the fabulous 44, which began at Burgh Quay and ended thirteen miles away in pastoral Ennis-kerry, in an entirely different county, the Glencullen bus was debarred from contention as a Great Bus Journey, in the same way that the number 1 was debarred due to the brevity of its route, allied to the fact that it left its terminus only twice each day and never on a Sunday, and was therefore regarded as non-existent by many, or legendary at least, the unicorn of buses. With the industrial estate far behind, and a heater blowing warmth around his ankles, and the prospect to come of shanks, slices, and many misread putts, Lynch felt nearer to bliss. He closed his eyes, opened them in time to see a light change to red. He lay down on the back seat with his legs curled, and when he tried to open his eyes again, they refused, and the bus rocked him gently, warmly, as it went on its way.

When he awoke, the 75 stood quite still on a ragged stretch of lane with a few cottages alongside one kerb only. The rain, as he had foreseen, had drifted, and the same weak sun shone one more time. He went downstairs to investigate and found every other passenger had gone, vanished, along with the driver. No one had thought to check the seats for sleeping men, and so there he was, becalmed in an unknown lay-by. An orange triangle parked behind the bus signalled a mechanical failure of some description. In one direction the lane widened, like a tar river, and Lynch headed towards its mouth. The noise of traffic sounded almost suddenly, as if a switch had been flicked, and increased in volume as he walked towards its source. And there, at the end of the lay-by, he could see that the main road was not far away. Across a strip of rough land, a wire fence marked the border with the carriageway. It presented itself as a simple operation, merely to cross the scrub-patch and climb a fence whose height was not daunting for a man pretending to be twenty-eight. Lynch, instead, first sat down on a hard ridge in the full glare of the bright cold sun.

His formal clothes felt less awkward on him now, his leather shoes had ceased to pinch so persistently. He felt more tranquil somehow as the cars flung past him, thundering madly over the rumble-strips, so urgent, so necessary, all those lives careering past with the same sun flashing for a moment off every wind-screen, as if the occupants had been chosen. Extraordinary, he knew, to feel so suddenly content, with the noise of the motorway soothing him now like the pulse of a steady breath, the hard brightness all around him as if he, too, might be chosen for some purpose. He squinted hard as a single-decker powered into the distance, thought it might have been the 44B, but then the 44B never came this way – or did it, for where was he anyway, stranded in some lay-by he'd never seen before, where was he? Maybe, he wondered, maybe this was the mystical point where all the bus-routes crossed, like those sites where ley-lines meet which become shrines where people gather.

Behind him the 75 still slumbered, broken down, awaiting repair, and the thought crossed his mind that perhaps the bus had broken down on purpose, somehow aware of his low evaluation of its route, determined to become a Great Bus Journey no matter what the cost, to make a place for itself in his memory as the bus on which he had once been abandoned. That was stupid, he knew, that was so stupid it made him smile. The shouts of children came from a garden, and he heard them approach. He knew they had stopped, shocked or frightened by the strange man sitting on the edge, dressed in his best suit, so he pushed himself up, pulled a silly face for their amusement, then hurried down the hill through the bunches of weeds.

AIDAN MATHEWS

Waking the Jew

Then he realized that he was not dreaming and that the hammering was happening at his own front door. The other, browner beat was the sound of his heart in hiding, the sound of its startled darting. Where had it been all this time? It was broken yet it worked. He put his right hand over it, in under the eiderdown duvet, as if it were a baby whose breastfeeding would betray everybody.

'Wake up,' a voice was crying from out in the one-way street; and the voice was a woman's. But why were they using a woman? They had never used women before.

'Wake up,' she was calling. 'Wake up.'

So he lay still and inhaled through his mouth to listen, listen closely, listen carefully, because of the bluebottle noise of his sinuses. And if he lived, if he survived, if he went on existing, he would have them yanked out straightaway, those polyps in his nose, under local anaesthetic in the day-care clinic on the coast road, where there was no mortuary with a fake plaque saying Hospital Administration. Because it was not fair to be always stifled, always suffocated. He had never smoked. He was the only boy in the building who didn't scavenge for fag-ends. Yesterday he had traded tobacco for aspirin, brilliantine for biscuits, and brought them home in his underpants to his mother who had kissed him on the forehead like an important corpse and told him, her Solomon, her sweet King Solomon, that he was responsible.

'It's time,' the woman was yelling. 'Are you in the land of the living?'

Am I? he thought. Am I responsible? Lord, rescue my soul from their destructions, my darling from the lions. I have a right to breathe easy in my seventies, for Christ's sake. I am tired of all this shit.

'Bring out your dead. Bring out your dead.'

That was not her, the woman. She was down at the door by the wooden washtub where crocus bulbs grew upside-down among the winter pansies and where he had buried the last of the dollars in oilskin when the border closed. The baritone whoops had come from the corner, the house with the trellis. But the house with the trellis was Christian, a cross in the toilet.

'Say if you're there,' she implored him. 'I'll take No for an answer.'

By now they would have blocked both ends of the road, the lane to the grass courts of the tennis club and the alley in which a eucalyptus was patiently uprooting the hydrant. He could hear the trucks clearing their throats, gunning the motors to blot out boots and shouting, the garbage chucked like children into the stainless steel of the pig's snout. Yet no one would look out; no one would look up. They would stare instead at the softly boiling eggs as they evened the nooses of their neckties and their wives slipped studs with gold initials through the holes in their shirt-cuffs. Mass bells should be pealing too, cassettes of a carillon spooling beside the tannoys in the church tower. That would be heaven.

Solomon sat up. He sat upright. He was a man who knew what day of the week it was. It was Friday, and Friday was bin day. One thing followed from another if you let it. Had he put out the bins? Had he bins to put out? Come to that, had he bins? He had a black bag. Perhaps he had two black bags. You never could tell what you might stumble upon in your own backyard. That was what it meant to be a widower, to be a man without a woman. For the first time in forty-two years, you found out when the rubbish was collected.

'Mr Blatt.' It was Number Seven, his next door neighbour, the indefatigable one. 'You asked me last night to rouse you this morning. Rouse me early tomorrow, you said. Well, it's early, and it's tomorrow.'

Thunder of the knocker, lightning of the bell; and after the din of its bitter dentistry, fists on the frosted pane, first gloves, then gauntlets. There was an order to everything, even to urgency. But was it night or day? The blind he had drawn was the colour of morning. Its black had begun to go grey. That was a plus. That was a surplus.

'Rosen, it's me. It's Tess. Tess of the Dodder Valley. I'm in my dressing gown.'

Wait, he thought, wait a minute, you bloody woman. Wait until my heart stops; wait till I find where my eyes are. And he went searching behind him, roaming the hill of paperbacks on what had been Melanie's side, the window-side, the white east of the bed, and frisking finally the tinfoil jackets of the antacid tablets he received on the tongue like a Catholic between killings.

'Don't break my door down,' he said. 'The novelty has worn off that one.'

His glasses were hidden in Jane Austen, at the page where he had stopped when the Judy Garland midnight movie season started at ten to the hour with the star in blackface for Harry Rapf's *Everybody Sing*; and when he put them on, the room arrayed itself around him, tidy and detailed, like the way it had looked when their granddaughter spring cleaned at the child-minder's rate because she was saving for slacks and a scooter. Now he knew where he was and who he was. He could leave the why to the rabbi and the how to the interns; but he would take great care to be buried with his tortoiseshells. He had been right as well to leave in Melanie's contact lenses. After all, they had not removed her aluminium hip. They had not hacked at her bridge-work with mechanic's pliers.

'Mrs Cassidy,' he said, as he came down the stairs, one by one, to the hall. 'Mrs Cassidy, you would wake the dead. Do you know that?'

'I have a hard enough time waking the living,' she said back. Her hand was in through the hairy letterbox, wagging at him. Where were her rings gone?

'I was in the shower,' he said, and he sat himself down on the bottom step, beside the pampas grass, where he had levered out a carpet-rod to stow beneath his bed in case of burglars. He was not about to open the door in a pair of boxer shorts and a scar from a duodenal ulcer.

'You were in the shower?' she said, and her shadow blew its nose at the glass. 'Be careful in the shower, Mr Blatt. You could do yourself an injury. Where would I be then?'

Her breasts were soft and spacious. He could write on them, like vellum, with a ballpoint pen, smiling at the sink of the nib in the spring of the skin; and she had studied it, upside down of course, with a double chin from straining, saying: Solomon, Solomon, Solomon Rosenblatt. My solemn man, my happy man, my roses and blather. What are you doing to my breast? What are you doing to my heart?

It was the first and last time he had written the Lord's name in Hebrew.

'I can't let you in, Mrs Cassidy,' he said. 'I am more or less in the image and likeness of God. It is no fit state to be seen in.'

Four phones rang at once. Rang in the hall, rang in the kitchen, rang in the bedroom, rang in the bathroom. The klaxon in the bathroom was for strokes, falls you could not rise to. A bathroom was a breeding-ground for embolisms, thromboses, cardiovascular gnashing; for clots, vomit, stoppages, prayer, incontinence, embraces, choking, piss. Where there were taps and tiles, the Red Sea would not part, the Jordan would not ford. Sand would flow from the faucets.

'Are you not driven demented?' said his next door neighbour.

He reached out. Lifted the handset like the dressing on a wound.

'I don't mean dementia,' said Mrs Cassidy's shadow. 'I mean annoyed, like.'

'How did you get my number?' he said. 'I am ex-directory.'

'This is your wake-up call,' said the phone. 'Thank you for using the service.'

'Thank you very much,' he said. He had tugged a plume of pampas grass across the brown of his breasts. The indefatigable one might be seventy-odd, but her corneas came from a long line of snipers.

'I hope you did not think I said dementia,' said Mrs Cassidy's shadow. 'Did you think I said dementia?'

'This is your wake-up call,' the phone said. 'Thank you for using the service.'

'Anyway,' the shadow called. 'Happy anniversary.'

'Thank you very much,' he said. 'I can hear you. I heard you the first time.'

'How many years would you be married?' said the shadow at the door.

'It is not that sort of anniversary,' he said. 'It is more history.'

'Everything's history now,' the shadow said. 'Look at me.'

'This is your wake-up call,' the phone said. 'Thank you for using the service.'

He swung the receiver down like a club on the cradle. Then, after a moment, hoisted it to hear again. Had he broken the bloody thing? But the distant air-raid siren of the dial tone was there still, still low and clear.

'Hello?' said Mrs Cassidy. 'Hello?'

And he had thought at the time it was strange for a Soviet soldier to say that, as if he were a Yankee, as if he were Johnny Weissmuller meeting the first Europeans, but the man had gone on saying it from the doorway of the hut, hello, hello, hello; and Solomon had said the only Russian word that he could remember. He had said da; he had said da, da, like a baby dragging itself behind the corduroys of its father. And the soldier spreadeagled himself at the door frame to protect his boots while forty papery corpses watched his breakfast of yoghurt and coffee steam in a parallelogram of January sunlight.

'Are you all right for bread and milk?'

'I am all right for bread and milk,' he said. 'Are you all right for bread and wine?'

'You're a terrible man.'

She was right. He had come from a malodorous drop. He would have to change. There was no two ways about it. His shorts were stale. He could smell his penis. If he had a coronary on the dual carriageway and they saw the state of his underpants in the morgue, he would die a thousand deaths. So he would strip off,

stand in the shower, and soap himself. He might even sing the
Shema. Why not? Every man was a tenor in his own toilet. As long
as he said Adoschem instead of Adonai, what harm could there be?
Hadn't Melanie sung Kiddush at the ironing board like a second
Sophie Kurtzer? Besides, his granddaughter danced with the Torah
at a feminist minyat in a Tel Aviv sports hall, and she dwelleth in
Israel even unto this day; she had not been smitten in the knees,
and in the legs, with a sore botch. To be sure, her convertible had
been daubed with acrylic paint from a spray can, but that was the
old people for you nowadays. In the dormitory suburbs of Zion the
just did not sleep. They kept vigil. They were vigilantes.

'I am going to Mass now,' Mrs Cassidy called.

'I am going to wash now,' he told her. 'In ten minutes I will be a
new man.'

'You could be talking about baptism,' she said.

'No,' he said. 'I am not talking about baptism. All baptism is
baptism by fire. I am talking about sprinklers.'

'Shalom, Rosen,' she said. The shadow lifted; left. Blue
brightened at the mortice lock.

'And also with you, Tess,' said Solomon Rosenblatt.

When they had come back from the hospital, Melanie went
upstairs to the bedroom and lay down. He made her a cup of tea
with a tea-bag, but there was no liner in the pedal bin, and he
stood there in the middle of the kitchen, not knowing what to do,
while the bag burned his fingers.

In the maternity hospitals they would give you the X-rays.
They would give you a parcelled miscarriage, even. They would
not file the breaking wave of your torso in a plain brown envelope,
like a frothy calendar. They would not incinerate the ruin of a
breast that had fed the mouths of her children, the hands of their
father, a breast that had grown with its quiet sister through the
early nineteen thirties while the sun danced in the sky. And when
Jean Harlow's knitted bathing suit scampered across the screen
behind the Yiddish subtitles, he had pressed his calf against hers
in the turreted church-pews of the neighbourhood cinema and
asked her was she saving her milk for her honey?

'I am saving my milk for my son,' she said to him, 'and my honey for my beloved.'

He knocked and went in.

'Room service,' he said.

'Why did you knock?' She had taken off her shoes and her earrings. She lay on the bed with her bare feet side by side as if she was at the chiropodist's.

'I don't know,' he said. 'I don't know where I am.'

'The door,' said Melanie. 'The door into the room; the door out of it.'

She had opened the window too. The long lace curtains blew like a bride's train.

'You're not going to see anything you haven't seen before,' she said. 'There is no mystery left. Come in.'

The radio was on, but it was low-down, whispering about orgasms. Orgasms are a shared responsibility. What sort of shit was that to be airing when the children were fresh home from school, spelling the morning's words for their mother, lamp, ramp, camp, and cutting out pictures in the *National Geographic* for their project on Tutankhamen?

'I should have thought of a biscuit,' he said. 'I never thought.'

'The tea is grand.'

'You like the biscuit with the sombrero on the wrapper.'

'I went off it,' she said. 'It was too noisy.'

He sat on her stool at the dressing table and looked into the three of him in the mirrors. They were not the three men of Mamre, those flickering triplets in replica buttondowns, and he, he was not Abraham. Neither was Abraham, either. My Lord, he thought, if now I have found favour in thy sight, pass not away, I pray thee, from they servant. Do not let them gut her like a halibut. Her breast is a kitchen. Dynasties victual there.

'Do you know what?'

'I don't know anything any more,' he said. 'I know zero.'

Why did he not have cancer of the prostate? Every male child of a certain age was supposed to, and he was certain of nothing on earth except his age. He had been born in the twentieth century, in the waiting room of another millennium, and he had drunk cocoa there until the stationmaster made them stand on the platform in the train's incense: so he was at least a thousand years old, if not already posthumous. Yet his prostate, whatever it was, was still working away at whatever it was meant to. He might even outlive the criminals in the Kremlin and the scented Vatican fat cats, though by then the kids in the cul-de-sac where he lived would skedaddle when they spotted him, a gangster gone gaga. His mother had settled as soot on the branch of a birch tree, but her son was a perfect specimen. The genito-urinary girl had written it down, and the cardiologist fellow had written it up. He could dress now.

'You can dress now, Doctor,' he had said. 'My girlfriend would kill for those braces. They are very in.'

'I am not a doctor,' Solomon said. 'Everybody doctors me.'

'Being a patient doesn't stop you being a doctor,' said the heart specialist.

'I am not a patient, either,' Solomon had said. 'I am neither animal nor vegetable.'

'There is nothing else to be except a patient or a doctor,' the doctor said patiently, 'unless you believe in the communion of saints. Do you believe in the communion of saints?'

'When I close my eyes,' Solomon said, 'I can hear the sounds inside my mother's stomach.'

Then he was so confused that he put his vest on back to front, and paid with Visa. In the car, in the rush hour traffic, in the red lights flaring their fireballs out of the darkness and the downpour, the neck of the singlet chafed his Adam's apple like the gloved finger of a hand tracing his throat.

'One. Four, one, five. Two, one, two,' she said.

He stared at her now in the vanity mirrors. They had taken off their watches and their glasses and gone to bed together, back to back, night after night, year in, year out, since the time the scientists sent monkeys and dogs into space to see if there was any hope of escape; but the capuchins and the poodles had brought no olive branch back to the ark, and, year in, year out, night after night, back to back, they had gone to bed together, shut out the light and practised dying, while their watches crawled like insects over the carpet and the spectacles folded their wings.

Eternity was a waste of time. He had wasted so much time he might be eternal.

'That's the code,' she said. 'Ring Joseph. Why don't you?'

'I am not in the mood to confess to a beard,' he said.

'He's not a beard; he's a shoulder.'

'A cold shoulder,' Solomon said. 'An older, colder one.'

'But a brother's, first and foremost. He doesn't stop being a brother because he's a psychiatrist.'

'No,' said Solomon. 'He is always and everywhere a beard.'

'He is not a very good beard,' she said. 'Be fair to him.'

The radio was gossiping about a celebrity who had autographed her panties for Rwanda. Each knicker weighed in at a king's ransom: the bottom line was a round figure, a cool K. Also, some chaplain at a Mickey Mouse technical college would shave half of his head for five hundred smackers. If pensioners could twist in the plaza of a multiplex, so could anyone. The Third World depended upon us. Do it now. Do it this instant.

'What time is it?'

'I don't know,' she said. 'I am never sure about America. I think they are just waking up.'

Her feet had never been barer. Ancient varnish dirtied a few toes. That was from when she had worn the espadrilles; but when had that been? He wanted to turn round, go back to her, to hold them in his lap, heavy and hard as candles, the parts of her that he had never pet-named. But it would shame him. He hadn't held her hand since the last photograph; and when had that been? How could he hold her feet? Yet he had followed her footprints through deserts and dust bowls. Where there was sand in his life, there was sight of her steps, two by two and side by side, the unoffending bedouin houseshoes.

'Listen,' she said.

Outside in the garden, the wicket gate whistled on its hinges. He had oiled them once, and lost the advantage of seconds.

'It's Number Seven,' he said. 'It's citizen Tess.'

'Pretend we're dead.'

They were Mrs Cassidy's blows as well, a Beethoven's Fifth at the hall door. The woman had militia in her blood.

'Don't,' Melanie said. 'Pretend we're dying.'

'Jesus was a Jew,' said Solomon.

'She told you too?'

'She told me too.'

'What did you say?'

'I told her I thought he was a Roman Catholic.'

They listened for the gravel and the gate; for her gate and her gravel. Then there was only the wind.

'She has hair from a saint,' Melanie said. She had drawn the duvet over her, but her feet were not hidden. They leaned like tennis shoes she had whitened and left on a ledge to dry. The binmen would pick them out and shake off the eggshell.

'You put it under your pillow,' she said. 'You sleep on it.'

Powdered milk would be provided by fourth-class pupils from a primary school. The girls were line-dancing in relays until the cows came home; and word was in that drag queen Gloria Mundi, appearing in cabaret nightly plus Sundays at the Enigma, would contribute the blouse off his back.

'If there's a miracle, you place an advertisement in the saint's magazine. It does not have to be a huge big one. It can be a little small one. "Thank you for your wonderful work on my melanoma. You're a saint. Love to all the dead"; and your initials and the postal district.'

Then he did get up and go over to her, and he did kneel down and gather her feet into his arms like stove-wood. He had seen it happen in the old proscenium picture houses and on video cassettes. Now it was happening here: to him, to her, but not to both of them. Rain on the high electrified fence made slick sounds like cigarette lighters. Brown drool from the bunk above him dripped on his navel; but his sunken umbilicus was a faraway place. It was at least a day's journey from the waterhole of his nipples across an impossible wasteland where even the bacteria had evaporated. He would run out this minute to where the dachshunds were patrolling and throw himself on the children's high voltage climbing-frame.

Calls would be answered before midnight, the radio was announcing. After midnight it would be too late. Pledge what you can while you can. Principles won't be worth pumpkins when the clock strikes twelve. Think crystal balls, not glass slippers. If you want to be in with the smell of a chance or, in the case of those celebrity unmentionables, the chance of a smell, ring-a-ling-ling instanter. People were waiting to hear from you now.

'My parents should have called me Sarah,' she said from the bed behind him. 'I am dying of my own name.'

His tears ran down his nose onto the twenty-six bones of her foot.

Then he told me, this black American soldier, to choose a pair of spectacles from the mountain. Well, at first I was afraid to. I was afraid I might start a landslide around me, and be buried for ever under the downward drifting mass of a million prescription lenses, a great, glittering ice-cap of glasses. There were glasses for reading Victor Hugo and glasses for walking a punctured bicycle, glasses for baking what hadn't been bottled, glasses for watching Westerns when the whole parterre hurrahed if they saw their misspelled surnames in the end-titles of the Hollywood shorts: best boy, key grip, bravo! But better, best of all, there were glasses for boys to take off before kissing their girlfriends, and glasses for girls to put on before teasing their boyfriends with: I thought you came here to stare at Jeanette MacDonald.

'Jesus Christ,' said the soldier, 'you are worse than a woman choosing a hat.'

Then I reached up to my own height, you see, and I stretched out my hand, and I pulled a pair of eyes from the glacier. Very gently, very gingerly, in case the hill would flinch and avalanche.

'Hosanna in the highest,' the soldier said.

Their frame was tortoiseshell, which you cannot buy now for love or money because it is too inhuman to the tortoise, and the wings were made of thin wire with flexible grips. The previous occupant had padded the left grip by winding a tiny strip of bandage around it. I imagined he had an ulcer on that ear; but why not on both? Why not on both at the same time?

'Can you see with them?' the soldier said.

I breathed on the lenses and his fingerprints appeared.

'Well?' said the soldier.

They were like the markings on an aerial photograph of a lost archaeological site.

'I can see everything clearly,' I said.

'You haven't put them on,' said the soldier. You must understand he was American. 'Put them on,' he said.

'I can see everything,' I said. 'I can see.'

'Jesus Christ,' he said, 'you couldn't see the writing on the wall when you walked into it.'

It came to me, there and then, out of the blue, why the person had padded the grip. He had leaned his head on his left hand while he wrote with his right. He was tired, you see. He's been studying for his last examination. His father hides the sherry in a bookshelf behind *Diseases of the Breast*. His mother notices nicotine stains on the moons of his fingernails. His sweetheart will open her mouth, open wide, open wider, her tongue slippy with strawberry ice-cream, so he can spot the new filling, a dull pellet of silver where the gum bristles with stitches. And he leans his head on his left hand and he writes her a letter with his right.

I can see him fifty years ago through the peephole of his glasses. Through the magnification of his lens I saw him today, this Friday, the twenty-seventh of January in the year of our Lord, Five Thousand, Seven Hundred and Fifty-Five.

Solomon stared at the students and the students peered back at him. Some of them squinted through the cage of their hands. Children had scratched at the whitewash on the inside of the windows of the tram with the compasses from their geometry sets, and sometimes he had seen their pupils at the slits as the car shuddered through the forbidden district. After that, the authorities had coated the outside of the windows with a dark preservative.

'Fifty minutes,' said the teacher whose perfume smelled like aftershave. 'That was beautifully judged, Dr Rosenblatt. We have time for a couple of questions.'

The children were so tall. They could all be basketball players,

Ethiopians leaping about. The desks were designed for old-fashioned humans. Where had these femurs been cultured? Was it diet or hormones? The girls were budding and bleeding in rooms full of dolls with real hair that thanked you when you truncheoned their mechanical stomachs, and the boys woke at night to the pool of their salmon, a water mark of tree rings radiating outward, ripples that stretched and sank and ceased like the last creases in the freshly laundered bedsheet. They in their light years, he in his heavy, what had either to say to the other? The time of their life was not the life of his times. He was a widowed man with the pong of old age and few cranky anecdotes. They were Isaac and Rebekah, lifting up their eyes in a field in a far country.

Solomon peered at the students and the students stared back at him.

'Anyway,' he said. 'Enough of Bindermichl Displaced Persons Camp in Linz. All of us lived happily ever after, once upon a time.'

They gave him a glowing ovation, some of them standing, the desks like binlids, more of them now, feet on the floor, all of them then, until it became a prank, and the teacher beat on the table with the duster, and the chalk-dust made Solomon want to sneeze, but he stifled it. His polyps would punish him later, his sinuses start up their horseflies in a lampshade.

'Thank you,' she said. 'Thanks very much. I won't forget that.'

'Not at all,' he said; but she had been talking to the students, so he worked his other hand deep into his pocket to tug at the tight elastication of his togs. They had been biting into his scrotum since he arrived at the school, but what alternative had he had? There wasn't a clean pair of underpants in the house, not even in the laundry bin. He had had to make do with his swimming-trunks.

'On behalf of us all, I would like to thank Dr Rosenblatt for sharing his life-story with Three B today. We're very privileged. We're mindful too, Geraldine O'Connell, that this isn't any ordinary day, and not because it's Friday, no, I heard that loud and clear, but because it is of course the fiftieth anniversary of the liberation of Auschwitz by the Allies.'

'The Russians,' Solomon said. 'I am not actually a doctor, you know.'

'I'm terribly sorry,' she said. Her poor cuff was streaked with pink chalk. She had made it worse by dabbing at it. That was from writing on the blackboard while he spoke. The names of his family and his friends were listed in columns behind him, under the crucifix with a missing shoulder, and the names of two of them had been spelled correctly: David and Joseph. She had not had so much luck with Mordechai and Moishele, with Yossele and Zavel, in their pale red approximations.

'You were thinking of my brother. He had that effect on women, actually. He is still a doctor, but he's no Doctor Kildare.'

'Doctor who?' she said.

'Absolutely,' said Solomon. 'He is the living image of Doctor Who.'

Their eyes met for a moment. Then the tramcar sparked, swerved, moved on. As he crossed the tracks, with the four arrowroot biscuits in one pocket and the three stamped analgesic tablets in the other, the breeze carried a slipstream of eau-de-toilette from the passengers on their way to the Easter ceremonies.

'Jordan has a question,' the teacher said. 'Haven't you, Jordan?'

The lad had written it out. He smoothed the page with the side of his banana.

'Can you find it in your heart to forgive?'

'I would,' said Solomon, 'if I could find my heart, but I cannot remember where I left it the last time. They have given me a cardiac muscle to replace it, with a pump-action component that is all Greek to me. It does a grand job.'

He ought not to have talked at such length about his family. He had been invited to discuss Hitler and the Holocaust. What had Hitler and the Holocaust to do with smelly Esther, a cot death in the spring offensive? What had Zindel's autograph book for stellar signatories to do with the statutory guarantees of minority rights in multiculturalist polities? Jack Haley, Ray Bolger and Bert Lahr meant no more to these third-year teenagers than the names of the patriarchs. Yet Hitler and the Holocaust was the sum of all these subtractions.

'Deborah,' said the teacher. 'You have a question.'

The child had beautiful, bare arms, like the missing limbs of the Venus de Milo. Her mouth and her eyes were the same age exactly: there was not a day between them. She had been born by Caesarean section. He was sure of it. Caesar babies were cherubs. The smiles had not been wiped from their faces in the dumb maul of the birth-canal.

'Would you like to be an Israelite?' she said.

'What a wonderful question,' Solomon said. 'Thank you for asking it. Yes, I would love to have been an Israelite. I would like to have been with Joshua at Jericho. That was before King Solomon, you see, and so I would not have had to endure the comparison all my life. My name has been the source of some not inconsiderable unpleasantness.'

'I'm sure that Deborah means Israeli. Don't you mean Israeli, Deborah?'

'Yes,' said the Venus de Milo. She stuck out her lip and blew her fringe from her forehead. 'That's what I meant. Sorry. Would you like to go there, to Israel? Is it your fatherland, sort of?'

He thought about this while he groped at his groin. They must have shrunk in the sea. He would buy a dozen or so shorts on his way home through town; that would do for a month. Anything was better than asking citizen Cassidy to kick-start the washing machine, and drying them in the microwave had not been fruitful.

'My fatherland is Mother Earth,' he said to the cherub, 'and my motherland is Father Time.'

'Is that Kahlil Gibran?' the child said.

'No,' he said, 'it isn't. I would have thought it was a bit beyond Kahlil Gibran. It is something my father used to say when people talked politics at the dinner-table.'

Who was the boy at the back of the class, leaning his head on his hand and toying with a ballpoint? And the old, ordinary woman frowning at the state of his fingertips: who was she? The light was against him. He closed his eyes to see, but her bulky housecoat hid her. He could not be sure if her breast had been butchered and burnt like a plum-pudding with a blue halo of brandy.

Now the class was turning round to look as well, and the boy at the back made a face at his friends in the front; but he sat straight, twirling his pen like a baton and beaming interest. He was another of God's incognitos.

'John Paul has a question which John Paul is too shy to share,' the teacher said. 'I shall ask it for him, and Martin Brennan will give it his undivided attention. Shall I ask it for you, John Paul?'

The boy bowed his head.

'Don't make it too hard,' said Solomon Rosenblatt. 'I am no Einstein; I am barely an Ein. Once or twice I have been able to say Amen in my life. Once or twice I have been able to say Amen to it. Alleluia is another matter; alleluia is a long shot. *Dum spiro spero.*'

'I know what that means,' said the cherub.

'I know you do,' he said. 'It's a call to arms.'

'John Paul's question is this,' the teacher said. Really, she stank like a bouncer. 'What is the last thing—'

But the bell was ringing suddenly its oriental, ululating all-clear call, the kids were rising up in their places, striking their breasts like baboons, jostling, rejoiced; and the teacher made a bullhorn of her hands to be heard in the hubbub.

'Quick march, one, two, three. Quietly, quietly, quietly, please.'

Basketball candidates stooped over him for a handshake. Their palms were as clammy as his from the cotton pockets of their trousers, from juggling lunch-money and testicles while the addled grandad wisecracked through his Western History module. 'Shalom,' they said to him, 'shalom,' as if he were a Christian charismatic at a prayer-in, as if he were a folk-singer with a ukelele strumming the psalms of David to an air from *Oklahoma!*. 'Shalom.'

'Goodbye,' he said. 'Goodbye.'

A plaster-cast leg lurched at him from the left-hand corner of his field of vision. He autographed it with a flo-pen, block letters in burgundy, while the invalid dispatched cheese-sticks between the herpes on his lips. On the far side of the cripple, at the head of her handmaids, Praxiteles's masterpiece smiled slyly.

'Goodbye,' she said. Her face tilted to interpret his upside-down signs on the mould.

'Shalom,' he said. 'Shalom.'

Boots thawed on a radiator. Windcheaters slithered with a noise like nylons from the bentwood backs of chairs. On the loud industrial floor among woodshavings and cycle-helmets, tupperware cylinders bewildered him. He had drilled a rival's initials in the desk lid with a corkscrew and filled the borings with blue octopus-ink. The cantor from Krakow unstrapped his arbutus leg and hopped from the changing-room. Somebody had abandoned a pair of tortoiseshell glasses on the window-ledge. They angled like the discs of a desert observatory at the dead masses drifting in space.

'Coffee,' said the teacher. 'Coffee and a ciggie. That is, if the secret police don't come to take me away, ha-ha.'

She had rolled up the ivory sleeves of her blouse and was slowly effacing the names on the blackboard. Mordechai was missing, Leib and Lorelei, Tadeusz the arriviste who preferred to be Tadeo, and Zavel who married out, gave up the synagogue for the tenor sax, and wore a yellow star cut from a sheet of watered silk. He covered his nose and mouth with kitchen paper so as not to trigger catarrh, so as not to breathe the smell of their chalk dust.

'Happy enough?' she said. She wiped her hands elaborately. The board was pitch-black, with a small swirl of gas in the upper atmosphere. Megaphones in the corridor summoned assembly. Ash settled on his shoulders; pollen from a pinewood clouded his watch-face.

'Happy as Larry,' he said.

'God,' she said, 'you have the lingo.'

'Amn't I living here for years?' he said to her. 'Since before they launched the ape in a spaceship.'

'Go way,' she said, and she steered him through a labyrinth, lockers and lights, left, right, left again, towards the land of caffeine, the coast of mocha, where the substitute teachers would be dunking their wholegrain ration in polystyrene cups while the veterans broke soluble codeine tablets from blister-foils like discount Communion hosts. For he had discovered the same staffroom and classroom the world over. Only the corridors were different; and even then, if there were light and time enough and no official was dragging him by the elbow through the milling children, he could still identify each boyhood friend behind a Bunsen burner from the streaming faces of the swimming squad in the coloured photographs among the college trophies.

'Out into the firmament,' Solomon said. 'I am telling you the truth. He came back a better beast, a much more manly mammal, with backbone in his spine. Only, his spine was lighter. His skeleton was lighter. The bones of his foot were lighter. You would expect the opposite, of course; but that would be a great mistake. The greatest mistake of all is to expect the opposite.'

'I'm afraid it was all before my time,' she told him.

'You're right to be afraid,' he said. 'Everything that was before your time is before you now. Sooner or later, you will be old before your time.'

'This way,' said the teacher. 'This way is quicker. The stairwell at break is just bodies. You'd never get through them. It's Dante's Inferno.'

She stopped for a moment to smile at him; so he stopped and smiled back. Somebody should speak to her about the aftershave. She was a nice individual.

'Between ourselves,' she said, 'I am so relieved. I was terrified they would start asking about the Palestinians. One of the Religion teachers was winding them up. All last week he was at it. I put my foot down fast, take it from me. But they're at the age when they love to embarrass you. Plus there's this boy who is black, very black-is-beautiful, black is the be-all and end-all, the only black in the school, in fact, so obviously we're delighted to have him, but. I thought he'd start his thing about the twelve million slaves, et cetera. Then his sister rang today to say he had hepatitis, thank God.'

'I understand,' Solomon said.

'We did Anne Frank for starters. They loved that. The girls did. Half of the girls are writing diaries. The things you find out about the families. Dear Jesus. Anyway. Then we saw the film. You know the one. For the life of me I cannot remember the title. I don't know whether it's amnesia or what. Maybe it's Alzheimer's.'

'I understand,' Solomon said. He was beginning to sound like a beard.

'I don't seem to be able to remember anything any more,' she said. 'Zero. Isn't that terrible?'

He had seen too many films in which stout and stocky gentiles played the stinking inmates shrinking to italics in the middle distance; too many films in which the final credits assured an exiting audience that no alsatian had been abused in the making of this motion picture. His early twenties could only be imagined because they had never been photographed.

'I don't know what to tell you,' he said to her. 'I don't know which is worse: to forget our memories or to remember our forgetfulness. I don't know which is better. You should talk to my brother. Once he looked like Jesus Christ. Now he's God the Father. His ultimate goal is to be an American.'

'Ditto the delinquents here,' she said, 'but I don't want them to be American. I want them to be European. You know.'

'Know what?' he said. 'What do I know?'

'I try to be positive,' she said. 'You know, to be proactive. But.'

'As far as I can see,' said Solomon, 'the only aim of education is to teach people to read silently.'

'*On y va*,' she said. 'Open, Sesame. Welcome to our safe house.' And she held the door for him as he passed on into the sniggering, gregarious staffroom. 'Or at least it was our safe house until the secret police decided to stamp on the civil rights of smokers.'

'That's all right,' he said. 'I don't smoke.'

'It's all wrong,' said the teacher. 'I do. You can't say a cross word about homosexuals nowadays, but if you light a cigarette you're a Nazi war criminal.'

'Actually,' he said, 'most of them didn't smoke, either.'

She sat him at a table full of open exercise-copies with jolted, slantwise writing down the wide margins. Lists on grey graph-paper scrolled at his feet. Mugs over many weeks and months had printed noughts in profusion wherever he rested his wrists. His coat-hairs snagged in stickiness, in circles within circles, cells in metastasis. He put his hands on his knees and played 'Chopsticks'.

'Coffee in a momento,' she said. 'Then, with your kind

permission, I'm going to disappear for two minutes and twenty seconds. It is not to powder my nose, et cetera; it is to perform some rudimentary breathing exercises in the disabled toilet, which is more like a torture chamber than a restroom, to be honest, but the alternative is to puff in the car-park.'

And she was gone before he could tell her, sugar and milk. Because of his accent she would bring him black, bitter coffee; because of his faith she would be afraid to offer him food, milk or meat in case he went stalking off like a sulky Ezekiel. It was no wonder he'd lost weight since he started the lectures. Even his hands had shrunk back. Now the ring on his finger moved up and down as if it had grown more gold.

'I never heard such shit,' said the man beside him, the man who was twisting straws from a fruit-juice carton round his finger. 'Even when you meet them, you know who they are. I mean, they don't have to be togged out. You can almost smell them. The way they talk, the way they move, the way they shake your hand. The way they shake your hand would make you sick at times.'

'The point is,' the girl beside him said, 'you wouldn't leave a dog with a baby, would you? I don't care if it's the nicest dog in the world, even a labrador, say, that someone who was visually impaired would adore. No, you'd have more nous. So the same thing applies with children. I wouldn't leave a seven-year-old, any seven-year-old, boy or girl, alone or on their own with one of them for five minutes. Listen, I wouldn't leave Justin, and he's seventeen, almost.'

Her hand had not stopped marking the botched copies in front of her, X after X in a brilliant, blood-red ink, like the dye his mother had pricked into letters on longjohns and on pillowcases lest they be mislaid in the place where the train was to take them.

'I don't know,' said a third man. 'I'm not sure.' He prised the last of the raisins out of his scone and began to butter the halves while his colleagues ogled the ceiling in a show of outrage at the imbecile's dithering; but the bread was soft, the margarine hard, and the nine fresh raisins by themselves would be convertible currency. How could he roll them in his fingers like balls of

mucus? For nine fresh raisins there were women on the landing
above who would let you feel them all over with their clothes on,
and one of them was pregnant, with a craving for mint.

'Listen,' the man beside him said. 'Not a million miles from
where we're sitting now, there is somebody we are all agreed
upon.'

'Who?' said the man with the raisins.

'You know who he is, that's who,' the woman said. 'Someone
whose name begins with an S. Someone who thinks he's God's
anointed.'

And his teacher appeared out of nowhere, out of a puff of
smoke, with a matching cup and saucer in her hand. She set it
down unsteadily, the black, bitter coffee and the small seedless
grapes on a stalk.

'This is not "So Long, Farewell",' she said. 'It's more *Auf
Wiedersehen*. Back in a jif.'

He sweetened his mouth with the grapes to brace himself for
the other.

'What about God's anointed?' said the man with his mouth full
of scone.

'He's always bringing girls into the audio-visual room, that's
what,' the woman said. She had stacked the copies to one side and
was drawing lines through names on a list.

'Pastoral care,' the scone said.

'Pastoral fare,' said the man with the straws.

'Well,' the woman said, 'I hope he uses a pastoral letter.'

Solomon leaned over. The coffee had made his eyes water.

'Excuse me,' he said. 'What are you talking about?'

He had darkened his accent a fraction. That impressed people.
Often it made all the difference. Restaurants without room in
them rearranged tables. Shows that were block-booked found
seats in the circle. Even motorists at parking metres had awarded
honorary degrees to the elderly German gentleman who could not
reverse so readily in a right-hand model, Volkswagen or no. He
had been amused by it, bemused by it, beholden to it. He had
accepted the space, the seat, the table, with good grace and the
odd guttural. Besides, to be taken by strangers for a German was

proof, if any proof were needed, that God is not near-eastern but far-eastern, a Zen master, a smile and not a scowl, the Buddha of the ludicrous. That, at any rate, was what his brother had been saying for forty years in five remaindered ebullitions.

'What are we talking about?' said the straws. 'Do you ever read a newspaper? We're talking about parasites, about perverts. About Roman Catholic priests. Men who dress as women and prey on children.'

'I understand,' said Solomon Rosenblatt. 'I could have sworn you were talking about Jews.'

'Melanie. Is that you?'

'Speaking. Is that who I think?'

'Who else?'

'How are you?'

'I don't know. I'm here.'

'You'll have to speak up,' she said. 'You're very far away.'

It was like a language lesson. He was learning English again from the *Beano* and the Bible. His tutor was a Tommy who had been seconded with shingles.

'What time is it where you are, Melanie?'

'Israel is two hours ahead. If your clock has gone back for daylight-saving, then we're three hours ahead.'

'So it's what?'

'Late. Dark. It doesn't matter.'

He listened to her breathing in a house in Tel Aviv. Cars sounded their horns behind her, below her apartment balcony; but it could not be a wedding. It must be the traffic lights again.

'Are you not at the Sabbath service?'

'I am,' she said. 'This is a pre-recorded interactive answering-machine with mail-drop.'

'What about your feminist prayer group?'

'I am going through a heterosexual phase at the moment. His name is Benjamin.'

How could she suffer the horns? They were worse than ambulances. It was where she lived, of course, among Yemeni riff-raff.

'Benjamin is all right,' he said. 'Benjamin agrees with Melanie.'

'Yes,' she said. 'He goes down very well in certain quarters.'

She breathed like a mystic. Her lungs were so light. And he would dip his fingers down into the cot to make sure, to be certain, to feel her swift, silent exhaling on his hands like a twitching cricket in the wickerwork lantern of his bones.

'Melanie,' he said.

'I'm here.'

'She's in hospital.'

'Good. That's good. That's as it should be.'

'She's on her own. She doesn't have to share. It's private.'

'I know. I know. I understand.'

'She watches television.'

'Nothing changes.'

'She likes the children's television.'

'I remember.'

'They've brought back programmes from thirty years ago. You'd recognize them.'

'Of course I would.'

'Off the top of my head I would not be able to tell you the names of the programmes, but they have given her so much morphine that now she is a morphine addict.'

'I know, I know. I'm here, I'm holding you, here in my sitting-room in Tel Aviv, I'm hugging you. Can you feel me hugging you? Can you?'

Silence streamed from the satellites like the seraphim. Their cries went up to Heaven and came down again, at the international rate.

'She walked ahead of me through the twentieth century,' Solomon said. 'Like a pelican of the wilderness, an owl of the desert. Now she watches cartoons. She waits for her morphine. The houseman injects her and the hippo sings the alphabet. Zee is what they say now, not Zed. X, Y, Zee.'

It had taken him an eternity to master the subjunctive. The Tommy with the shingles had mouthed it for him as he sat on the floor with the other fellows in a half-moon round the teacher's tea-chest.

'It should not be,' he said. 'It should not be.'

'Sshhh,' said the Tommy. 'Sshhh.' And he made a Caruso pout while the class nibbled with their nails at the lice in their armpits. 'Sshhhould.'

'It's for the best,' she told him. 'Sick people should be in hospital. They feel better there.'

'They don't get better there,' he said. 'In among the conifers is a block called "Hospital Administration". It has nothing to do with either. It's a make-believe; it's a morgue.'

'You're healthy. Healthy people hate hospitals.'

Her breathing could not blur the snarled allegro of the traffic. It was hell on earth. Benjamin would want to be Cary Grant to keep her happy in that grubby Babel; and she would need to be Audrey Hepburn to stoke his snap, crackle and pop. He had seen the sabras windsurf on the lake of Galilee with their army walkie-talkies dangling from the strings of their bikinis and the men watching like Zulus in under the parasols.

'Hello?'

They smoked in the shade and drank out of reach of the terrible ultraviolet. They were healthy folk who hated hospitals. Because hospitals were for sports injuries and abortions, for the donor queues in the plasma unit when the sandbags were being filled. What could the topless centrefolds in their comics make of a mammograph? It is clouds descending and the birth of stars.

'Hello?'

Let them stick to the shoreline. Let them clean out their face-masks while the Christians write postcards. There is a time for being profoundly ignorant; and if there isn't, there is at least a time for being ignorant of your own profundity.

'Hello?'

'Melanie hates hospitals,' he said, 'and she's dying.'

It was the first time he had said it. At any rate, it was the first time he had said it in English. So he sat for a moment, thinking about his thoughts; and the Lilliputian lanes of downtown Tel Aviv seeped from the handset onto the eiderdown.

'Are you there? Can you hear me?'

'I can hear you. I can hear the Circus Maximus too. It's like *Ben Hur* over there.'

'Dearest,' she said, 'have you been drinking?'

'No. That's my sinuses.'

'You must be strong,' she said. 'I know it was never one of your weaknesses.'

'I am strong. I'll survive.'

'Survival is not strength. Survival is length. Length is no yardstick.'

'Melanie,' he said, 'are you growing a beard?'

'I'm growing impatient, that's what. Your wife is more anxious about your laundry than about her lymph glands, and you're sitting on your bottom feeling autobiographical.'

'You get it from my aunt,' he said. 'Nettle and dock in the same sentence.'

'I have to be hard. If I'm not hard, I'll cry. If I cry, I'll wreck my make-up and I've just put it on to go out.'

'You're too young to wear make-up. Brush your teeth and you're a beauty.'

'Except for my forehead.'

'High forehead, high intelligence. The fringe hides it.'

Above and beyond them, a hundred miles out, in the blue-black stillness of space, the satellite waited for word. Green tendrils of silence climbed like the limbs of a vine; twirled, twined; and quivered toward the world again, while the circuits worshipped.

'How does Benjamin feel about family?'

'Please don't talk about offspring. You know I don't want offspring. I want children.'

'At my age, it amounts to the same thing.'

'Then you're a knave as well as a fool.'

'First Hitler, and now the contraceptive pill. The Ashkenazi will be like the Amish. The tourists will pester them with their polaroids.'

'What is wrong with being Sephardic? Tell me.'

'They're not the people of Einstein, the people of Kafka, the people of Freud, the people who created the world in seven decades. All the visionaries are gone. Only the opticians are alive.'

'What do you know about Einstein? Bugger all. That's what you know about Einstein. Kafka and Freud, my kidneys. You know about Betty Grable. You knew about her before and you knew about her behind.'

'Arse,' said the Tommy. He tapped Betty's bottom in the life-size pin-up, and the hunkering students hooted lewdly, even the two who had passed blood in their stools.

'Arse,' they said. 'Arrsse.'

'I know what it is,' she said. 'You're giving those lectures again.'

'The odd one,' he said.

'They're all odd. They're all pathological.'

'Tit,' the Tommy said. 'Tit; or boob.' The tip of the billiard cue bobbed at the Victory sign of the starlet's cleavage.

'Tit,' said the man with the frostbitten foot, the few teeth, the pelvis like antlers. 'Tit. Orboob; orboob.'

'Why do you do it?' Melanie said. 'Why?'

'I want them to remember,' said Solomon.

'You don't remember,' she said. 'You repeat what you read in books.'

'The veil of the Temple,' said the soldier with the shingles. 'A bit of all right.' His stick triangulated the vaginal region: up, down, across; and across, down, up again, as if he was sketching a star of David.

'I'd better go,' she said. 'This must be costing you a fortune.'

'You'll get what's left. You'll get what's right. I hate to think of you wasting it on blazers for boyfriends.'

'Briefs,' she said. 'When will you call me?'

'You don't mind?'

'Of course I don't mind. I love you.'

'I love you too,' he said. 'So at least we can agree on one thing.'

'Cunt,' said the class. 'Box, snatch, hole.'

'You see,' he said, 'there's no one else I can say Melanie to.'

'You say that to all the women.'

'I do,' he said. 'I am not able to say it to a man.'

And when the tutorial was finished Solomon had gone out into the camp, into the grey sea of its choppy canvas, burlap and tarpaulin, the breeze-block walls, the executed shirts on the guy-strings of the windbreaks, the waterbarrels staring at the salt stains in the sky. Flies flew, birds landed, men stood to urinate, and women crouched in trench coats to lick soup bowls like a lover's genitals.

'Have a child,' he said. 'A child has twice as many bones as an adult. Did you know that? Did you? There are a hundred and one reasons to have a child.'

'Sshhh,' she said. 'Sshhh. I'll have a hundred and one children. Sleep well.'

All over Europe, Europe was all over. People were pitching tents in their own country.

'Goodbye, Melanie,' he said.

'Goodnight, Solomon, roses and blather. Goodnight.'

But he held the phone to his ear when she hung up, although the beau Benjamin would be ringing through his battle-plan for a secular sabbath, free sex with expensive wine, and although the automatic exchange would continue to bill him in its deadpan, digital way if she lifted it off the hook for the late-night picture-show or a bath and beauty sleep or a bottle of pills, perhaps, that would start in pins and needles and end in sutures and stitches.

The satellite was moving in a blue daze over the face of the deep.

The way home brought him past the hospital to the docks, and in the dead centre of that diameter, between the chlorine of the ward and the iodine of the estuary, he could go no farther. The road ahead was blocked at the level crossing.

'Shittim,' he said. 'Shittae, shittae, shitta.'

He slowed in second, the engine stalled, and the presentation plant he had been given by the aftershave angel at the school fell forward from the front passenger seat onto the floor. Clumps of compost stuck into the soaking carpet square. Now he would have to stop at a service station and pay the boy a pound to valet the mess. Manure was still manure by any other name, nitrate or stardust. He should have stayed in bed, behind his eyelids, when Tess Cassidy called.

'Christian dignitaries will also be attending,' said the medium wave to the knuckles on the knob of the gearstick, 'among them the Polish primate and the Papal nuncio.'

Cars had been driven onto the sleepers of the railway track. That was the long and the short of it. He could see by stretching the skin at the corners of his eyes. People were gathered in groups at the barriers, clapping and chanting. He could not hear their palms or their mouths, but the motorists around him were turning off their dims, and so did he. Had there been an accident? He did not wish to witness another fatality. On the other hand, there was no reversing. The traffic was bumper to bumper. In the rear-view mirror above him he could see the rear-view mirror behind him, and a woman's angled gape as she flossed briskly; behind her, a sudden, incongruous cortege; and beyond it all, at the back of everything, the floodlit towers of the hospital.

'Back again, sir?' the porter had said. 'What can I do you for this time?'

Because he had left that night when she died, not taken the elevator, gone down the stairs, the cold flights, one Madonna, two Madonnas, three Madonnas, more, and out the hall, avoiding the chaplain with the budgie, standing at the payphones till the priest had passed, watching the workman frost the windows of the kiosk for Christmas, and then the last heave, pushing the revolves of the door over the stiff, resisting horsehair, to find himself surrounded by the smokers on the steps, by duffel coats and dressing gowns, their fragile incensations, the breath of a body going up in smoke to a sky without stars.

'You too,' they said to him, smiling. 'Aren't we terrible creatures?'

'Communists,' the announcer said, 'defectives, gypsies, homosexual persons, Jews, Muslims, pacifists, prisoners of war, Quakers, Christian Scientists, and a large part of the indigenous German transvestite community whose sufferings have never been acknowledged adequately by our polarized, either-or Euroculture.'

The man's voice on the car radio was a kindly counter-tenor's, though the atmospheric interference hissed and booed him until his blurting was a ruined aria, shouts on acetate, shrieks pelted by sleet; and when the neighbours had carried their armchairs and antimacassars into the very best room in the house, the room that was always empty, always aired, the room where his father had told him about love and the uterus, then his sister would serve sodas and spa-water, and the street would sit and listen to the clarinet concerto on the wireless; sit and listen and breathe through their mouths while the elderly relatives shut their eyes and held their heads as still as if they were nudes being painted in a life class.

'Sshhh,' said his father. 'Please.'

His leg would fatten and fall asleep from his criss-cross boy-scout crouch in the forest of sideboards, but he could still applaud at the close of each movement like the costly, cushioned front row of the theatre a hundred miles away where they were clearing their throats now, the regional oligarchy, and the men were using the programme notes to fan their moustaches and the women were picking fibres of wool from their gloves off the stone in their engagement rings.

'Sshhh,' said his mother. 'Sshhh.' But she was speaking to her lap, to the strange stomach noises that squabbled inside her like a radio being tuned.

'She won't stand in a line and let a doctor look at her,' said his father. 'It would be worse than death.'

'The line or the look?' said a voice in German, and his father sighed back at it in Esperanto. So his grandfather must have been present, prickly and elongated, a public statue with a prayer-shawl of pigeon droppings and a place in his heart for Lillian Gish; the tubercular shofar-blower who had gargled violet phlegm for the first time on Rosh Hashanah; that bigot of a bookworm with his agitator's bulletins and his rainbow rhetoric of a new life in a new land, yarmulkas in Kenya, Echt Deutsch in an African yeshiva.

'Shittas, shittarum,' Solomon said. 'Shittis, shittis.'

If a suicide had been guillotined by a commuter train, drivers would have sprinted from the booths of their cars to inspect the deceased. Bystanders would have chattered among themselves as if they had been on Christian name terms all their lives. He would have seen starbursts, flashes of light, and a debonair photographer handing his fedora to a detective as he draped the black hood of his camera over his inflammable hair-do. Then the onlookers would have scattered and sped home, settling the children earlier than usual – the bedtime story, the night prayer, the light on the landing – to make love at last in a new endearment, an altered tenderness, grace beyond faces, the landscape of their flesh without a name to it, a space to be held and handled and handed on, the place of all pasture.

'My waters are breaking,' she had said, but that was the morphine. He bobbed his head at the oxygen tent and the nurse made him a cup of tea with a tea bag in it.

No one had blinked; no one had budged. Nobody raised an eyebrow, raised a hand, raised the matter, raised the dead. In the lanes to left and right, the incoming, the outgoing, overgrown adults aged at a standstill in the sashes of their safety belts. Even the toddler in the car ahead of him had tired of trying to exasperate Fatty Arbuckle with his plasticine grimaces, and the girl in the rear-view mirror had given up grooming her gums.

So he fumbled at the tufts of hair behind her ear in the way that she had liked him to, and he left the oxygen tent, the tent of meeting, the airy, prayerful tabernacle; but he had come back again, stepping in his stockings lest his parents look up at him from the oil lamp in the pantry, to tweak the pleats of the muslin cone over the cot where his new brother was smelling of cloves and privies. It had been his own idea, the enormous wedding-cake cover, to ward off greenfly in the hot months.

'Hello, bareface,' he had said. 'Hi, buddy. Hello, hello, hello.'

'And the European Parliament observed a minute's silence at midday,' the radio said to the handbrake, to the hairs that were hers in the space between the seats, to his four relenting fingers, the ringworm years, the years of worn rings, a white wedge in under the wedding band, a weal, really, almost a lesion, before he gave them both up, sugar and starch on the same day, at the shame of the sight of his eighteen-carat coil split open like a seal on a bottle of medicine.

'I'm not the lady with the lamp,' the motor mechanic had said. 'In case it goes and ulcerates, you should see a doctor. I don't know about seeing your wife. She might ulcerate you more.'

Then he put away his pocket pliers, the long-haired boy in overalls, and they stood in the smell of surgical spirits at a ramp where iron chains hung from a cross-beam.

'You know where to come,' said the motor mechanic, 'if you ever want your fillings out.'

And his mother had been so embarrassed that she excused herself, stood up and walked out as the first phrases of the adagio lifted the parlour like a row boat; and he, he had slipped out after her, round the back of the barley-screw stools and the lowered, listening heads, holding his pockets with his fists to hush them, the chinking nickel change, the cigarette cards of the great aviators, glycerine sweets in the shape of comets, and a damaged stylus he had played in a garden on the grooves of his own thumbprint.

'If she wanted to join her cousin in Canada, she'd have to strip to the bone and let a stranger inspect her,' said his father. 'That's not public health; that's veterinary medicine.'

'Sshhh,' said his father's father. 'Sshhh. Let me listen.'

The music rose and fell, Rosenblatt, rose and fell.

When they came for him, he went with them quietly. A budgie flew in front of him along the corridor. At the end of the room the tent had been taken down. She lay with a look of astonishment on her face. He breathed through his mouth so as not to disturb her.

'Would you like to say a prayer?' the nurse said.

Her feet had fallen apart like a ballerina. Between the big toe and the second toe he could see the pressure mark of her flip-flop from the odysseys of a suburb.

'Pardon,' he said.

'A prayer,' said the nurse. 'But only if you'd like to.'

The only prayer he could think of was the prayer for orphans. His mind must be going. He was starting to wander, like his father before him, his mother before him, and Melanie now, now Melanie, before him in the flesh.

'I said a prayer,' he told the nurse. 'My prayer has been answered. At least, there has been a reply.'

Where were her contacts? He could not imagine where her contacts might be. If she lost them again late at night, in the small hours, in a power cut, she would have to bump down the staircase on her bottom, trudging the carpet with her buttocks and heels like a stalled tobogganist who has cleanser on his face and a cavity in his nightgown. Yet if she left them in for too long, she would destroy her corneas. She would be blind, and where would he be if he were blind, hunting for the string of the light-switch in the toilet, urinating on his ankles in the darkness? Because she could never have a guide dog. She was afraid of alsatians.

'I'll leave you alone now,' the nurse said, and he stared at her, stared at the holes in her ears where the drop-earrings would hang for her first date, her boyfriend, her lover, her husband, her helpmate; but she would take them off, her earrings and her shoes, when she went upstairs to the bedroom to lie down, to free her swollen breast and nurse a baby, because a child would be thrilled by the sight of it, the beautiful brightness at her throat, tick-tocking glimpses, and he would reach up to touch it, yes, to tug it, no, to tear it, stop, from the soft droop of her lobe.

'Sshhh,' he said, stroking her hand, the fingers and bone, not the sog of the bruise where the drip had been leaking. 'Sshhh.'

Two beds down, they were pitching the tent again.

'Clear skies and stars galore for any armchair astronomer,' said the wavering medium in the stalled cabin, 'but groundfrost and black ice on the back roads, so my advice to you plural is: lock up, lie low, and avoid all unnecessary journeys.'

Yet he had followed his mother out of the chamber music on the public address system in the hospital and into the car-park, her Solomon, her sweet King Solomon, and he had sat there, such a running-board, picking grime from the steering wheel, such an automobile, grime that might have been sweat or dead skin or soot from the leavings of the city.

'Isaiah, 43,' the chaplain said, and the budgie ran up and down his shoulder. 'I have called you by name and you are my own. I have engraved your names on the palms of my hands.'

'They called us by number,' Solomon said, 'and tattooed our wrists. Auschwitz, '43.'

Then he slept.

She had not died in her own language, Yiddish of the aureole, pidgin of bibs and milk. Yet the paperback he had studied said that she might. He would write to the author on a point of information. He would tell him to his beard that she had brought the booklet into their home and left it for him in a plain brown wrapper on the west side of the bed at the luminous hands of his clock.

Why had she done that? Why had she done that to him?

There were no answers at the back of the book. There was only an advertisement for another work by the same chat-show physician on post-natal depression. Still, Solomon had read it from the end to the very beginning, from the appendix to the acknowledgements, as if he were back at the brand new classroom radiator, cribbing mnemonics in a Hebrew primer, and the eight-year-olds were rowing like frogs, face down on the rafts of their school desks, practising the breast-stroke for a visit to the baths.

'All aboard for Berlin,' the teacher had said. 'We haven't won a medal since the fifth century.'

'But thou art he that took me out of the womb,' the boy wrote in the slow, stiff, matchstick letters he had never mastered; 'thou didst make me hope when I was upon my mother's breasts.' Would the teacher return the confiscated copy of *Hollywood Heights, Hollywood Lows*? And he watched the letters dry, the page discolour, the wood disintegrate, until he was far removed from a room where radicals had put typing skills and Talmud Torah on the same curriculum because they were dying, all the women in trousers, all the men in open-neck shirts, to be part of the new order of life.

He knew what he was dying of. He was dying of a pain in the breast, of a place called Melanie. He was dying of a growth that had brightened inside him and gone on brightening until he could not look at it through his tortoiseshell glasses. It would show in an X-ray of his chest as the birth of a nebula, gases and gravity, a seven-day wonder; but it would not show the star at its right hand side. It would not show a seat in a bus in North London where a woman from the east of his life does not get up as usual and gather her groceries and walk to the stepwell, though her stop is near, is next, is now; and yet she's still sitting, and her stop dwindles behind her, smaller and smaller like the letters on a wall-chart in a doctor's surgery, but she hardly looks, she hardly looks back. For the first time in ten years, almost ten years, nine years and seven months, she can feel the slightest seepage in her, ooze of a freshet from her, blood stencilling her lips.

'Are you all right?' said the man.

But Solomon could not lower the window. It had been jammed for weeks. So he opened the door a fraction. The radio had been right about groundfrost. Coldness felt for his skeleton like a housewife frisking a chicken's carcass.

'It's not my fault,' he said. 'I can't go back.'

'Animal Rights,' the man said. 'They're blocking a train.'

'Animal rights?' said Solomon. 'I'm an animal. I have rights. I have the right to go home.'

'Don't look at me,' the man said. When he spoke, you could not see his face. The words were mist and fog. 'I thought you were dying. I thought you were dead.'

'I couldn't be both,' Solomon said. 'Dying is the opposite of death.'

He must have drowsed; he may have dozed. Half of his leg had gone to sleep in his shoe, in the pins and needles of amputation, and his waistcoat buttons were still twitching in time to the blows inside his body. Perhaps his heart would steal a march on his prostate. That would be perfect. Then they could tow him to the ties, and have done.

'I was daydreaming,' he said.

'Thanks be to Jesus,' said the man. 'I like my mouth-to-mouth a little later on a Friday. Beer before bubbly.'

Air from his nostrils steamed and smoked in the moisture of beasts, the venting of cattle. How could an eskimo suffer the sight of it, this heat-haze from his ribcage, a pent-up, panted thing, the ghost of his bloodstream going before him through the seventy

words for wasteland? It was something else he would have to ask
Melanie, because he did not know any Inuit or Aleut, though he
had seen one in the zoo photographing a waxwork of a hunter
with a harpoon; so he must jot the question down among the
other queries on the sheet with the Roman numerals, like the
checklist that he drafted before phoning his brother the beard in
the promised land of Palo Alto, California. Otherwise he would be
speechless when he woke in the morning to find her up before
him, and gone before him, to find that he was lost, and then to
lose what he had found, a tiny corkscrew hair in the ransacked
hollow of her half of the bed.

'Who are they?' Solomon said. 'Over there, at the railway
tracks.'

'Right animals,' said the man. 'That's who.'

'You are a voice speaking out of a cloud,' said Solomon. 'Do you
know that?'

But the man was walking away from the crank in the car,
shaking his skull at the dusk, at the hocus-pocus of people and the
hardened arteries of the city around him. His hands swayed sky
high in the sign of surrender, but no one looked up and no one
looked out. They were mouthing contentedly the chorus line from
the same rock song on every wireless; on every radio the same
amplified slogan at a rally in a stadium. Some of them skimmed
through the evening editions, speed-reading advertisements
for attic insulation and articles that downsized the estimates
of yesterday's massacres, while their children's fingers quick-
marched along the headrests. Outside, in the wind, up-ended
toddlers pissed against a tree trunk.

'It was only a dream,' Solomon said to the steering wheel. 'You
do not wake from a nightmare.'

He felt his face, the new growth, stubble like stitches in a
hospital. At night, each night since 1936, his skin had bristled.
The hairs had stood up.

'Please,' she would say. 'I can't close my eyes with the light
on.'

He had not petted her breasts for ten years; but would he have
felt it, the stone in the apricot?

'The girl in the physio said she'd walk on my spine if I wanted,' he told her.

'People have walked all over you for years,' she said. 'Why pay for it?'

'It was probably my accent,' he said. 'Of course we'd end up sleeping together.'

'You'll end up sleeping on a plank,' she said. 'The same as you started.'

Pillars of salt had soared around him. The overhead halogen lights whitewashed the car-park, the perimeter fences, the igloo where the attendant incinerated lungs. All the watercolours of cholera matted the huts and outhouses, the radiography ramp, the smoke-stack, the shingle roof of the cell count clinic; and beyond the square of shadowless sodium, its terrible detergent glare, he could imagine the fringe of the forest, glints of tinfoil from a picnic, the pine trees waiting for the solstice when the Christians would come with their hacksaws and their hatchbacks and their hands smelling of resin like toilet freshener.

'I will survive this,' he thought. 'I will go on from here to be married for more or less forty-two years; for forty-two years I will go on from here to be more or less married. But I will change the names on all the forms at all the frontiers. I will call her Sarah, though she was not a Sarah, really, and neither was Sarah herself; but at least it does not rhyme with anything awful in the seventh edition of the *Home Guide To Good Health*; and I will call myself something other than Solomon, since I am not majestically wise or majestically well-off, even if I do on occasion allow myself to believe that I am the shakings of both, the delusion of brains, the illusion of cash. The majesty I abdicate to the son who drowned in my semen.'

Birds that had lost their bearings sang for seconds in the blinding rectangle, and gave up. Pylons loomed to left and right. A field-grey sleeve threw down a cigarette which fell three feet inside the line they could not cross, dropped there between the wire and the walkway, landed and lay a yard outside the boundary: and the sleeve waited then, high above them at the clapboard parapet, its buttons on the belt feed.

'Amen,' said Solomon Rosenblatt. 'Alleluia.'

When he stood out of the car, he had as many shadows as a soccer player. They walked him like bodyguards across the quick-dry tarmac of the overflow corral to the hospital's red revolving entrance. Ashes and butts festooned the horsehair mats, but the smokers had disappeared.

'I'm sorry,' he said.

'Sorry?' said the porter, and he turned down his Walkman.

'I need change to get out of the car-park.'

'The barrier's up,' the porter said. 'The borders are not closed. As well as that, it's free after midnight. Even the coffee is free after midnight. Everything's free after midnight. Did you not see the signs?'

His thumb was already fumbling at the volume.

'Give us an N; give us an O!'

The wind from central Europe shifted a hair's breadth, a compass point, and Solomon heard their outcries gust into earshot. Under the signal-box by the turnstile, men and women stamped their desert boots on the chippings to stay warm. Children peered from a thicket of ski-pants, the muted, queuing kids in their kindergarten gabardines, their mittens made from ankle socks, the balaclavas blazing out of loose ends and leftovers: and his mother had told him, this, this is amber from a bonnet; indigo from a prayer-shawl, that; and there, in the cut-off caterpillar colours, is burgundy from your grandmother's oven gloves. Now you know three things more.

'Give us an A; give us an H!'

For a moment he imagined they were throwing their arms to heaven, the children wading in their parents' Wellingtons, the roly-poly tot with the seven sweaters for asthma, and the boys' cauliflower ears taped back for the bar mitzvah studio portrait; but they were only hauling helium balloons down out of danger from the high overhead wires, the skull-and-lightning legend, and snagging the strings in the picket's cardboard placards that he couldn't, for the life of him, decipher.

'N.O.A.H. What do you have? Noah!'

German was breaking through the English on the radio like the stalagmite of a tooth through a cheap enamel shell. He leaned towards it, listened for it, his lips parting, his mouth opening to block the rumpus of his nostrils though the cold air quickly sketched the chink in his bridge and the scald on his tongue from the bolted coffee. In a high-fidelity studio somewhere in Hamburg, say, the calm, contralto tones of a woman with headphones guided through the blizzard of a bad transistor his language of special occasions: of weddings, of erotic novellas, of the telephone. So he shut his eyes and everything went red, the amniotic pastels of blindness, and then he could almost make out the little obliterated letters on the tongues of leather shoes, names that had melted into sweat stains, lips that the snow had smeared like ice-cream.

'No! No! No! No! No!'

He was homesick for the worst years of his life. When he had been sick-at-heart, he had been single-minded; when he was sick-unto-death, his hopelessness had passed almost for peace of mind. Without these things, without his unhappiness, man is a beast of the field.

'Yes! Yes! Yes!'

He was a sentry in a cemetery. At night he pushed a dustcart among the beehive headstones, tucking hot-water bottles in the blankets of gravel.

The voice in Hamburg welled and swivelled like a warp on vinyl, a backing-track to the sing-along on the home service. Yet she was right to be righteous: the supermodels had indeed behaved splendidly when they hurled their rabbit-stoles, their fox-furs and their ocelot leggings on the charity bonfire in aid of all threatened species. They had stood up; they had been accountable. Perhaps they had not yet given their lifeblood in a blood-bath, but they were donors already, with pins in their lapels.

> From the adder to the zebra,
> They were all in Noah's Ark;
> The A to Zee of you and me
> Does not exclude the shark.

They had printed the lyrics of the hymn on banners and sandwich-boards. Small children tapped on the passenger window, gesticulating wildly at the message on their chests; and the crowd hooted and honked around him, waving their fists and flashing their lights in hail-fellowship with the funny juniors. Yet the soldier who had stood in the doorway of the hut, the Soviet who had said hello, hello, hello, to the silence, the stillness, the woodwind of their pleurisy, covered his mouth with a cloth from his pocket, with linen from the lost kingdom of napkins, from the ruined empire of the handkerchief. He was not a Jain out of India, afraid of inhaling house-dust mites lest he swallow the molecules of Elohim. He was a Russian. He was afraid of inhaling.

He stood at the door of a place that began with A and ended with Z, and his tears ran down his nose onto the twenty-six letters of the alphabet.

'Who is the dumbest of the animals?' a woman called as she roamed among the cars with pamphlets, petitions. Her enormous earrings were Spanish question marks; her vanilla buttocks abounded. He worked his wipers to be invisible, squirting the last spurts of Melanie's washing-up liquid onto his windscreen. Now nobody would notice him. Now he could yank at his swimming trunks where they gnawed at the fold of his flesh.

Now he could wait.

First the photographers; then the policemen. You would expect the opposite, but that would be a mistake. Whoever they were, these demonstrators, liberals or Jehovah's Witnesses, the toyboys of Utopia or the gigolos of Eden, they knew which level crossing was closest to the television station. Ecstatic protesters would preach to camera, and call their *au pairs* on a cellular phone to video the newscast. None of them had understood that only the virtues which ruin us are real: the rest is history.

Why were they playing the chorus of the Hebrew Slaves on his radio? Was it a tribute? They should be playing Sirota. They should have sent Sirota's Edison cylinders up into the firmament instead of man's best friend or his first cousin. Then the Lord would have come out of hiding, like a Jew from the raftered ark of an attic after a pogrom, and been seen face to face for the first time

since the death of Moses. A satellite in outer space would be
his footstool, the international calls occur as love-cries, and the
universe declare to the world of earth that this was the promised
hour, the sabbath rest, the feast of day fourteen.

'Back in your cars. Stay in your cars.'

But the Hebrew slaves had been hired out as decoys in a thirty-
second commercial for life insurance. The hewers of wood and the
drawers of water were lilting Pharoah's lullaby. Solomon's hand
reached out and switched them off all by itself, the undertakers
and their siren from Egypt.

'Stay where you are. Go back, go back.'

How tall and stately the policemen were, stately and tall. You
would know from the way they walked that they had driven cows
to a milking-shed when they were only boys, when they were
barely breastfed, batting the spattered flanks with tennis racquets
as the foreigners stood up out of their sun-roofs, adjusting the
light meters on their cameras; and you would know from their
boots and their batons that they were not accustomed to lowering
their voices at a car window or to raising their heads at the
visitor's hatch in their headquarters. Yet nothing had prepared
Solomon for the smell of grapefruit on the gauntlets of the
motorcycle escort, for the sting of citric acid on his lip and the
sight of himself in the convex visor of the helmet, an obese and
bulbous medallion, neither image nor likeness but a billboard
caricature; and he had made the sign of the Cross in front of them,
the three militia pistols, made it deliberately, elaborately, up,
down, across, like the patriarch in Petersburg blessing the
bayonets of his conscript uncles, while the whole patrol chortled
in the style of the silent movies.

'Here's a Yid who thinks he's Euclid.'

Now they were lifting the vegetarian joggers at the level
crossing, shifting the cars that had been left there, until he could
see again the dull apron of tar and arrows where the railway
tracks thinned into tramlines.

'Maybe he thinks he's Archimedes. Do you think he thinks he's
Archimedes?'

Yet the veterans of the ashram went on chanting mantras in

their saffron parkas with the luminous armbands, and his mother passed him on the other side of the street, not watching, not wanting to watch, studying the longitude of the footpath, stepping with care, cautiously even, as if she had found herself among many snails mating, the pained antennae on the crazy paving, their lonely, foaming unions.

'What is the sum of the squares in the Star of David? Can you tell me that?'

'Move it, move it. Keep it moving. We all want to be home for *The Late Late Show*.'

'The sum of the squares in the Star of David is shit. That is what it is.'

What would the child with the glitter on her face do now? Her balloon was sinking without trace in the depths of the sky. She would have to look for a smaller child with a bigger balloon to browbeat; and she already was.

'Move, I said. Are you deaf?'

This time Solomon remembered. He opened the door wide.

'Don't be aggressive with me,' the policeman said. 'Are you one of those troublemakers?'

'I'm sorry,' Solomon said. 'It's the window. The window is kaput.'

Why had he said that? Why had he said that word? It had come out of nowhere.

'What's the name?' said the policeman.

Capo, yes. He had once said capo, but that was different. That was about Italy, about baksheesh or blackmail. He had never said the other.

'I asked you your name. Do you know your own name?'

The waiting was over. He was almost at one.

'Rosenblatt,' he said. 'Solomon.'

The policeman angled his torch at the windscreen, at the paper disc with its stamp, its smallprint, its star. Solomon looked up to him, the curt and vertical deputy whose feet would overshoot the bars of the bunks in the guardhouse. With a diver's leaded shoe on his good foot, he could kick you to death in twelve seconds. Twelve seconds had been the record. Nowadays, of course, the

divers wore flippers. The contestants would have to cast about for
an ice-skate.

'Well, Mr Solomon,' the policeman said, 'do you realize you've
been a bad boy?'

'Yes, I do,' said Solomon. 'I have lived long enough to learn that
I am the greatest problem in my own life.'

'I mean,' the policeman said, 'you have not been paying your
proper taxes.'

'My wife does all the paperwork,' he said. 'She is wonderful at
paperworking. You should see her. It is lovely just to watch.'

'Tell her to wake up and get a move on,' said the policeman, 'or
we'll be knocking on your door one of these days.'

'I will talk to her tonight when I see her,' Solomon said. 'When I
talk to her tonight I will see her immediately.'

'Are you all right?' said the policeman, but he did not shine the
torch in Solomon's face in the way that he should have, really.

'If the truth be told,' Solomon said, 'I am not myself.'

Yet his sinuses had cleared. He could breathe carbon monoxide,
fumes from the diesel buses, and the saturated bark of the birch
tree at the barrier.

'I think I'll have to bring you home with me,' the policeman
said.

'Pardon?'

Out of the nightfall, out of the street lights, he could sense it
now, shape it now, the immense, intended, uneventful thing.

'Listen,' he said.

'You listen to me,' the policeman said.

Listen for the low bronchitis of the locomotive, for the slow
arousal of its breathing; listen for the shorter, swifter gasps, the
respiratory spasm in the lungs. Hear this, O Israel. For a moment
he caught sight of her on the station platform; but the steam
became mist, and the mist became a cloud, and he could no
longer make out the hatbox with the sanitary towels and the
bottle of syrup for her stomach noises.

'Home is where you should be,' the policeman said.

They had walked away without looking back, the two parents,
the two grandparents. Side by side and two by two, they had gone

along the gangplank into the hull of the dark. The trainspotters had watched it from the embankment while they sharpened their pencils with their marvellous Swiss knives.

'I've been to the market to buy a fat pig,' the policeman said.

And the panting, pent-up wagons begin to trundle past, the shackled stockyard boxcars clattering on the rivets of the tracks. Even the pedestrian with the Mickey Mouse headphones covers his temples at the sound of their wailing, at the rocking, clockwork length of a whole train howling up out of blackness and back gardens and blackberry bushes and a short cut to the church. The campus cyclists are wheeling away their racers while the bolted carriages shudder through, all chalk and creosote and the locked smell of sheds, solid with livestock silent as the tomb, the speechless, shitting cattle in the fog of their lungs and the children grinding their faces into their mothers' genitals.

'What?' he said. 'What are you telling me? What?'

It was gone. The barrier was lifting. Urine glittered on the sleepers.

'Home again, home again,' said the policeman. 'Jiggedy jig.'

DEIRDRE SHANAHAN

Talking to My Father

At the end of the back gardens a muddy track runs between the Victorian houses opposite and these hard-edged ones where, beneath the floor boards, cavernous and deep, trains roar. If you follow the track beyond, there are allotments identified by odd, flimsy sheds half falling down. Quirky, with a door loose, a wall lopsided or a plank dangling, they scatter where there must once have been fields on the outskirts of town.

I push the buggy along the muddy path but there is no sign of anyone except a woman in a headscarf at the far end working on one of the allotments. The air is so chill you could knife it. Stones hit my shoes. My hands are numb but I had to get out. I could not stand the pressure of the walls, so pale and lifeless. Sasha cries. The cold hits him but he will settle, as he always does. His fat pink face is like my father's, and like him, he is happiest outside.

The figure at the far end walks this way and I see it is Mr Abdi, who often stumbles along his plants. How did I ever believe it was a woman? My brain can't think. It had been falling out of my head ever since Sasha came. Mr Abdi nears, his dark eyes, like jewels, flit and catch me, dance like the eyes of one I knew once but no longer do, one who is the father of my child and with whom I spent nights and days in bars in Berlin when I was a student and there was nothing else to do but to go back to rooms in shambling houses once in the east and now standing gaunt and naked.

'Hello.'

'Hi.'

'You've brought your young man?'

'He likes to come out.'

'Puts roses on his cheeks. You want to see what I have been doing?'

'Can we?'

'But of course. Come through.'

I bang the metal frame against the gate and judder Sasha. For a moment I fear he will burst into tears but he doesn't as he's so well wrapped in every conceivable layer that the knock does not register. Paint has chipped off the lower edges of the buggy but it will only match the other marks so I don't mind. It was third-hand for only a few quid and I will be pleased if it lasts until he walks.

'See here. I have these.'

'What are they?'

'Sweet potatoes.'

'They're huge.'

'Margery swopped them with me.'

'Did she?'

'She grew these too.'

'Kinds of pomegranate? I thought they only grew in hot places?'

'She has a greenhouse thing. Not the big ones but the kind that fits anywhere. You need one. They give a person a head start. Do you want to come down to the end? You could leave him there. He will see you when he wakes up.'

Mr Abdi trundles ahead down a narrow path between distinct squares of ground. One has a washing-line and many have little fences or runs of low hedges as if they were front gardens.

'They are ridiculous. Why don't they leave the land open? You can get more out of it, like my potatoes. See them here.'

There are green shoots and stubs of flowers in the open.

'I have spinach and cabbage and further on I will grow my beetroots.'

'It's very impressive.'

'Not as good as the garden in Bombay.'

'Garden? I thought it would have been courtyards?'

'There are gardens. I had one outside the city and a man to tend it.'

I listen, though he has told me before how he arrived here having been a bank manager with a nice house, and found on arrival that he was not considered seriously for any position more than counter clerk.

'Even though I was busy I always tried to grow things though my girls never liked much the vegetables.'

'Maybe they do now.'

'I don't think so. What about your young man?'

'He'll eat anything.'

'You have no problems then?'

I shook my head.

'No. I'm lucky, so far.'

Mr Abdi stamps the ground with his hoe.

'Hard as rock.'

'The weather will change. As the days pass the earth will warm.'

'Never in all my twenty years in England have I had an easy winter. It chills my bones, picks at them like a knife. I am driven into my house like a hunted man and I hate it.'

He rubs his hands. I turn the buggy round out of the sharp winter glare. Four boys about fourteen or fifteen kick a ball around the rough ground next to the allotments. Their cries cut the air.

'Get it, ye headcase. Go on.'

A lolloping boy with a thick quiff of black hair trails after the ball and gives it a long full kick. Two run elbowing each other.

'Ye bugger, it's mine.'

The small blond groans forward, grabbing his knees.

'Fuck off, you.'

They rush with ferocity and obsession, in the same way as my brothers had, filling days with the run and roar of excitement as the ball went to and from them.

'Will you come to the big shed?' Mr Abdi asks.

'Your temple of earthly delight.'

He turns slowly and edges a smile for a moment and I wonder if I had not been tasteless for Mr Abdi is a particular man, formal and restrained, always pleasant; he made me welcome from the first time I ever went snooping around the allotments, entranced by the geometry and the wealth of lush plants, so I do not want to annoy him.

Every year, in the big shed at the entrance to the allotment site I

have been told authoritatively by him, there is a Summer Show
with lavish cups as prizes of which he has won six for all the
categories he has entered. We move quietly, he with a purposeful
step. There is an aroma of compost, old water, a sweetness and
composure as he watches his cuttings emerge into the light.

'My daughters think I am crazy. They want to keep me in the
house, but it would kill me.'

'I suppose they worry.'

'Worry?'

'You might overdo things.'

'Impossible. Anyway, there is always someone around. Margery is never far and her friend, Sylvia, is always creeping about
trying to get samples off me and lecture me on details of plants as
if I did not know already. I was taught Latin in school, you know.
I know the generic names for plants,' he snaps.

'It would be natural for them to worry if they haven't been
here, they'll think . . .'

'Let them think what they want to. I am their father but they
take no notice of me. Everything I have is here, though sometimes
I think back to before we came and when it was so easy and the
girls were young.'

'But you are proud of them, you said they have done so well.'

'Ah yes. Caroline is finishing her pharmaceutical course and
getting married, Yasmin is married to an optician so that is a good
thing, but Tahrah has still not made up her mind and flits from
job to job. She cannot settle. Shasmi has tried talking to her but
she will not hear of it.'

'You'd like her to settle?'

'If she met some nice young man whose family we could get to
know and exchange gifts with, it would be a relief. But I fear she
won't. She thinks I am old-fashioned. There now. That will do.'

He plumps down the earth in a large tray with seedlings. He
told me the name once but I have forgotten.

'That is all I can do for now. Oh watch . . .'

Sasha's pudgy hand goes towards a tower of plastic flower pots.
Just the thing he would like to have tumble down on his head.

'I'd better take him home.'

'I will have my other vegetables ready for you tomorrow, if you would like to call.' He pushes some stones away with his feet and pulls off his right gardening glove.

I walk the long way back, past a phone box. It is two weeks since I have rung my father. Though I try to make it weekly, other things like life or shopping get in the way. It is almost twelve. If he had been down in the fields where his ragged crops of beans merge with cabbage and carrots as was usual, he would be up for his meal by now.

Propping the buggy up in the open door of the box, I dial.

'Who is it?'

'Dad.'

'Yourself.'

'How are you?'

'Not too bad. Not considering the old cow got herself out of the long pasture last week and was stumbling by the seashore.'

'Good heavens. Did you get her back?'

'Did I hell? I had the boys out looking for hours till we could rope her in but she came. In the end, she came. How are you?'

'I'm all right.'

'You've settled yourself?'

'Yes.'

'Good, and have you a fridge yet?'

'Yes.'

'A decent one, not like that other old thing you had?'

'It works very well.'

'But does the door close on it?'

'Of course.'

Silence.

'Did you get your pension seen to?'

'I did. And a devil of a job it was too. A fella in Newcastle West is dealing with it. I'll definitely be due an increase.'

'I'm glad to hear that.'

'What was it you said?'

'Nothing. How is Connie?'

'Connie's fine. Her appetite is much better and she's eating like a horse or she was the day I was up at her when I went along to see the television and the big American Senator that is over again. They must have nothing to do in their own country to spend so much time here, flitting all over the place. What was that you said?'

'Nothing.'

'It must be the line. Have you any notion of getting a phone of your own?'

'Yes but I can't manage it yet even though I need one with him.'

'What?' he bellows.

'I'd like a phone because of Sasha.'

'Oh, yes. And you need the use of one for yourself too so you can phone up when you like and I can phone you.'

'Yes.'

'Have you any more news so?'

'No.'

'That's it then. I won't be keeping you. You must be busy.'

'' 'Bye Dad.'

'Look after yourself.'

'I will.'

'Goodbye.'

The phone goes dead. I put down the receiver and it looks at me as I edge the buggy away from the open door. Sasha's tiny hands in mitts lie on his blanket. Why does he never ask about him? Not once. Not ever a direct question. He wouldn't, the mean bugger. He wanted all that part of my life concealed because in his mind I had done wrong, but I wanted him to be interested, to know, to understand. At least Sasha is mine and no one can take him away. I can still hear Amy and Jem warning me of a fractured life with teething and nappies. They said I had always said I'd make sure I'd never get stuck this way. Yeah, I did in the days when I didn't know what I was talking about, but as the thing grew, whaling my stomach, I could not face the alternative, so now there's just me and him. Him and his bobble hat over his fat face with splurges of pink cheeks and lashes so dark and long he could only have got them from his father. I go up by the park and turn to the shops. Whatever Amy and Jem thought, and sometimes I did feel as if my brain was not functioning, I had not completely gone to pieces.

The rattle goes in, the dummy, nappies, wipes, tissues, a bib, cotton wool in case. In case of what, I could not think but it was better to travel with it. A beaker, a bottle of juice, some water, a change of clothes in case he spews up all over himself, me, or even worse, somebody else, and a cloth to wipe his face. I shoved the lot in the tray under his seat and set off round the corner to the park.

My fat bundle swings to and forth, moving in waves out and towards me. He loves it. The park is the one place he can have fun outside the confines of the flat, though more than once I have thought of taking him over to my father. He could toddle on his fat legs, be safe with only the soft fall of ditches to worry about. But the trip had not happened. How would we have been greeted? With interest? Acrimony? It was too uncertain and I had never been brave enough to try. Yet he could be a good man. He was once. There were times when we were in the fields in the summer and my mother called me to take him some tea. I ran as fast as I could through the reedy grass and boggy pools to deliver the bottle, while he stood with his fork to one side and embraced me when I gave it to him.

Other mothers leave the play area and gritty-eyed boys with padded jackets and black trainers take over.

'Come on Sasha. Let's see if Mr Abdi is around.'

I bundle him, fat as a loaf, into the buggy and speed along through the iron gates with a broken bit until we get to rough land backing the allotments and creep down the path. A row of terraces was knocked down three years ago and the council still have not decided what to do, so boys just meet and run there. They dart cursing the air, hard as glass.

'Hello there.'

'Hello, Mr Abdi.'

'I have some gourds for you.'

He opens his hands.

'Kaela. I managed to grow them all through the winter. Feel.'

I press the green skin, leaving a dark impression with the back of my thumb.

'They're lovely.'

'I hoped you would like them. I am cutting some for Caroline and Yasmin. I planted them for the first time a year ago.'

My fingers rub the hard edges and I think of old boots and those of my father, worn to the fields, going out or coming in, caked with mud, dust flying off like flour. What would he say about these vegetables with names he had not heard of, strange exotic biographies?

'You can take these with you.'

'You're sure?'

'The girls will not eat all this, besides I have Mooli too. You said you liked it last time.'

He holds out a plastic bag and drops one in, the slim creamy length curving ever so gently.

'They will do you good. Feed you up. You need it.'

'Do I?'

'Yes, a good big meal.'

He thrusts the full bag into my hands.

'Thanks Mr Abdi. Thanks.'

'The boy will enjoy them.'

'It's a great life being a baby. He just sits there getting fat.'

'He will lose it when he runs around. My girls were the same, very chubby when they were small. Let me show you these also. My geraniums and stocks cuttings. Margery is very good. She gave me those. And azalea and forsythia. What do you think?'

I bend to smell.

'You could open a nursery.'

'I will put these in here for you.'

He plucks up two pots and lifts them down safely. He likes watching things grow, and so do I, though I do nothing about it. He has the knack, nurses and cares for his plants, as tenderly as if they were children. He wants the best. I could never do this but I like watching him stride the aisles of the big hut, stroking the shoots of gangly plants with luscious drooping leaves. His life is lived with a dizzying array of smells. All interior. He spends hours here, and when he doesn't, leaves notes for Margery like, "Water the small Magnolia." "Check the shoots." "Please do not overfeed the rose-cuttings."

'I do not really like being in my house. Here I am free to do as I like. It is wonderful.'

'What about when you worked in Bombay? Didn't you miss your garden?'

'Not really. I had a nice office with lots of plants. I made it green and pleasant and was doing well there with the job but Shasmi was eager to leave for England. She thought we would have a better life.'

'Mr Abdi, have you ever been to Kashmir? What is it like?'

'Ah, there is nowhere so fair. Its beauty sings through the lakes and mountains.'

'There's somewhere called . . . Sringa?'

'Srinagar. One of the most lovely towns. I have always wanted to go because they say there is a spirituality about it. They say birds sing, and the songs are reflected in the water. There are the most exquisitely landscaped gardens built for the Mughals and emperors. You could only ever dream of such buildings, palaces and pavilions, with marble and fountains. The garden of India it was called once.'

How much more would I rather have met Hari there, where according to Mr Abdi it is possible to walk along the terraces of the palaces with flower beds laid with intricate designs, and the heat of the day swelling.

'You are thinking of going?'

'No, I just . . . met someone from there once.'

'Ah, a friend?'

He follows my gaze.

'His father,' I say.

'Sasha's?'

I nod.

'He is not here?'

'We met in Berlin when I was studying for a year. I had to leave but he is an actor, so I don't know where he is. He could be anywhere.'

I close my eyes, recalling how two years ago it was easy to see only to the end of the next Strasse. Nothing much mattered but going out for the night. I was young, unwilling to be tied down. Now I have aged decades so that I almost no longer remember those days, except I still recall that night, those eyes, the father of my child.

'You look like one dreaming,' Mr Abdi says.

'I suppose I was once.'

'Do not sound so glum. You cannot help love or the places it takes us. It's a strange, murderous thing.'

'Is it?'

'There is a story of a prince who lived in Poori, where the great temple of love is. He loved the wife of another but she pleaded with him to leave her so that she could stay with her husband. The prince persisted with his attentions and in the end killed the husband, hoping to win the woman, but she was so shocked by the death, she fell down in a heap on top of her husband and later would have no more to do with the man but would rather spend the rest of her days alone.'

'How sad.'

'But you have this young man.'

'Yes.'

'He is great company?'

'Yes but . . .' I pause. What the hell did he want to know about my difficult, cantankerous father, making tea for only himself no matter who else was about.

'My father isn't interested in him, doesn't understand. I don't mean he hasn't got a heart.'

'You just haven't found it.'

'I suppose not.' I wonder if this is not a veiled criticism. 'I'd like to talk about Sasha but I can't. When I start, he changes the subject, so I don't say anything.'

I turn so that Mr Abdi does not see how low and disappointed I feel and so I do not see his watery grey eyes reminding me of pools my father fished, wandering his way across the landscape on his bicycle, scratching the old blue metal, catching ferns and stalks in the spokes, manufacturing dust until he reached a good stretch of road. After my mother died, he went far to reach water as if it drew him, gave him peace, but he must have let it fall away or given it back for he rarely brought it home. I yearned to go with him, longed to journey into the heart of the country, but he left without me, without any of us, eager to get away for a day's peace while we were left alone to bicker or occasionally play.

'If you keep trying you will reach him. I am sure he would like it. I often think that if Tahrah married I might have a grandson.'

'But you have grandchildren.'

'Girls are not the same. A little boy. I could teach him . . .'

'To garden?'

'Yes and be out with me. Girls, you know, are always within. A boy and I could explore.'

Mr Abdi tiptoes to the end of the hut.

'My most prized possession.'

'What are they?'

'A rare kind of orchid.'

'It's lovely.'

'They will truly be when they grow. I have made the right conditions.'

He lifts a glass lid.

'I wish I could do this, but I can't. There is so much to know.'

'We have to try to find out for ourselves. That's what I did. I read all the books and tried many times to set these and for several winters they were killed off or I had used too much fertilizer or too little. Eventually you get it right.'

And how he had. Little delicate drops of petals like sumptuous fabric fall down from a dark centre. He picks up one and brings it close.

'You are so clever.'

'It took me years but every day was worth it. I learnt such patience from my wife. She was quiet, with a slow wisdom. What I could not have done without her. She gave me the strength to come here and courage to stay when times were difficult. She dwells in my heart like one of these.'

I had never heard such praise, such honour, yet here, where it is warm and dank, his remarks seemed natural. Maybe once I had heard something like this from my father in his odd, truculent way, but it was after our mother died fifteen years ago. 'She was a good woman,' he offered, when looking for a new tablecloth and rummaging around amongst laces and chairbacks, doilies and embroideries in the trunk in their room. He missed her, though he rarely admitted it. He turned in on himself and I had to get away as soon as I could. My father was lost and strange, taken out of himself, as if a wind had blown through him. He huddled in the kitchen but no words travelled between us. We were locked into the deep frozen north. Afterwards we laughed at the songs he bawled out, and found bottles empty and hidden behind the septic tank. He was never the same again, but grey and meek, dozed and sad, while we escaped to school and later to college. The well of silence was never broached. Her memory pervaded our lives quietly as a tea towel hanging to dry on the back of a chair, just as she left it.

Mr Abdi gives me one of the flowers.

'Keep it nice and warm and there is no reason why it should not survive.'

I turn to the door expecting him to follow.

'I will stay. There are a few things I have to do.'

I shut the door and pushed Sasha up the path. The sky is darkening later than usual but I still have not got used to the nights falling down. It is always a shock, yet I always hope it will stay light but find myself treading homeward and considering whether to make egg or Marmite sandwiches.

A few days later I push the buggy holding my coat close while a breeze blows. It is cold and getting colder but I have to get out. Washing flings itself around in the gardens. A good blowy day my mother would say, her arms going up and down in a sink of suds. It sounds quiet around the allotments and there is no sign of anyone.

'Hello. Mr Abdi.'

Perhaps he is in one of the smaller huts, though he did not possess one, preferring to have the use of a rented space in the big hut.

'Mr Abdi,' I call, louder.

No sign. Never a day had passed but I had found him. The wind blows across flowers, brushing the tops of sprouts and cabbages. I rumble back with stones hitting the wheels and in the big hut I see Margery.

'Hello there,' she says.

'Have you see Mr Abdi?'

'He's gone to live with his daughter. Didn't you know?'

'No. Why has he gone there?'

'His house got broken into.'

'Oh no.'

'Not badly, but he was very upset, poor love. Well, anybody would be.'

'Was he hurt?'

'No. I don't think he was even in at the time, he was up here, but he got awful shaken.'

'What happened?'

'The police think it's local boys. Whoever it was managed to get in through a window but they didn't take anything except some change left out. Well, what would he have to take when all he loved was here? He was sensitive as a flower, wasn't he?'

I pull back the buggy towards the door.

'He's taken his plants.'

'Oh yes. Said his daughter was going to put up a proper greenhouse. They can do that in Richmond because they have huge gardens. He was a very nice man. Such lovely plants, I never saw the like. I don't know where he managed to get them all. I'm blown if I could ever find some as nice as his. He could plant anything, couldn't he, Sylvia?' Sylvia comes in, holding a pair of light brown suede gardening gloves, the fingers sticking up as she tries to fit them on.

'I found these, Margery. What do you think? They fit.'

She pulls them on.

'You know, I think they must've belonged to him. But as long as me fingers are covered I don't mind.'

I wander down to his patch, vegetables creeping forward in the

light, but I cannot look at any without wanting to hear him
instructing me in their origins and purpose. There is a great hole,
a loss in my day, and for an instant I do not know what to do so I
turn the buggy around and walk up past the plots and get onto
the track to the shops. I wonder what his daughters are like and
see them, slim, creamy-toned with gold earrings and exquisite
manners in a courtyard with white splashed houses and the
dappling smooth breasts of temples they had lived among. There
are buildings touching the sky, and a vague impression of cloud,
translucent, almost gone, and drifting like Hari who has slipped
out of my life. It had been so easy, his coming and going and
leaving this bundle behind.

Sasha sleeps, his fat arms across his chest like an old man as I
go down the track to the shops. There is the phone box. I hear my
father's voice coming across miles of waves. It is about midday,
and days since I propped open the door of the phone box with the
buggy and rang him.

HOWARD WRIGHT

Harbour

O ne of the brightest and best, Moira reasoned all by herself the
time for getting out. She had had enough of the extended
family, the penguins to anoint her wounds, wipe her nose and
mend her looks, so one night she escaped with a zippered holdall
packed the day previous when all the other girls were attending a
sex-education slide show, a friend's money on loan to add to her
own in the seat of her pants. She caught the first bus out, travelled
north and south and a long way west, until finally, after two
months in hostels, men's flats, and public parks, she replanted
herself in a casual fishing village on the eastern peninsula among
the nets, clinking masts and the pervasive rank plutonium salt-
smell of nuclear Britain.

She rented a wardrobe, a bed and a table in a mouldering
room at the top of a house dark and cold whatever the weather,
and, giving nothing away, through sheer power of personality
wangled a job at a seafront chipper, graduating the following
Monday to a clear view of the grease-stained main street, the
thuggish arcades and rubbishy flowerbeds. By the second week
she had found a routine. She took up serious smoking and tied
back her hair. She lost weight. She masturbated. And after
another month she was able to pay back her friend, sending the
postal order from a town at the other end of the bus route.

Then one day, as if some barrier had been breached, the
summer crashed into the village and the chip trade was good and
getting better. The customers were day trippers wanting a breath
of air and a clear view of the coast, the harbour, the curve of the
Earth. They walked to the end of the breakwater, then hurried
back complaining of the sharp light. They stood in uninhibited
groups or rubbernecked in tiny cars, the traffic increasing until

the main street and tributaries growled with metal lava and the thumping beat of heavy bass. Teenagers mauled each other. Drunks abused drunks. Mothers with babies roamed in gangs. By evening, many of the older couples had found safe sex and large meals in manky hotels, leaving the children free and vicious. The local women stayed back, or indulged in brief, loud liaisons, while their men built Liverpool or Glasgow, or hauled and gutted on the trawlers. Moira wasn't the type to mess around but, wanting to feel safe, she adopted a boyfriend, Rory, who kept a diary and listened to Fleetwood Mac. At first he was all talk. Then the talk petered out, and polite if firm groping ensued, much to Moira's consternation.

Her room, at the top of the grand slice of Victorian ruin called the Villas, offered a sky-view through a cracked and spattered casement. As well as that, the wallpaper peeled and rotted, the cornicing detached, and the bed unstable, the partition walls were so thin she was forced to listen to conversations in other rooms, with the grumbles and groans of the inefficient plumbing, all of which made her realize she was not yet free of her fear, a fear which, among other things, compelled her to check under the bed and in the wardrobe before going to sleep. When Rory called, the pair of them spent less time on the mattress and more on the torn carpet, which she cosified with pillows and a blanket.

Occasionally, he brought the blue-backed diary he was keeping especially for her, and which she added to from time to time. She did this with enthusiasm, enjoying the embellishment of what she was; Rory explaining he had spent ten years and ten volumes doing the same for himself even though no one would read them.

One particular entry covered the telephone of the house, how it only took incoming calls, and worse, clung to the wall near the front door (which, of course, had a doormat), and resembled nothing more than a tiny flayed possum surrounded by scrawled numbers and abbreviated messages where all kinds of eavesdroppers could make a point of earwigging on your business.

So no surprise, on the Sunday in question when the call came through, Alfie Burns, the spriteliest of Moira's unsavoury 'neighbours', got to it first, shouted her name, and she came running,

clattering down the echoey flights to grab the receiver from the fat
man who was always offended when the call wasn't for him –
which, of course, was always.

Hastily repositioning her clothing, Moira put the receiver to her
ear, heard the voice and visibly straightened. She cupped a hand
over the tobacco-sweet mouthpiece. It was a man's voice, familiar
and knowing, which, after a few pleasantries, asked to meet her
somewhere – she could name the time and the place. Moira
explained she worked most evenings, but finished at nine on
Tuesdays. OK, said the voice, after nine – where? She described a
spot on the outskirts, in the open and within running distance of
the harbour. He would find it, he said, and after giving her a
warning about not turning up, said goodbye. Moira gently
replaced the receiver and, deciding not to rush, not to fall into
his trap, slowly climbed to her room and cried for the pleasure it
gave her.

Glass had been recruited to find Moira and bring her home. He
was inexpensive, stubborn, had an eye for detail, and dyed what
remained of his hair. For his own reasons he concluded that
Moira, though wayward, was worth pursuing, and in time
gradually moved over to her side. His employers called her
'ungrateful and disobedient', which he agreed with, finding it
sexy. And though he liked Moira, he had a job to do – professional
and, by reputation, pedantic, he was trusted. He had even talked
to her on several occasions over the intervening weeks while she
continually gave him the slip. However, Glass was so confident
this time that he began to cultivate a moustache to add to his
thinning quiff; this time he would get his reward.

He retraced his steps and spoke again to her friends about bus
routes and date stamps. He discovered some astonishing errors
(chief among them staying too long in the fishing village), and
was soon travelling in Moira's wake, using brutality and gentle
diplomacy, at turns coolly arrogant and charming, until he
reached the harbour's clinking masts, the main street, the
rubberneckers, and was throwing his own litter in the flowerbeds.

He booked into a B & B for its en suite and satellite TV, and dutifully chatted up the landlady, thinking himself the spy, the debonair hero, the sly chameleon. He checked out the shoe shops, the newsagents, the supermarket, the whole street, and finally the chipper. It was then a short step to staking out the Villas, and (timing it to perfection) making the phone call.

This was a piece of bravado which surprised him. The journey, the questions, his growing proximity to Moira, had filled him with expectations and made him take chances he might otherwise find disagreeable. Touring the pubs, he was the seasoned drinker, a raconteur standing his round, getting to know the barmen and matching anecdote with anecdote, colouring his fictional life for the genial five-speed, two-fisted imbibers. He made friends and discovered their nicknames and sporting favourites. By Tuesday, he had thoroughly enjoyed himself, and was eager and waiting. He re-dyed his hair, trimmed the tache, and promised himself to learn a few jokes.

Until, at long last, finally, there was Moira.

As he watched her, stretching in a white nylon coat, doling out orders to the obese and sullen, shuffling the hot golden mass from the tank of fat into scoops of paper, taking the money and giving change, Glass realized she belonged there as much as anywhere – not bad or mad and, regrettably for her, not yet invisible.

Ten past nine, and the chipper full, Moira left by a side door. She took off her coat, rolled it into a ball and stuffed it in a shoulder bag. Glass drove ahead to the place by the road on the outskirts, past the hubcaps and thistles, where the sea was always calm and the crumpled landscape lay uninterrupted.

True to her word, Moira followed, for she knew Glass and his methods. She lit a cigarette to cloak the smell of the evening's work. Her skin reeked, making her complexion worse, a few pimples already breaking through the epidermis. The soft air was playful on her bare legs; her unwieldy if comfortable trainers scuffed the dry road. She kept her hair up in clips. Glass, she knew, noticed these things so she had to be careful.

As it turned out, whether intentional or not, he was visible a long way off like a crease in the evening air, tinged orange by the late sun, taking in the panorama, then wiping his eyes and putting something in a pocket of his jacket.

Anger getting the better of her fear, Moira slowed to finish her cigarette, discarding the butt in a defiant gesture as she came up close. The sky deepened to a planished blue. Smoke plumed against a faraway hill; a smouldering wood, thought Moira, or a livelihood disappearing molecule by molecule. Higher up and approaching, a diamond jet scored the graduated perfection, passing over and away towards the ship resting on the horizon.

Glass stepped forward and nodded, uttering something suitably banal.

Moira coughed and lied, saying she didn't recognize him with the moustache and the tint in his hair. He suddenly became self-conscious, scratched his face and hesitated; she had landed the first blow. He wouldn't be drawn. Glass said she looked fit and healthy, the sea air must be agreeing with her. Moira ignored his sweet talk and got to the point. She wanted to know how he had found her and what he was going to do about it. Glass gave her half the story from middle to end, and offered a cigarette which Moira refused, saying she only smoked American. Trust Glass to get that wrong; details were supposed to be his strong point. He made a note: she wore tortoiseshell clips, the skirt was short, skin greasy, and when she was tired she annoyed him.

He tried sympathy, said running away was no solution, she would always be found. She wasn't as clever as she thought. Round Two to Glass. He was here, he explained, to bring her back, though he knew she wouldn't go. He reminded her that she had once called him 'consoling'. Moira said he didn't suit the moustache or the hair colour; made him look pasty, translucent – she saw through his vanity a long time ago. And Glass, though hurt, thought it a good sign she criticized his appearance.

OK, he said. Game over. No 'consolation' this time. She could leave when she liked, and he would still be there or there-abouts.

Moira shrugged and said he had to earn his money somehow. With no obvious skills he was now a tout, a snitch, a bounty-hunter; the lowest of the low, an arselicker. She felt sorry for him. Glass didn't care what she thought – a job's a job; she could keep running and he would still get paid. He wouldn't lose out.

On the pig's back, aren't you?

That's right, replied Glass, happy at last to agree.

Moira asked how long he was going to keep up this cloak-and-dagger act, the secret agent escapade.

As long as it takes.

She knew he enjoyed his job but this was ridiculous. She smiled at the facetious moustache, if in her head she had doubts about its motives.

This isn't a marriage and I'm not going with you or anybody like you, even without the facial hair.

You'll never marry; I'll never marry; we're both of us destined to be on our ownios.

OK, OK, she said, suddenly feeling outmanoeuvred. Where's the catch?

No catch. Either you come with me or keep running. I'll be with you either way.

The plane vanished, leaving a chalk trail dissipating overhead. The hill was smoke-free, and the freighter dozed against the last of the sky.

Of course Glass knew the girl wouldn't be amenable; something else was needed. He had tried all the moves and still she wouldn't see sense. Moira hesitated; her legs were cold, she wanted another cigarette but her hands were shaking.

I found you because you were stupid, Glass continued. The way to lose me is to live nowhere, have no friends, be self-sufficient. You depend on people too much.

She had been stupid, Moira admitted, though she would not accuse him of being clever; she eluded him before and would do so again. At least she learned by her mistakes; she had him on a leash and could let go any time. She too had tricks up her sleeve. And with that she turned and began walking back to the harbour.

Now Glass was trembling. His one big chance was getting smaller by the second. His voice wavered slightly with the excitement. It would be enough, he shouted, to have a kiss and I'll let you go. I'll say you've gone across the water or your trail's gone cold. Let me kiss and hold you, Moira, and I'll make you disappear.

Moira paused at her name, lit the much-needed cigarette and, realizing he was joking, laughed.

Life isn't that simple, she said, and congratulated him on having an imagination and a cock.

No, really, he said, that's the deal.

Moira put her hand over her mouth and coughed violently. He was serious.

Look, she said, swallowing her breath, you're old enough to be my da, if I had a da. And I would kill you if you so much as touched me like a da.

He held out a hand. Well, that's the deal.

Moira sighed. Just go away, she said, knocking his hand aside. Or do something useful like annoying someone else. I want nothing to do with you. She pushed past him and carried on, with greater speed, towards the village nestling at the bottom of the road, the masts and lines protruding above the rooftops.

Like the professional he was, Glass wouldn't take no for an answer. He hadn't run for months, yet here he was cantering after the girl, her thin legs, the swing of her arms, and reaching out to seize her by an elbow.

Last chance. The elbow was cold, the skin dry and rough.

Moira whipped her arm away. No! she shouted.

He grabbed both shoulders. Yes, he said.

Moira spat in his face.

Though smaller, Glass was stronger and heavier, and ignored her venom. He gripped a fist of hair, and loosening the clips which fell on the road, pulled her head back, forcing Moira to drop her bag and expose the intimacies of her throat.

Yes, he repeated, clamping his mouth onto hers, pushing both hands away as he pressed against her breasts and stomach, his own hands struggling beneath her skirt and over her buttocks.

Moira swore and punched and wrestled, tearing his fingers from her flesh only to have them reassert themselves. Glass squeezed and cuddled, his suit protecting him from the blows. Then Moira landed a punch to his stomach which stalled his advance and allowed her to hear a clink in his jacket pocket, a chink in his armour. Instantly, like a snake shooting out its tongue, she retrieved his car-keys, and slithered away from him.

You can't run, shouted Glass.

Just watch me.

Moira swung her arm back and threw the clump of smooth steel as far as she could into the dark and kelpy sea. Glass, winded, red, angry, disappointed, followed the trajectory to the muted splash, turned and watched the girl scamper away. To himself as much as anybody he said, I know you, Moira. I know all about you. Reassured, he pocketed the clips, secured her bag, re-established the faint strands of his much-maligned coiffure, and took off his socks and shoes to wade out over the slippy stones, destroying his suit.

It was nearly midnight when she got back. Her money and stuff were back with Glass. She went to Rory's for replacements, and used Rory's key to clear out the essentials and tidy herself. Rory got a slap for not being around when he was needed; of course, he blamed himself for his weakness, then shrugged and went on his way to catch a few of the fish swimming, he rather optimistically thought, in the great sea of Fleetwood Mac enthusiasts.

Next time I'll get a woman who wants sex, he said.

Impossible, Moira told him. Sure you're only a prick from the neck up.

Her final words were a warning about Glass; however, Rory had already met the man. With no time to kill her former groper, she threatened to break *Albatross* if she wasn't given the blue diary, then stamped on the record anyway, and smashed it against the door, and took to the road with Rory's money in the seat of her pants, a half-empty book under her arm, and a bag of nothing over her shoulder.

Glass, of course, followed at a healthy distance, keeping his masters informed, though they, it must be said, were already forgetting Moira and regretting Mr Glass.

MARTIN MALONE

Where the Sun Doesn't Shine

Harry Kyle dreams about thorns of Christ growing briary on the roadside, of air sweetened by orange and lemon groves, of banana plantations, fruit bagged in garish blue plastic, protection against heavy winter rains, yellow sand storms, the sea's withering breezes, and an added bitter coldness that falls with the darkening of day. Of mush terracotta soil, drying under the wild caress of a Mount Hermon wind. Of a pale sun in grey-white cloud, hundreds of seabirds raising a cacophony, feeding on the remains of a harvest reaped by gelignite fishermen.

His dream eye sees grey Israeli patrol vessels bobbing on a shoreline not theirs, passing the gaping eye socket of a Moorish keep, its sun-scorched walls soaking in the smoky aroma of mint leaves burned by loved ones for loved ones who can love no more, in a Muslim cemetery that reaches as far as tall iron gates set like black teeth between marble columns. The cry of the gannet, the shush to shore of stormy waves, the first time to see another's blood on his hand, and how it hurt, without actually causing him physical pain.

By the time he parks the Chevrolet jeep and unloads his pistol, returning the Browning to stores, along with Joe's Stengun, night has drawn in. He wakes with a wide-eyed jolt, and a constricting sensation in his throat. His sweat rich, thick and warm on his forehead, his temple veins throbbing. His dream ending as it had begun, with soap staining his hands a bright red.

Harry Kyle stares at the darkness until the darkness stares back. A stiff wind blows, sweeping across the Currah Plains, blowing flecks of rain against the new PVC windows. June's naked buttocks lean in to his, and for moments he snatches comfort in her heat, before easing from bed.

In the kitchen he makes tea and brings the steaming mug into the living room, and sits on a fireside chair, a breath of cold ash catching in his lungs. He sees the darkness and the amber streetlights of the Camp through the quarter of window revealed by the blind. The wind plays down the throat of the chimney, and sometimes it falls silent. Its silence is a silence of the ages, of wisdom garnered from the four corners of the world. In its silence Harry Kyle feels truly alone.

June's trying to figure out what the hell has got into him, why he has a mourning bell for a face, and why, sometimes, when disturbed by the kids, he yells at them, and at her, and what happened to his relaxed, easy-going manner. He asks himself, too. Continually.

He was home from a place he couldn't wait to leave behind. And now, by night, and when not otherwise preoccupied, by day, he found himself in his combat boots, reliving, and thinking, and when not thinking . . . seeing.

He was weeks back from the Middle East, the tan starting to fade in the late autumn coldness. He'd put on a little weight that June said suited him, had given her something to hold. He hadn't been training, he said. He was twenty-eight, and liked to pump iron, see the muscles flexing in his forearms, feel the perspiration trickle down his spine. But now, only lately, the inclination to train had deserted.

He could never wash his hands enough. June appreciates that, the new ultra hygienic Harry. You could eat your dinner off his hands, if you didn't mind the smell of Dettol.

He finishes his tea and rubs his hands together. He was raised on a small poor farm in a corner of Kildare. Land and livestock he'd come to hate as much as the father who, although not a hard man, but neither an especially loving one, he'd come to detest for tolerating poverty, for expecting his son to do likewise.

He was home, but not home. His mind elsewhere, his grey eyes on Lebanese soil, his nostrils taking in the rich red earth, baked by the hot Khamsin winds, and freshened by the early autumn rains, and sea breezes that chased and drove cracks in the hot winds, making crevices for the rains to come through.

This Saturday, three of them ago, he woke in his prefab accommodation and lay on for a few minutes. A brown army blanket tacked across the window blocked daylight, except for a tear in the middle revealing a single bright eye. Reaching a hand from under the green mosquito netting he thumbed a switch on his Sharp radio, and listened to the BBC World Service News. The air smelt of last night's mosquito coil lying as ash under its small aluminium plinth. In spite of the deterrent, one buzzed by his ear in the middle of the night, and fattened by his blood had paused long enough for him to snap it dead with his hands, its burst carcass staining the netting.

The Ghanaians guarding the barracks kept wood fires going in braziers they'd fashioned from barrels, and stood around these at nights with their FN rifles slung over their shoulders, chatting with the Lebanese army sentries who showed up on parade most mornings, and left the soldiering on the streets to the Amal militia.

The Military Police detachment operated from a long building with an eaveless verandah. On ground level, the sandbag parapet soaked in rainwater that streamed down the valleys of the corrugated tin roof. Some of the bags had burst, spilling sand, and others were beginning to unstitch. Replacing them would pass the time, and afterwards he'd type up that Final Traffic Accident Report and get it off to HQ.

Joe the Fijian was on the Duty Desk this morning, taking weapons in from some French UN soldiers who were visiting the ruins of Tyre.

He read last night's journal, checked the ablution area for cleanliness, and the dry toilet for emptiness. He was the oncoming Duty Desk, and if there weren't enough buckets to flush away the waste the toilet got blocked. Sometimes the off-going Desk didn't bother to replenish the buckets, and people just dumped their loads and walked away. Then if you wanted to crap you'd to use an Arab toilet and squat over a hole, and it isn't easy to read a newspaper in that position.

Knocking on the kitchen door, he entered. You always knocked beforehand. This was done to let the rats and mice know you were coming in. He checked the cupboard above the sink. If there was a rat or a mouse pinned he'd only have coffee for breakfast. By rights he should leave the traps until after breakfast, but that affected his appetite too. He couldn't sit at the oil-cloth-covered table and eat, not with the image of a dead rat next door, its black eyes glassy, its ringed tail hanging limp, its piss and shit staining the newspaper laid on the shelves. He rapped on the long press and, eating a breath, swung the double doors open. Blankety-blank. The trap set, its rasher missing, its blue sowing thread frayed.

Joe said a Ghanaian had eaten the rasher. Probably the rat, too. He doesn't like Ghanaians. It's a racist thing with him. He doesn't like blacks. He was serious when he said this, and he a dusky colour himself. A true Fijian with no light colouring the Indians had brought to the islands. Harry was sure he meant he didn't like Africans, but didn't go down the road of asking him. The whole colour issue can raise its ugly head and refuse to lie down. But he derived great craic from the things Joe said to the lads, things no white man who wanted to own wrinkles would ever say.

That's how the day started. Checking rat traps, eating break-fast, listening to Joe locking the French weapons away. Bitching about the Ghanaians singing jungle songs by the braziers last night, eating the donkey they'd skinned that evening. Going on to say that he'd checked with Ops, and the Area of Operations was quiet.

Harry sighs, eases the cabinet's drop leaf down and screws off the brandy top, filling a small glass. Something to hold and stir, to catch his stare, rather than to drink. The wind moans and dies. Traffic begins to fill the roads, headbeams on.

The radio set crackled with activity. Ops telling the various battalions to go into Shelter. Some place in Nepbatt was hit. He picked up the gist of it as he entered the duty room. Joe was already in flak jacket and helmet, carrying his Stengun, the Investigation Box sitting at his feet, saying he'd called the others out of their beds to man the desk, and as backup if they need them.

Joe wasn't too sure what had happened, but something had, and Tyre MP had to respond a.s.a.p.

Harry gets up, sips at his brandy, and tugs on the blind, revealing the full window picture; beyond the road the Curragh Plains flare into a broad expanse of lush green carpet, patterned with furze bushes the last of summer gold on their pine. Grey skies, pylon wires holding chorus-lines of birds, racehorses nudged to gallops by jockeys collar-zipped against the cold, a spill of chips, and tree tops of distant woods. He wasn't in Lebanon . . . but telling himself that, and showing his eyes the proof didn't keep the bad dreams away.

They drove quickly along the coastal road, passing sand quarries, a half-built hotel someone's second thought, and twisted railroad tracks that once carried the Orient Express, before wheeling a left turn up Burma Road, hearing gunfire in the distance and the sound of a tank loosening its chamber.

Harry bites his lip, fingers sleepcrust from his eyes, and returns to the armchair. They didn't speak much in the jeep. He drove steadily, not rushing. All he could think about was Ops sending the Battalions into shelter, and the MPs out in a soft-top jeep to investigate an incident of which they knew nothing. The unknown mission. It mightn't have been as bad if he'd had time to steel himself.

Reaching a checkpoint they were flagged down a narrow, rutted road by Nepalese soldiers. Harry knew the village but its name escaped him. Joe said Kafra. He was right.

He parked in front of the UN post and was met by an officer who brought them to the scene. A soldier's broken body lying on the ground by a whitewashed wall, his severed right hand beside a railing guarding an aged olive tree, bullets spilled from his rifle's magazine, the weapon's buttstock shattered. And cats darting in out of the small square, feeding on flesh. An old man carrying a black bag shooing them away, picking up pieces. There was more. Joe touched his ribs to show him.

A woman's foot wrenched from her body lay close to Harry. Upright, blue leggings, bone and sinew − blown off her feet. Her foot forgotten about in the rush to get her to hospital. The officer had mentioned that, hadn't he? Eighteen years old. She'd a name but it passed by Harry.

The old man's eyes met his. Harry thought how they had no depth. The bag opened. Harry Kyle eased to his hunkers, pinched the girl's foot and lowered it into the bag, and then watched Joe go through the same procedure with the soldier's hand.

For moments Harry stood there, feeling a numbness in the pit of his belly. Gathering his thoughts he went about his work.

He took photographs, and measurements for the sketch. Names of witnesses for the statements that would follow. On the way to Tyre they stopped in Nepbatt HQ and snapped photographs of the body for the Final Report. It wasn't his first time to see a dead body. But the others were of old men, and it seemed sad but natural that they should die.

This was wrong. Bodies torn, the souls wrenched from them. The Nepalese soldier a week left to go home, home to a wife and four-year-old son who would only have a scant memory of his dad. The young woman . . .

He'd always known that some day this would happen. His eyes would be called upon to see such a sight. He didn't believe he'd handle it so badly. Didn't think for one moment he'd wake up in a cold sweat, that the sight of bloodied limbs would haunt his nights and his waking hours. Seeing them in the ordinary things he did. Imagining June's foot in a blue legging, seeing the kids missing a hand; horrific thoughts sailing across his mind. And cats crying in his nightmares in a demented craving for the taste of human flesh.

The weapons logged in, the blood on his hands, and the washing, the constant washing, because his hands can never be clean enough. And he tells himself he washes not because the girl's foot was dirty and covered with the dust of her day, but because he is fearful of being tainted by the evil done to her, while now and then he acknowledges it is the sight and the feel of her foot he wishes to scrub from his memory.

He hears the door opening, but doesn't look up. Its hinges need oiling.

'Harry?' June says.

His 'Yea' is low.

'What's wrong?'

He sighs. 'Nothing.'

'It can't be nothing.'

Tell June? He hadn't told anyone. He and Joe went back to Tyre, rang Ops with their findings, and while he typed up a report Joe sieved cava into a basin, and later they drank it, and beer, loads of cheap Lebanese beer. Getting sick, and Harry knowing that his vomiting had nothing to do with mixing his drinks.

He tells her. Inching the words out, and June waiting for the bits to fall with an eagerness in her blue eyes, as though with his words she could piece him back together and make all the nightmares go away. June believes in building bridges with words.

Her fingers stay on her lips. He'd finished and he waits for her to say something. Anything. He can tell by her eyes she doesn't know what to say. Then he catches the smell of that day. It breezes into his nostrils as June goes outside to the kids. A smell of death, of war, perhaps of Hell. Yes, Hell. And he has a little corner of it in his mind all to himself. In the shade, where the sun doesn't shine.

FIONA O'CONNOR

The Break

A small thatched cottage with a crooked path leading to a wooden gate. Behind lay a neat wood and tidy hills and cypresses mounting in strict order. The scene duplicated over and over across the expanse of nylon curtain. And each scene a closed universe unto itself, corralled by a bleached ring of daisies, the whole as white as a Communion veil.

She sat alone in the breakfast room drinking her tea. Around her the tables were laid. Cold cutlery silently admonished the missing guests. Above her a lost-looking man stared out from a framed apostolic blessing upon Michael and Deirdre on the occasion of their wedding in Clonkeen, Co. Kerry, 1975. The lost man was the Pope. Dead now, he had been a familiar stranger all her life. Sounds of cooking and radio were coming from the kitchen next door, but she preferred her isolation in the chilly room full of down-turned cups.

The others would be along soon. Frank would wander in rubbing his sore head or his hands, cracking feeble jokes. Eileen, his wife, would soon follow, manoeuvring her bulk between the close-set tables, frowning on Frank, averting her hostile eyes from the swollen-faced young woman. Danny too, last up, would not be able to look at her. They would tuck into their fried breakfasts, slurp their sugared tea. Frank would talk in a feigned shocked tone about the amount of gargle they had got through last night. Nothing would be said about the incident. Afterwards they would go to their rooms, pack up and head home. They had intended to spend their last day sightseeing but that would not be possible now. They would drive home in silence. And she would not see Danny again. At least not outside work. He would avoid her at the factory too. Perhaps she'd look for another job. Perhaps London. Who could say?

The evening had started out well. Winter break. Nice restaurant. Sirloin steak and chips and Irish coffees at the finish. She had felt relaxed, watching Danny beaming at her. He was pleased with how she was doing. Frank was smiling too. Eileen she was not sure about. She wasn't hostile exactly. In fact, she was being friendly, to all appearances. But there was something there, behind her smiles. Still, she'd come around eventually. Anyway, she'd have to put up with it, now that Frank was on her side.

Danny went off to order the first round – pints of Harp for the men, the girls were on vodkas and Coke. Frank eased open the top button of his shirt. His moon face blossomed bright red from his collar. He patted his fat gut as he eyed her across the table, his loud Belfast voice filling the restaurant. Apart from two other tables – parties of weekenders braving the weather – the large restaurant was empty. This made the impact of Frank's booming voice with his loud laughter all the more noticeable. Frank was telling the joke about Cinderella washing her knickers. His eyes kept resting on her breasts, his little tongue kept wetting his purple lips; he liked her.

She brushed her long hair from her face, laughing at the joke she had heard many times and anyway was not funny. But everything was funny now in the first mellowing into drink as their faces warmed, and they pushed back their chairs from the table so that they could lean back, cross their legs and eye each other with lowered guard. She lifted her vodka and Coke and smiled at Danny and Frank. Eileen swivelled her corpulence uneasily in the hard chair, managing to turn her back to the girl. Frank ignored his wife, winked at Danny.

Danny was wearing white socks. She noted that with pleasure. White socks emblazoned with a little Irish tricolour. You could see it because his flannel trousers were too short. The tricolour was enough to get him shot on the Shankill. Down South Danny was indulging himself in a little patriotic belongingness. You wouldn't think he was fifty-five. He looked much younger than Frank or Eileen but in fact they were all born in the same year, 1944. That seemed a reassuringly real year. A year for history books, for war, real war, with a beginning and an end, and where people knew

what they were supposed to do. Not like her year. Born on Bloody
Sunday, 1972, in a flat in Kells Walk, her mother's screams in
labour insignificant in the noise of gunfire and panic on the street
outside in a war that was not a war at all, but a slow bleed.

Danny wore his age well. He didn't eat too much, looked after
his hair. She'd found aftershave in his bathroom, though she had
never known him to wear it. It was only when he was naked that
you could see. Her white body slim and young touching his tired
skin. She liked his eyes on her nakedness, his heavy breathing
that was immediate when she touched him, his quick erection
that would not last, his gratefulness before sleep and the snores of
sweet oblivion. And she liked his old man's smell.

She knew they were being watched. Their bantering hard tones
were alarming the soft-bellied Free Staters. For years they'd been
hearing accents like theirs. On the evening news mostly, linked
with atrocities, with murder and hatred they couldn't fathom.
Now they were uneasy at the loud laughter, the odd picture the
group made – the beautiful young woman with the fat couple and
the smiling man with thinning hair and shortened trousers. She
leaned over the table to collect the empty bottles and Danny
patted her bottom fondly and Frank winked at Danny again. She
liked that.

Eileen had gone to the toilet as she went up to get another
round. They were settling into the main body of the evening, the
drinking hours when they would labour through many pints and
glasses, reaching ever deeper into the well of deferral, forgetfulness, postponement of pain. She knew what was being said while
she was away. Winking again, Frank would be edging forwards
and, lowering his voice, would ask, 'Are you enjoyin' yerself,
Danny boy?'

And Danny would smile enigmatically and nod that he was of
course.

'How did you ever manage it, ye wee bastard? She's lovely, so
she is – Jesus sweet Christ, what I'd give for a night wi' that.'

'Shush up, you fat bastard, she'll hear you. Ah, there you are –
did you manage that all on your own – sure I was comin' to help
you.'

And they drank another round and laughed louder. The driving rain against the window and the black night outside drew them closer to each other. Frank went on and on about his engines and Eileen even made a joke about how Frank would smuggle engines into the garage like fallen women. Danny didn't say much at all, just leaned back and laughed at his fat friend's jokes till his eyes streamed with tears. Everything was funnier here where they were different – strangers in the place of schoolday legend. The belonging place that gave them a point of reference. The place of soft vowels and smiles that held them just outside acceptance. But they didn't care about that now. It was enough to be here. The food and the drink were good and Derry was a long way away.

Derry, how she hated that place, and yet it was home. How could you hate your home? Easy, she thought, if home hates you. Danny made things better though. At the factory all the men eyed her, licked their chops. She knew that. But they wouldn't touch, only look. She knew that too. They were scared, so they were. As though she was a booby trap. Danny now, he wasn't afraid. He laughed at the threat that hung over her. There he was, waiting around the gate every morning, waiting for her and she was always late, rushing up the street from the bus stop with her coat and scarf blowing open and her make-up a mess from trying to apply it on a jolting bus. He'd be shy. His voice would come out all forced.

'Morning Sheila, you're lookin' well.' It was all he could think of to say. Every morning the same thing.

'Morning Sheila, you're lookin' well.'

Until one day, in the dinner hour it was, he made himself speak and asked her out for a drink. She had pretended to go all coy herself. She was a good actress, having learned early how to lie. She could see his mates watching, disapproving. And he like a big puppy in front of her, eager for her answer.

They met in a bar out in the suburbs, where they'd not be known. She wore a pale, flowery dress and put her hair in two plaits so that she looked like his daughter rather than the woman who went home with him that night and quietly fucked him until he bawled out with an animal's ecstatic distress and lost himself in her.

'Are you enjoyin' yerself there?' Danny said, leaning over to her with his eyes glowing, his arm circling her back.

For devilment, because she knew Eileen was watching, Sheila drew herself up to Danny's ear and whispered to him until he broke into a horse's bray of laughter and sought another wink from Frank.

'You're a witch, so you are. A white witch.' And he pinched her waist so that she said in mock admonition, 'Stop that now you. Behave or we'll be thrown out altogether.' She glanced over at Eileen. 'Don't you see how they're all watching and listening and getting their thrill.'

'Aye,' said Frank, 'youse two'd better be careful. You know what they're like round here, they'll have the priest down to yis any minute now.'

Sheila smiled at Frank and Eileen saw and said, 'Huh,' opening a packet of crisps and turning away from them to watch the rain out of the window.

'We've no need of any priest,' said Danny, pulling Sheila towards him. 'I'll be doing any blessing of the sacraments needs doing tonight. Isn't that right, eh? eh?' He tickled her until she cried out in her laughter, 'Danny Boland! Stop that you wee shite, GET OUT TO FUCK!' and Frank nearly burst himself with laughing and spluttering. But Danny continued tickling her until she screamed all the more so that the waitress stepped out from behind the cash register to see what was happening.

One of the other parties got up to leave then, throwing glances towards them, and Eileen said, without looking around from her perusal of the weather and her crisps, 'Like mother, like bastard.'

The laughter stopped. Danny sat back in his seat, ran his fingers through his hair, crossed one tricoloured leg over the other.

'Ah, Eileen, don't start that now,' Frank appealed to his wife.

'I was at school with her,' Eileen continued. 'Bet you didn't know that. She was famous, your mammy was. Known down our way to all and sundry. Known especially to the soldiery. Oh yes. Known especially. We called her "the filly". Guess why?'

Sheila pulled a cigarette from the box. Her face looked nonchalant.

'Frank, gis a light there, will ye.'

Frank picked up the lighter, reached across the table towards her at the same time as she raised herself from her seat and leaned her body forward so that his hand brushed against her breasts. She laughed shortly.

'I said a light, pet, y'know?'

She spoke quietly, intimately, knowing Eileen was watching them in the reflection of the window. She laughed again as Frank lit her cigarette.

'Steady,' she said, taking hold of his proffered hand.

'Because she was a ride,' Eileen said. 'Though that was nothin'' to what she turned into, aye. Filly was a compliment compared to that . . .'

'Eileen!' Danny said.

'An' that's the truth of it.' Eileen scrunched up the empty crisp bag, let it fall to the floor.

'Oh, sweet divine fuck,' said Frank.

Sheila merely blew smoke from her cigarette.

'But then, fillies and grass, you know? The two go together, don't they?' Eileen stressed the word 'grass' lovingly.

Sheila reached across the table and stubbed her cigarette into Eileen's face.

'You fuckin' wee informer's cunt,' Eileen hissed, throwing her considerable bulk at Sheila, grabbing her hair and yanking her head back for what Sheila knew well was coming. In one hammer blow, Eileen smashed her big head down into Sheila's face. Chairs were flung to the ground. The two men tried to separate the women. Staff rushed out from the kitchen, then stopped, not knowing what to do. The women bawled at each other. Blood was running from Sheila's nose, filling her mouth as she shouted, spitting from her, turning the front of her jumper to browny red. Danny held her back but she was struggling and straining from his grasp, her anger bringing strength to her limbs which Danny could not contain.

'You're dead so y'are, y're dead, d'ye hear me, fucking dead as a pig,' she cried out in a strange, disconnected voice, pulling away from the hold on her, kicking out her legs at Eileen and landing a solid boot in her stomach at which the big woman gasped and collapsed slowly to the floor. Behind them another woman screamed.

Danny shook Sheila hard. 'THAT'S ENOUGH!'

It stopped then. Eileen sat heaving on the floor, surrounded by upturned chairs, spilt drinks, broken glass. The two men stood looking stupid, looking away. Sheila wiped the back of her hand under her nose, saw the blood.

'Where's the fuckin' toilets?' she said, turning and stumbling away down the restaurant. It dawned on her as she went that she was very drunk and that her nose was broken.

The cool tiles against her face were sobering. She sat in the cubicle, aware of the tang of vomit, mouth gaping, eyes closed.

She was humming quietly, trying to avoid the pain.

'I wish I was in Carrickfergus,' she sang.

She started crying. Big silent sobs welled up, spilled down her face. She sat on a toilet in holy Ireland, weeping, bleeding, foreign to any and every place on that belligerent sod stuck not far enough out in the sea. And there, on a hillside up North, the remains of her creator, her mother, lying beneath a Celtic cross, despoiled, spray-painted in green and orange by others who, like herself, could never belong. With *their* kin laid out too, uncertain occupants, around them. And none of them belonged. For history did not accommodate them. They were the dispossessed; forget the diaspora. It was them. Here lies Rosemary Morrison, RIP. Traitor. She continued to hum her tune, rocking herself on the toilet seat, tears falling off her chin and merging with the bloody mess of her jumper.

Somebody came in, banged the door.

'Are you all right in there?' It was a Southern voice, the waitress. 'They're waiting for you. Outside. Your friend said to tell you it's all OK now.'

Sheila could hear the disapproval in the woman's voice. There was a small window over her head. She stood up.

'I'm fine.'

'I've brought your coat. Your friend said . . .'

'I'll be there in a wee minute, tell them.'

'Are you sure now? They're waiting to go. Paid up and waiting for you.'

She waited too, unsure of what she should do. They never had anything like this before. It was a nice restaurant – family outings and visitors, Continentals, Americans. Nice people. Nasty crowd, these Northerners. Though weren't they all supposed to be reconciled now. The woman brushed back a stray wisp of her red hair and looked her face over in the mirror.

'Are you ready now?' she demanded.

'I'm coming in a minute,' Sheila roared back. 'D'you get me? Just tell them that.'

She heard the door slam. Cautiously opening her own door, Sheila saw her image in the mirror. She stood for a moment, her shoulders drooping, her whole body surrendered up to the failure of it, of her. Her coat was lying on the counter. She put it on. At least it covered up the mess. She got up on the toilet, climbed out of the window, out into the wind.

She could see the car park to her right, with the few cars, including their own, seemingly huddled together in the big open space and the surrounding trees being blown and beaten by the storm. To her left she saw what looked like a small road winding away towards the dark animal shape of the mountains, that looked, it occurred to her, as though they too were waiting for her. She headed towards that road, turning back briefly to make sure she had not been seen. There was nobody in sight.

She trudged off into the wind howling now in off the Atlantic, driven down through the corridor of valley between the giant bulks of stone. She kept her head down low, pulled her coat tight around her shoulders. The wind was whipping up her hair. Sheets of rain quickly soaked her through. She couldn't even feel her wet feet but her face felt clean in the rain and the coldness was good. The wind's force against her made her breathe through her

mouth in short tight gasps. Foreign air, legendary air. Not the
stuff of her turf. Of little terraced streets and black taxis and
chippies on rundown corners, combat jeeps idling alongside.

They'd go without her, she thought. The last thing they'll do is
come looking. Not out on these black slopes, no lights, no
signposts, no knowing what might leap out at you. No, they'll
pay up and head back to the cosy lights and central heating of
the guest house. Settle in for the night. Try to put her out of their
mind. She was trouble all right. They'd known that all along.
Sure that was part of the thrill of it. For Danny. It made his heart
lift, beat, become known to him again after all the years since his
wife had left. A mundane life of factory and empty house to come
home to. Pints down the club with the lads at the weekend. Then
her. Her body, the pall of provocation around her. Dangers to be
surmounted at every turn with that one, with the stink of history,
of trash hanging off her. And Christ, in bed she was dynamite.
But easily shed now. Her spell was broken now. She was only
trouble, so she was. And he was getting a wee bit too old for all of
that.

And just what was she going to do? Go for a wee stroll, she
thought. Eventually she'd find her way back. It was only a few
miles to the guest house. She didn't have a key though – the
landlady would be angry to see her in this state coming into her
tidy house, sullying her clean home with its Popes and Virgins.
Well, she could offer it up, so she could.

It was raining even harder. Not a star of light, and the wind
battering. She thought of Eileen's fat face, blistered from the
cigarette, and the groan out of her when her boot had found soft
resistance in her fat guts. Mortal groan, it was.

'Fillies and their grass, they go together.' Aye, that was true
enough. Grass all around her, wet fields, dark blocks of huddled
cows, coughing. Night yanked down over them like a blindfold
over a face. Night holding on to the storm, taking its time. Night
its own territory.

She would slip in beside the snoring Danny, warm her shaking
body against his warmth. She would lie still and wait for dawn
and then for the rising hour. She would wash her face and wait in

the breakfast room. They would cluck at her swollen, blackened face. Nothing would be mentioned.

A car was approaching, she could see its lights' diffused beam filling the black ribbon of road. She pulled into the ditch out of the way, kept her face down, held still. That was a habit she'd learned as a kid. Keep very still when you're caught in the lights. The car was coming fast, driving down the centre of the ribbon as they did in these parts. Enough to get you shot back home – driving with intent. It braked loudly in front of her. She squinted in the light. She could make out four or five faces. Young men, farm boys more than likely. Soft faces, expressionless eyes. She stared back at them. I bet I look a pretty picture to you, lads. You'd not take this home to yer mammys.

The car purred. She waited, thinking that a window would be rolled down and they'd ask her if she was all right, if she needed a lift. She was all right, she thought, safe down here in the soft-vowelled, soft-bellied South. The window was not rolled down. The moment lingered a fraction too long. Staring eyes acknowledged that. Nobody spoke and she became aware of her heart pumping. And then the moment fractured. The car accelerated in a burst of exhaust and screech of rubber and was gone. Darkness gathered around her again. Blotted her up.

She climbed out onto the road and walked on. She could feel the presence of the cows, occupants of the small mountain fields on either side. Swollen-eyed beasts melded into the landscape and the history, into the very air of the place. Cows and rain and grass. Not like her place, where the landscape colluded. Green hedges hiding things, crouching figures and guns. Landscape itself suspect. Grass covering secrets. Cement legitimizing conquest. And warm blood spilling; the only innocence. None of that here where the land lay on the right side of history. Only the howling of legend and the cows eating the flesh of the land, chewing the flesh, the land, the cud, the word. Swallowing. Not thinking. Swallowing.

Those faces in the car. What did they remind her of? Young lads, Huddersfield, Birmingham, voices, dialects – soldiers. Standing over a dead man, freshly shot. His blood a beautiful dark pool

gathering beside him. His head thrown back so that he looked . . .
what was that expression? Knowing. Like a doctor ready with his
own diagnosis – death – knowing it. The boys, soldiers, silent,
guns pointed at the ground. A couple of them chewing gum
intently. Their first shooting. They stood, concentrating on the
fact of it. She'd run towards the shots. Like people do at home.
She'd found them there in that still tableau, each in his role, as
though in conversation, silent communication. He knowing, dead
in his hot blood. They beginning to know.

The wind was lessening, the rain also. There was a river, fast
flowing in line with the road. She could hear the water running
and see the black shapes of mountain boulders strewn over the
river bed. In the west was now a pencil streak of grey light
between land and sky. Beyond the horizon she knew was the sea.

Something more. She stopped and turned, listening. Something
was approaching, from behind. Heavy running footsteps. A shape
appeared. A small figure jogging hard, coming out of the blackness.

'Hellooo!' a breathless voice called out. The 'o' of it flew up into
the air and echoed off the mountain. An old man, around sixty
maybe, and dressed in shorts, singlet and large woollen hat and
gloves.

'Nice evening,' he said in a high nasal tone, panting, stopping
just in front of her and half bending over, his hands on his waist
as he caught his breath.

She said nothing. She wasn't scared exactly, but this was
outside the range of her experience. She didn't know what she
could say that might meet the absurdity of the situation.

'Unusual to find anyone up here at this time of night,' he
panted, 'apart from a few sheep . . . or a wandering . . . cow.'

He was standing taller as he recovered himself, hands on waist
and hauling in deep gulps of air.

Still she said nothing. They stood for a few moments, listening
to the run of the water over everything about them.

Speaking as though to the horizon, the man said, 'No stars
tonight.'

'Not tonight,' she answered, surprising herself.

'Ah, well.'

'Where does this road lead to?' she asked.

'Into the valley.'

'And then?'

'Oh, out again,' he said. 'They told me there was a woman, walking. The lads, in the car. They said she looked . . . not too well.'

'I'm well enough.' She said it sullenly though she hadn't meant to.

'Good girl.' He rubbed his gloved hands together for warmth.

They stood awkwardly for a moment, not even facing each other. It would be too embarrassing to part, she realized, as they would hold each other in their sights for a long while were they to separate.

'Cup of tea?' he said.

In answer she began walking. He fell in at her side. He said his house was not far, just on aways. They turned after a while, off the road onto a rough boreen lined with tall hedges and trees. The ground was muck and pond-sized puddles they could do nothing but wade through. They walked for a good mile, mostly in silence apart from occasional comments he made to encourage her: it was not far now, just a last bit to go. They arrived at a cow gate which he opened. A lamp came on over the porch of the small house as soon as they stepped into the yard. He did not produce a key, just pushed at the door and walked in. A small red flickering light glowed underneath a framed picture of Jesus pointing to His exposed heart. Its light gave the room a strange tinge, intimate, like a church. There was a hall table, laden with paper clutter and a large statue of the Virgin. She saw him touch the Virgin's feet as he passed, then cross himself in a swift vague movement.

'Come on in to the fire, girl, and warm yerself.'

Tiny embers of turf glowed in the fireplace, a big old-fashioned fireplace with the irons still in place for cooking. She took off her sodden coat.

'Kettle,' he announced. He was pottering around, still in his soaking shorts and T-shirt, though he'd removed the hat and gloves. She saw that he was completely bald.

There were a couple of armchairs, newspapers laid on them for cushions. She sat down as close as she could get to the dying dust of the turf but there was no heat left in it. He came over, banked up the fire with fresh sods and sticks, then knelt down and blew at it like a bellows. A cloud of white smoky powder lifted. He continued to blow until eventually a tiny flame ignited.

'Drink?' he said, rolling the 'r'. Without pausing for a reply he brought out a bottle of whiskey from a wooden cupboard, then a couple of teacups which he blew into sharply to remove the turf dust. He filled each cup to the brim.

'Now,' he pronounced, 'see to that and you'll feel the benefit.'

There was something about his high voice and the weak-eyed look of him. His face carried defeat in it, and something else she was curious to discover. She sensed that he was luring her and the game was to resist. Let him try, she thought. The whiskey quivered at the rim of the cup as she lifted it very carefully to drink.

'God bless!' he roared and startled her.

'Look now, you've made me spill it with your shouting around,' she said crossly, thrown by the vehemence of his cry.

'You'll not mind if I put this on,' he said, 'before I die.'

There was a blanket laid over the back of the chair which he pulled around him. He said the words in a sharp, almost accusing tone, as if it was her secret wish that he would indeed die of cold. He sat nursing his drink with his blanket covering his head and shoulders and looking for all the world like a wizened gnome.

'You were fighting,' he said.

Sheila laughed.

'Bless me, Father, for I have sinned,' she mimicked a Southern penitent voice. He looked up from his pondering of the fire.

'You know?'

She didn't say anything. Know what?

'Ah,' he said. He took a long noisy slurp from his cup. 'You'll come to bed now?'

She could have snorted with derision had her nose not felt like a heavy brick impaled on her face. She thought of Danny's skinny white arse in the bed and herself pinioned against it. Why not this one now? Let him empty his wee sack into her. She could take his offering home as a souvenir.

'An' where's the fuckin' tea?'

His weak eyes crinkled into laughter.

'Right enough,' and up he went to the kettle which had boiled and cooled again, his blanket trailing after him.

'Have you ever seen a dead man?' she asked. The question just emerged, bubbled up and presented itself.

'Indeed.' He spoke without turning to her.

'I'm sick of seeing them,' she said. 'Young men's dead bodies. They're there all the time, in my mind. That's a bit sick, d'you think?'

He glanced over at her but said nothing.

'You know that expression on a dead man's face? What would you call it?'

She was looking at them; pale bodies, naked, grey, punctured with neat small holes, tagged, counted, and close together. And all in silent communication with it – the knowingness.

'It's only the flesh,' he answered, '. . . giving way. Animals have it too. Other animals. A young thrush, dashed against the roof in a storm, falling to the ground, eyes open, gives way to it. Flesh accepts, that's all.'

He was occupied with tea-leaves and water, his back to her. A deep groan tore itself from her, thrust up unbidden.

'My mammy!' she hiccupped like a child. Then wails started, deep down wails breaking through. He went over to her, knelt down and held her.

'Ahh . . .' He tightened his hold.

'Bullets,' she wailed, 'bullets. In her head, in her body, the place I came out of, bullets, holes . . .'

She began growling, rocking herself forwards and back violently. He shoved his hands inside her jumper and held her tight to him, feeling the warmth of her flesh.

'Soldiers. Soldiers first, then me. Bastard's bastard. She loved my hair, so she did. Curlers every Saturday night. Used to hurt. Her boyfriends would tuck me in. English accents. Kids spat at me in school. Pulled my hair out. She said not to mind them. Kept me home. Close to her. She was scared then . . . a knock on the door. She knew. Bang, bang, you're dead, that's what kids say.'

She began thumping his chest with her fists.

'Bangbangbangbang!' He pulled closer to her so that she couldn't strike.

'And they never let me see. Closed the lid, screwed down tight, lowered her in, me standing, never saw.'

'Whist now,' he half shouted, his hands clutching her breasts.

'Someone threw a sod, grass sod, then someone else, clumps of grass and earth pelting down on her. I couldn't move, couldn't, couldn't.'

'Come here,' his voice was pained. He put his mouth on her wet, contorted, snot-covered mouth and kissed her hard, biting her tongue and forcing his own into her. She slid off the seat, fell into him. He pulled at her clothes.

'Take them off,' he cried out, tearing off his own.

They rolled over each other on the floor, heaving, pulling at each other's flesh, biting and squeezing. He entered her, began fucking. She was still crying.

'I hate you, I hate you, I hate you,' she kept saying as he fucked her harder, hard as he could, her voice rising and rising, his face intent.

'Christ,' he shouted, coming in her. 'Christ!' he said again.

She cried out too then, a long deep groan that was both pleasure and pain. They subsided into each other's grasp, legs entwined, his head buried in her neck, panting still.

'You're a priest,' she whispered, 'that's what it is, isn't it?' It had just occurred to her.

He removed himself from her with a pained sigh. It reminded her of a teacher once who'd caught her cogging in an exam. That pained suffer-the-children tone.

'Ah, sure you knew that, didn't you? Knew all along.'

They lay on the lino floor for a long time, not speaking, listening to the little phuts of the firelight eating up the turf. His hand lay across her belly, she watched it rise and fall with her breaths.

After a while he said quietly, 'You're not to worry about those dead men. It will go. I see that as well, you know. The amount of bodies I've stood over in my time. Old men, women, boys and girls, babies just. Young men too, beautiful young men. I stand over them with my prayers, my book held up like some kind of protection. But I know . . . I know . . . nothing. Only that someone else will read the black book over me, but they'll be outside of the conversation too.' He chuckled to himself.

'Oh, yes, outside all right.'

A cock crowed close by.

'What was that?'

'Oh, that's the cock, right enough. Crowing for all he's worth.'

'And the hens busy firing out their eggs, isn't that typical,' she said.

'You're a lovely girl.'

Sheila realized they didn't know each other's names.

'You know what I think?' she said. 'I think you'se are just too polite down here. Because you'se are the ones holding the book. Always on the right side of it, always the innocents. It's not the British, the soldiers or the hard men. It's you'se, so it is, really. Holdin' on sneaky like, an' keepin' it quiet. While we all blow ourselves to bits and pieces.'

He didn't answer. She knew he didn't understand her. And he was tired now, tired out. She saw his eyelids close, his mouth relax. The cock crowed again and she roused him. She noticed that the light was beginning to pale out the curtains.

'That's twice,' she said. 'I'd better go before something biblical happens.'

She was dead right about the landlady. The expression on her face when she opened the front door, Sheila standing there with her finger jammed on the bell, bold as muck and looking like an accident.

'Nice morning,' Sheila said.

It was indeed a lovely morning, after the storm. Clear sky twittery with birdsong and cold sunlight strong on the land.

'What in the name of God happened to you?' The woman could not help herself.

'Devotions,' Sheila replied. 'Takes it out of you, doesn't it?'

BRENDAN GLACKEN

Out of the Ordinary

For a year and a half he had sought invisibility, yet the more remote the areas of the world he dallied in, the more he felt eyes turn towards him, the less secure he became. Two weeks in a Norwegian fishing village, suspicion sitting in the white sky above like a dead dog's belly, brought him to the verge of paranoia. A month's sojourn at the edge of the Casas Grandes of northern Mexico, where thirty inbred peasant families gouged an insane carnival living from traitorous land and fermented sugar, and he felt a marked man. Settled briefly in South Africa, in Richards Bay, north of Durban, his reluctance to flaunt his presumed wealth struck his neighbours like wilful arrogance, aroused their clammy interest.

Finally he travelled to Morocco, planning to make his way south to Marrakech, to Casablanca. By the desert edge he expected his life to blend into the wind and the white sand.

The fool. It was during his first night in the rotted-rose backstreets of Tangier that he first felt safe. In the love-comical embrace of a mute five-dollar prostitute, her guardian angel sister sleeping open-eyed at the end of the bed, street noise swamped his grateful soul, trussed his body in a white suit of splendid armour. At ease at last, he spent the winter in the screaming filth of Tangier. He floated untouchable, invisible, above all, and above all ordinary.

Summers took him north, to Majorca. He had learnt better now than to seek out dangerous solitude, remote foolish mountain villages, and instead settled each season in the northern resort area of Port D'Alcudia.

Cooking oil, hair oil, sun oil, sweat, sea salt, tang of hake, kick of liquor, basil, ketchup, all hung in the street airs, a permanent

nebulized haze over the bars, the pizzerias, the Chinese restaurants – fast-food emporia with multicoloured pictorial menus,
their language a photographic Esperanto. The people were
holiday-makers: intensely, they created this vast annual commu-
nal vacation, these shifting talking laughing weeping swarming
strangers: British, German, Irish, Swiss, Scandinavian, Japanese.

He moved through them daily, invisible. Crossed the steaming
road to the sea, threaded his way barefoot between the oiled
throngs on the stinging white sand. For one hour each day he was
beached. Then into the sea for twenty minutes, stripped to black
trunks, invisibility shockingly gone, and fear a fat cumulus cloud
slurping dollops of blue Mediterranean sea. He would dress and
make his way home along white seafront hotels, cool villas, shy
holiday homes.

Home was a vast hotel-apartment complex, more than three
hundred self-contained, air-conditioned boxes on five floors. Self-
contained, air-conditioned (after the first difficult summer), he sat
much of the day on the fifth-floor balcony of his box, observed his
neighbouring balcony boxes at right angles.

He rose early, ate no breakfast, had a light lunch indoors,
walked the streets, swam, showered, ate out at nine o'clock, sat
on the balcony from eleven to midnight drinking Malibu with
white lemonade, slept soundly, the more so when other guests got
rowdy in the bars below, drinking their glorious cocktails and
dancing the macarena.

His was the most orderly ordinary life he could imagine, though
he did not try.

Once a fortnight he visited Maria, a good prostitute and a bad
actress, all ambition and no talent, faking it, faking it. He called
her Sancta Maria, tipped her well. She laughed genuine laughter,
called him Johnny Thirty, this being all she knew of him, or
thought she knew, his name and age. His name indeed was John.
He was thirty-three.

At night the stars came out. He saw only huge filthy layabout
masses of compressed dust and inorganic matter and space debris
and God knew what else. He watched each black brittle night the
young couples who held hands on their balconies under the stars,

kissed, petted and not infrequently engaged in sexual intercourse, in full view of other guests, before the stars, above the pool.

The pool. A huge blue crater blasted out of the pink hotel garden, an enormous freshwater tear-filled eye of varying depth, shimmering under the sun. It gave its life daily to strangers, drew screams, laughter, heat from them. Dying a little each day, it was reluctant to release the last bodies each evening, drawing energy from them rather than giving it to them. Surface movement never ceased. It was alive, blinked in sunlight, moonlight, breathed always.

Early each morning he would sit on his balcony to watch the blue-clad poolboy release the long snake of his underwater vacuum cleaner into the blue water of the pool to remove the leaves, sweet wrappers and other debris of the previous day. And every second Friday during the season the pool would be completely drained at night. His spirit then shrank at the sight of the empty pool, the merciless deep blue eye-socket deprived of its shimmering eye, the blue-painted walls revealing the rather obvious deception of colourless water. Then refilling would take place and all was as before for the next plump batches of holiday-makers spilled from their coaches, the excited children, the languorous young women, the addled mothers and the vast threatening young male army that formed and reformed, advanced and retreated before the blue, blue eye under the hot, hot sun.

Latterly he had begun to get regularly drunk. This deliberation now began on his balcony in the early evening, pouring Malibu in triple measures, adding Coca-Cola instead of white lemonade. Coconut and Coke. A popular drink, a 'C & C' was what he asked for in the bars when he slipped out into the night's ink and shadowed his way down to Bellevue, a vast hot street of kitsch emporia and underdone pizza and cheap beer and tourists in gaudy shirts and angry shorts. The evening crowd swallowed him, he sank gratefully into its vast warm jiggling belly until regurgitated carelessly at some street corner.

There he would find a Britpub. The British were everywhere, or everywhere the Germans were not. This part of the island was colonized equally between the old foes, the Brits with their pubs, the Germans with their second-generation holiday homes. A holiday stand-off.

The Britpubs. Often someone was employed outside, to pull the punters. – Go on, ave a pinta funk, go on, put yer quid on the counter, ask fer a pinta funk, only a pound, inya go, go on, go on, besta British beer, itsa bargain, go on in, that's it, can't lose at that price my mateys, come on then, besta British.

– It's Johnny! Irish Johnny!

Johnny was known, it was the way he liked it. Strange bars were the only danger. The Brits were regular, compressed batch after batch, fortnight after fortnight, year after year. No one knew he spent the entire season there. He drank more C & C, talked sunshine and girls, beach and beer, football. Now and again he went back with Sylvia, or Jackie, or Sue. Their place. Not much usually happened after so much drink, nor did it matter. There was always fortnightly Maria, Sancta Maria, her bad acting, her blessed laughter.

Home alone, late at night, he watched the lights on the vast, regal Missouri, the enormous apartment complex which lay directly across from his own block, some 500 metres away, and towered above it. The lights he watched were not its own. In front of the Missouri, directly at right angles to it, was the Britpub, Raffles. Day and night it throbbed with desperate life and skinny laughter. On its roof were strung half a dozen long coloured strips of neon light, and it was these which reflected on the face of the Missouri, were thrown from there to its enormous pool, and reflected back again. The garish neon lights were transformed to a glow of pastel shades, shifting and changing, slapping the Missouri face with an old-maid luminous make-up under the yellow moon and creamy layabout stars.

Johnny would wake on the balcony in the morning, with the most ordinary hangovers. The pale face of the Missouri, its night make-up gone, stared at him insanely. So it went on.

– It's Johnny! Irish Johnny!

– It's Johnny Driscoll.

Would not be true to say he knew the day would come. Would be truer to say he hoped it would.

– Johnny Driscoll.

– Yes.

– I don't believe it.

– Believe it.

– So it is you.

– And you, Anna.

The extraordinary had come upon him, so Johnny plunged back wildly with Anna into the ordinary. They took the bus to Formentor next day, the attractive youngish couple.

– How did you recognize me?

– You haven't changed.

– I was told that's the best disguise.

– Pardon?

– Not changing. People's expectations you know. The passing of years. Time. I should look like someone you used to know, not someone you still know. Do you understand?

– I don't understand what you did.

– You know what I did.

– Yes. You stole from the company.

– Embezzled, yes. £300,000.

– I just don't know how you did it.

– Easily.

He explained the scam. A trained accountant like himself, with two years' more experience, the simplicity of it angered her. Two sets of accounts. Secret ledger. Third party cheques. Quotidian, mundane stuff.

– Not much novelty in your methods.

– No need, was there?

– No.

They swam. A well-dressed party of five people, three men and two women, walked down the shingle path from the hotel to the small jetty, a uniformed waiter bearing a large picnic basket aloft like a victory plate. A motor launch pulled in, took the party and their basket on board, raced fifty metres offshore to a proud cream yacht, unloaded its garrulous cargo. Tinkly laughter splashed to shore, glanced off white pebbles.

  – Your style.

  – Far from it.

  – You live simply then.

  – I simply live.

  – At others' expense.

Her seeing him, finding him, was extraordinary and he wanted only the ordinary, to be always among the ordinary. So they did the ordinary things. The trips to Puerto Pollensa, to C'An Picafort. The purchase of leather goods in the Inca market. The regular swim in the almond-scented sea. The bright cruel love made in her apartment.

The fact remained she was extraordinary in her being there alone, in her idiotic discovery of him, in her now unshrouded desire to appropriate part of him to herself.

Two weeks passed. Extraordinarily, she was not among the packaged, the bound, the chartered. She stayed on.

After a month he told her one night he was visiting someone called Maria and could not see her. She shrugged her shoulders.

He told her about Sancta Maria.

  – Good. Fine. Enjoy.

Maria was full of laughter and amateur dramatics. At midnight he left, buoyed up, prepared, determined. Anna was awake in her apartment when he called and they walked the almond-scented beach, five miles, returning by the Missouri, where Raffles spilled out its late, its last. All the besta British gone that night.

He sat later on his balcony, watched the pastel shades on the face of the Missouri, reflected from the Raffles neon lights, from the pool where Anna floated face down, and reflected back again. The stupid weak moon made slanted prison bars of light from his balcony enclosure. Soon the poolboy would arrive with his hungry plastic motorized snake, restoring the ordinary, his element, his true love, his only desire.

TOMMY FRANK O'CONNOR

Loose Head

When we were passing through the Library that Friday evening there was this lassie on stilts painting the inside of a gable wall. None of the team seemed to notice her or what she was doing, but I stopped as if I had run into the All Blacks.

Jackie, our hooker who also happened to be deputy County Librarian, had suggested the Video Room on the top floor as the ideal place to go through the tape and the game plan for our crucial match the next day. The whole idea of us in a Library seemed absurd. It was Jackie's line of work and seemed to agree with him, so that was OK, though we would still slag him about it: that smell of wizened skin and new paper being smothered in old classroom odour. Apart from a computer wizard in the reserves, the rest of the team were steelworkers, miners, brewery hands, truck drivers promoted to sales representatives like myself. We were the League Champions and five of us were Internationals, so we cut the right image for certain types of promotions.

Anyway, back to the gable.

I should explain that I've had this problem: when I'd look into space with a lot of distance or width, my brain and stomach would try to exchange places. The first time I noticed it was on a school tour when I was twelve. We climbed a mountain. Great; my face and the mountain nearly kissing as we reached the summit. Then I looked out on more space than I had ever seen in my life, down and up and deep never-ending caverns of mocking echo throwing me left, swinging me up and dragging me right, sucking me down, out into it.

I'll never forget what I now admit was terror, that entirely new perspective on the Bible story where the Lord sweats blood in an olive grove. It was like that dolly-out, zoom-in shot in Hitchcock's

Vertigo, only there was no cinema seat to cling on to and no shelter of darkness. To get down, I had to turn my back to the view and my face to the mountain, with Master fussing beside me as if I was the sickly son of a VIP. The sweat shivered out of me in rivers.

This was no emulsion job our painter was doing on the gable. That feeling reeled inside me again. I knew I should look away, but I couldn't. The wall was becoming acres of landscape, a hint of a mountain on the right, and a forest to the left, with streams trickling out of the horizon into a brook a run of trout would love – about twelve feet up.

'You like it then?' Her voice beside me broke into my thoughts of flies and bait.

Close up she was a mess: T-shirt, jeans, trainers spattered like a rainbow through a blender. I'm not sure if I said anything.

'The scale, the layout,' she prompted.

'I'm supposed to be somewhere else.' I wished I was, and was glad I wasn't.

'You're Dave Thomas, aren't you, the rugby player?'

'Yea, loose head. And you?'

'Muriel Joyce, Artist in Residence.'

We shook hands.

First touch, first contact must be decisive, Coach always drummed into us. Let them know who's boss. Something about her hand; smaller than mine, fingers longer. Not strength exactly; verve, full eyes more kind than an opposing tight head's, but no less positive. Five feet and maybe eight stone to my six-two and seventeen stone.

'Dave, you all right, boy?' Hooker had come looking for his loose head.

He dug into me going up the stairs about getting distracted before a match. I almost told him he should have mentioned that to his sister before she worked me over the previous weekend. Coach added his usual mouthful before we settled around the screen. Boy, those close-ups! You could smell the blood and the spit and the sweat. Great.

I looked in on the next Wednesday afternoon ostensibly to see

Jackie, though he had mentioned after training on Tuesday night that he'd be away. The developing mural had played in my eyes while I was up country the previous two and a half days.

Now I found that Muriel was no longer painting a gable. The work had grown onto the side walls, and she was up there on a makeshift scaffolding with the sky following her a couple of metres out onto the ceiling.

'Right man in the right place, Dave. Can you move me towards the mountain, please.'

After a few such moves she climbed down with the agility of a cat. 'God, you're strong, Dave. I had intended getting down to make it easier to shift me.'

'No sweat, you're welcome.'

'So what do you think now?'

'Looks finished to me.' It was so real that the old mountain-top feeling stirred again. Drops of ice slipped through my skin and beckoned on more to skip and tumble through the hairs on my body. 'If it was any more real I'd expect a scent of something wild,' I added as I wiped my face and tried to control the heavy-scrummage-machine tremor in my legs.

'Thanks. A couple of more days' finishing touches, a few light strokes here and there and you'll be surprised.'

I tried telling myself it was only a wall, but my eyes didn't believe me.

'Something wrong, Dave?'

I found myself sitting on the floor, my back against a wall of books. After Muriel returned with a glass of water I explained my phobia while she mopped my face. If the lads had seen me squelched out on the floor like that with a multicoloured moth flitting around me, I'd never have lived it down.

'Afraid of anything else?'

I shook my head. I feared nothing, I told myself. What was she suggesting?

'Then come in tomorrow or Friday; you're the one I need for this.'

Me, an artist's mate, in a library! I imagined opposing tight heads champing on that, the thought of it rucked and mauled inside my brain. More shaking of my head as she helped me to my feet, her voice like the touch of a masseuse after an International win.

'You need to touch it, to become involved in the work as it develops, and then it will hold no fear for you.'

I took a clammy grip on her advice as I had done to that cinema seat at *Vertigo*. She waited as I tried to consider the type of fly I might use to lure the trout in the brook.

'I'm not afraid,' I said.

'I can see that,' she said. She dipped her eyes into the silence of the truth, and slowly raised them back to mine. She placed her left hand up on my wet shoulder and took me on a tour of the detail that came together to form the heather and streams, the brook and the valley. There was a sadness on her face as she finished in the lowlands, and I tried to talk it off by asking if she knew a place that looked like her mural. She didn't answer, only asked a question of her own.

'Do you notice anything missing from the scene before you?' She took my hand and my elbow and guided me back a few paces to fill my hesitation. 'Take as long as you like. Time keeps a count of the dewdrops in a place like that.'

I had meant to mention that there was no house, but it looked grand without one. Anyway, I thought it might be bringing my work as a Builder's Providers representative to a place where it didn't belong.

'I wouldn't be much of an expert on these things,' I said. She raised her eyes to me. A look full of words suggested that I could do better than that.

'A house would look at home in there somewhere, a cottage maybe.'

'And where would you build it?' She looked as though she expected me to know the exact spot. When I noticed that there was no road and suggested that without access there couldn't be a house, she took something that was neither pen nor brush and seemed to uncover a track running along by the river and turning into a mountain pass exactly where it would fold itself around a cottage. I climbed up and touched the mural. I felt the wall, felt it but it was no longer there.

A smile banished her sadness. She reminded me about her request to join her in finishing the work.

'It will help you to face your problem. And I could really do with a hand.'

'Does Jackie ever wander in around here?'

'So you're afraid of him, then?' She tied me up with her eyes, and waited.

'Tomorrow, after three. It mightn't look like it, but I've work to do too you know.'

Thursday afternoon flowed over to Friday as my old tracksuit took on that spattered rainbow look. I found myself inside the mural as I lifted her onto the lower stilts from where she climbed to two heights higher. I mixed little tubs of colour and learned the difference between brush and knife and trowel as she helped me to paint my impression of the cottage into its place. It was single storey with a chimney at each ivied gable, clusters of flowering shrubs, and a log-cabin barn half hidden in the trees. On the mountain she created a stag with the demeanour of a winning captain. Just for me, she said. She finished the sun and fingered its light around the edges of trees and rocks. Something she did with her fingernails sent power rippling through the stag. I pointed out that our cottage needed her special touches to finish it, so I lifted her onto the stilts and watched blobs become a door and windows, and the front of a car peeped out from the far gable.

Now all it needed was people, I thought, but then they might spoil everything, so I kept quiet.

Jackie passed through twice with that stray demeanour he gets during opposition anthems. Just as well he didn't notice us; he'd have made some stupid remark about me spending more than an hour with a doll without laying her.

I remembered we had forgotten to eat, but I wouldn't break the spell as each part of her creation responded to her eyes, her touch. She even spoke to it at times and, I swear to God, it was as if she breathed a soul into the work and it whispered back to her. The opposite of what space did to me on that school tour way back.

While we were standing back taking a long view she touched my arm and asked me to wait. In a half run she skipped out of her earlier sadness, mounted the low stilts and began to work, with her back saying things to me. It was as if her whole body was in it, one moment moving, the next on the tip-toes of an idea, and then that all-in slow kind of wiggle before she jumped down and walked backwards to gaze with me.

Now there was a man on a ladder on the roof, thatching, and a lady poised with a brush admired her finishing touches to the front wall. Great. Something about the freshly painted couple played in my imagination, searched among my dreams. Two people, each absorbed in their own work yet one wouldn't look right without the other. Teamwork, true to a game plan without coach or captain.

I thought of the game plan waiting upstairs, the moves, the phases. Only a game. Anyway, we were on a winning roll and I was playing better than ever.

'It's not right yet, Dave, still missing something.' Her left arm was around my waist and my right hand rested on the shape of her hip.

'You're just like our coach, a pure perfectionist. Not even God or the Board of Works could find fault with that.'

She glanced at me and brought my eyes back to the mural. At any moment I expected a flock of birds to fly across the sky. And then I saw it. 'Children,' I said, 'they've no children.'

'Grandchildren, Dave, they need grandchildren.'

'I think we had better go and eat,' I said. 'This hunger is making me light in the head.'

She left the choice of restaurant up to me. Without thinking, I suggested the Steakhouse on the Pavilion rooftop. Even though I told her there was no need to change, she was into her flat, into a dress that snuggled into the surprise of her shape, and back in my car quicker than our pack would do a lap of the training ground. And she'd washed her face, and her hair looked different.

As we settled into dinner I realized that I was looking beyond her out over the city switching itself on for the night. An expanse of beauty without fear.

'Is this where you usually bring your girlfriends?'

'No. I mean I don't.' I swallowed a swirl of girlfriends like Libby

Vine and the amazing things they would do for me or for any of the lads. Tomorrow night our team would be back here and in the surge of the bar downstairs for yet more of that.

We heard Jackie coming up the stairs while still in conversation with someone below.

'Aye, Dave, I knew you were up to something. Didn't expect to see you here, Muriel.' He tapped her on the shoulder. 'And what's he got that I don't have, aye?'

His eyes were stuck to her. 'Pretended not to hear me when I invited her out last week.' He squeezed the creamy skin between her neck and shoulder.

'Leave it, Jackie.' I hit the table and startled the delft and cutlery.

'No funny business now, Dave. You know how important tomorrow's match is.' He was already half-way down the stairs.

Muriel tidied away the fat and gristle of her steak and laid her knife and fork side by side. 'What time is the game over tomorrow?'

'About five.' I hoped she wouldn't want to be involved in the after-match mêlée.

'How about if I pick you up and take you to *my* favourite restaurant?' Her words filled a hollow inside me.

'Great,' I said.

MARY O'DONNELL

Canticles

I saw Ottiline yesterday, for the first time in twenty years. The President had been ushered into the new Irish Conservatory of Music to unveil the plaque, flanked by the Director and Professors, the year's Performing Artist in Residence, the John Field Scholar, the Albinoni Scholar, and the sponsorhip organizer, when Ottiline glided past. She has risen to become Senior Lecturer and specialist in Twelfth-century Composition. I too am a specialist in Twelfth-century Composition. She inspired me to compose and play when all around me were damaging their tympani – blessed membranes of inner ecstasy! – to the sound of the Sex Pistols, Sid Vicious, the Boomtown Rats. She teaches medieval harp, fiddle and the organistrum. It is my privilege to mostly play these instruments. My diary is full for the next two years.

But before I became a music student, I discovered the *symphoniae harmoniae celestium revelationum*. Well, mother did. One day as she sat down to practise, she casually tossed a soiled wad of music sheets at me.

'You might have some use for those,' she muttered as she opened *59 Best Loved Piano Pieces* and grimly flexed her fingers. She had discovered them inside the lid of her piano-stool, a treasure for which she had trawled Francis Street, up the hill from where we lived. Having lobbed the yellowing manuscript into my hands, she began to attack Rachmaninoff's Prelude, Opus 3, No. 2, as it should never be attacked. I said nothing and brought the pages – fine as young skin! – into the kitchen. My bag lay on the table, bulging with Leaving Cert. books. We were having boiled bacon and cabbage for dinner. I remember the clatter of saucepan lids that foamed and sizzled like lava while mother ran at Rachmaninoff. But old Rach would not be hers that day, despite her lusty *multo agitato*. I turned the knobs on the electric cooker to three, then, at the window – propped open by mother's hazel wand from her water-divining days – I examined the manuscript, holding it to the light, separating the sheets. As I scrutinized each one, and certain phrases sprang to life, something awakened in me – an excitement, a sense of being a link in a random chain of events that I might have the capacity to complete.

Outside, leaves lay in crisp stacks against the walls of the opposite terrace. Crows cackled above chimneys. In the dining-room off the kitchen, mother reached the climax of her Prelude. The dark lower notes growled their *fortissimo* and I knew that our neighbours would be hammering the walls again.

Father would sleep until half-past four, despite the racket. He was working that night, as he had done every night since Les Trois Canards had taken him on. 'Holiyers next summer, girls!' he would say, rubbing his hands together. We ignored father's predictions. For one thing, anxiety made him exaggerate, and for another, in the middle of an oil crisis he refused to sling hash. He worked only in classy joints, with a foreign menu in ornate writing and an interesting wine list. So while father slept and mother played the piano, I trembled as I read the phrases, *O vis aeternitatis, O virga mediatrix, O viridissima virga.*

Six months on, my parents were able to tell their acquaintances that I was studying for a 'Bee Muzz'. Within a week in college, Ottiline became my tutor, Ottiline of the fleecy, shimmering hair, the undulant walk across any room, the trail of cigarillo smoke despite her asthma! She encouraged me. She hectored me. I thought of Richard Bonynge working Joan Sutherland, or von Karajan bullying his finest soloists. This was *it*, I thought, how it had to be.

One day as I practised the harp, she interrupted mid-phrase and broke my A string.

'You did that on purpose!' I gasped.

'And you're out of tune!' she screeched. 'For God's sake keep

your instrument tuned! If you can't hear properly, then you've no
right to be here . . .'

I resented that. I knew I could hear. Later, she apologized.

'It's just that I'm working on something – a version of an
Oswald von Wolkenstein, it's –' her voice dropped, she chewed
her lips – '*difficult.*'

'Von Wolkenstein?' I felt giddy. 'I have something too – a find –
a real find!'

She didn't ask what it was.

That night, I removed the manuscript from a box inscribed
Taken from Old Waterloo Bridge, London, one of mother's antique
treasures which father, in an effort to 'brighten it up', had painted
blue, inside and out. Ottiline would be able to tell me about the
manuscript. She would help. I thought of her sensitive face, I
imagined her humming the Antiphons and Responsoriums, the
Alleluias and Lieder, the way she had of tilting her lovely head as
she tried to hear the music. I had hand-written some of the words,
which my old Latin teacher had translated into passable English.

> *The Spirit, life that gives life,*
> *and moves all things*
> *and is the root of every creature*
> *wiping away pain*
> *and anointing wounds:*
> *this is the radiant and admirable life,*
> *awakening and reawakening all things*
> *to their most natural ecstasy!*

Whoever wrote those words, that music, was an artist, a
visionary. Certain phrases were worked and reworked, as if to
induce an ecstatic trance in the listener. She – I always felt it was
a woman – addressed the Virgin as a *virga* or 'branch', or even a
viridissima virga, 'a most verdant branch'. Ottiline had to see this.

Eventually, I brought her home. As we pushed open the narrow
front door and negotiated the tiny hallway, I sniffed the air. To my
relief, mother wasn't cooking. Instead, she was waiting by the

piano – poised in fact – one elbow resting on the cracked inlaid mahogany, dressed to kill in mauve and turquoise satin. She swept towards us, arms outstretched.

'Oh, you're *here*! You're here, at *last*!' she cried.

'We're here,' I replied casually. For a while that afternoon, her need for art and culture made her lose her sense of judgement. Because Ottiline was in the house, mother was charming and funny. The effect would last for weeks, before the little black balloons that often trailed above her head descended again. Ottiline was pleasant enough. But she coiled herself back in the sofa as if she did not have to make any effort in our home. Her eyes swept over the piano, over mother, around the little room. As mother struggled in the kitchen with the fresh Java coffee, bought for the occasion in Bewleys, she looked faintly amused.

'What's funny?' I asked.

'Oh.' She wheezed a little, sliding fine hands into the pockets of her jeans. 'All this, I suppose. Not quite what I expected.'

Mother staggered in with an overladen tray, piled with cream slices, Danish pastries, and our silver coffee-pot. 'Oh Mammy,' I whispered. 'That's heavy! Anyway, Ottie and I were going to make dinner soon.' Inexplicably, Ottiline fixed me with a long, approving stare.

But she took what she felt to be her due, waiting as her coffee was poured, as mother spooned in the sugar, added a drop of milk. We sipped our coffee, made small talk. Outside on the street buses tore past in a whirl of dust. Occasionally, one of the sellers would come down from Thomas Street market, her cartload of toilet-paper, or chocolate, or flowers, rumbling below our front window.

At eight o'clock the bells of Christchurch rang across the darkening city, the bolognese was simmering and Ottiline had opened a bottle of Blue Nun. Mother nudged me.

'Show her, Anna, show her – you know!' she urged, excited as a child. I wanted to. I really did. Yet if mother hadn't been there, I would have wriggled out of it. She sat happily, as if that manuscript marked my natural admission to a world that had been denied her. I laid the manuscript on the kitchen table.

'You know what I think this is?' I was bursting to tell her. The silver eye-shadow she often wore made her lids ripple as she glanced quickly over the top page. Something in that glance made me wary, but then her amused look slipped back in place, and she shrugged.

'It's – sort of – it's connected to Hildegard,' I stammered proudly. She put the page down, lit a cigarillo and reached for the whole manuscript – as if it was some old magazine. Nervous of that cigarillo, I gently removed it from her hand.

'Somebody's keen!' she whispered. Again she stared at the top page, eyelids glistening. Mother perched on the edge of the sofa. But something in Ottiline had sealed itself off from us. I watched as her face became an unlovely mask, bland with cunning.

Then she spoke. 'That's not from the Sibyl of the Rhine, or any of her sibylettes either.' She actually chuckled. Her eyes fell again on the manuscript, 'It could be anything. It could be – some menopausal Victorian – having *fun* with vellum!'

I heard mother's gasp. She began to pat her hair into place.

The words came slowly from my mouth. 'I don't – think – so.'

'Have you tried to date it?' Ottiline asked then.

'No.'

'Well then.' She looked relieved. 'And what have I told my Anna-banana about the value of a little research, hmmm?' She smiled warmly as she tapped the back of my hand with her index finger.

'You're probably right,' mother cut in.

'I have a friend –' Ottiline drew breath, '– who knows about – such things – if I could –' she chose her words carefully, '*borrow* it?'

Mother was frowning. Then I stood up. 'I don't think so,' I said a second time.

'I *could* try—' she went on.

'No.' Mother was firm but gracious. 'Thank you.'

Slowly, I gathered the manuscript and replaced it in the blue box. Ottiline understood. Minutes later, an unfamiliar coolness possessed me as she moved calmly, rapidly down the street. Her cigarillo glowed red as she slid into darkness.

She was right about the value of research. Mine eventually

confirmed that the influence of Hildegard von Bingen had, by the late twelfth century, reached the shores of Ireland, where a woman in the forests of Laois put ink on vellum and as a means of raising herself to ecstasy composed her own theology.

When I saw Ottiline yesterday, I thought of mother's efforts to exalt the bizarre turmoils of *her* life. She now plays in grand style at her own grand piano. As most of the neighbours are gone, she makes plenty of noise. Developers have planned apartments on the street, with electronically operated gates. Father still waits on tables, in an Italian restaurant that employs the mature type of Maitre d'.

But time transforms us. A single disappointment finds a lifetime's compensation. One is able to observe from a distance the average humanity of a former god or goddess, whose feet of clay allowed us to go on. Yesterday, Ottiline and I ignored one another. We clapped, one of us with joy, the other with an asthmatic hiss, as the Director read from the new plaque: *'This is the radiant and admirable life, awakening and reawakening all things to their most natural ecstasy!'*

BIOGRAPHICAL NOTES

FRED ANNESLEY was born in Strabane, Co. Derry, in 1940 and educated in Foyle College and John Prior School in Lifford. He became one of the youngest recruits ever admitted to the RUC training depot and was posted to a station on the Fermanagh/Cavan border. He emigrated to Canada in 1960, working as a reporter or editor in many cities there, and is now on the *Toronto Globe and Mail*. He has had five short stories published in Canada.

HARRY CLIFTON was born in Dublin in 1952 and educated at Blackrock College and UCD where he took a Master's Degree in Philosophy. He taught for two years in Nigeria and also worked in other places in Europe, Africa and Asia, and administered UN/Concern refugee aid in Bangkok. All his early poems and short stories were published in the *Irish Press* 'New Irish Writing'. He has had a number of poetry collections published by Gallery Press and in 1981 he won the Patrick Kavanagh Award. Last year Macmillan published his *On the Spine of Italy: A Year in the Abruzzi*, and this autumn Lilliput will be bringing out his debut short story collection.

MACDARA DOYLE was born in Dublin in 1965. A UCD MA graduate in Irish history, he won the Irish Schools Creative Writing short story prize in 1984. In the early 90s he worked for a year in Mexico and also for *In Dublin* and *Magill* magazines. He is now a Communications Officer for the Concern organization.

BRENDAN GLACKEN was born in Co. Mayo and educated at Rockwell College, UCD and the University of Reykjavik. He is a staff journalist with the *Irish Times* where he writes a thrice-weekly satirical column, 'Times Square'. He has published a collection of these pieces and has also had three radio plays broadcast by RTE.

PATRICIA HICKEY was born in Dublin. A sociology graduate of Trinity College, Dublin, she has worked with Aer Lingus and as national secretary of an educational organization. Her stories have been broadcast on community radio and she is now working on a novel.

FRED JOHNSTON was born in Belfast in 1951. In 1969 he moved to Dublin where he worked as a journalist and in advertising. His first stories were published in the *Irish Press* 'New Irish Writing' and he won a Hennessy Literary Award in 1972. Founder of Cúirt, Galway's annual literary festival, his first story collection, *Keeping the Night Watch*, was published by the Collins Press in 1998.

PAUL LENEHAN was born in Dublin in 1962. He has had stories in anthologies in Ireland, England, Australia and Germany. In 1998 he completed the MA in Creative Writing at the University of Glamorgan and is now writing a novel.

MARTIN MALONE was born in Dublin in 1957. A Military Police NCO with the Irish army, he has served five times in Lebanon and once in Iraq. A prizewinner in RTE's 1998 Francis MacManus Awards, his stories have been broadcast by RTE, BBC Radio 4 and World Service, and his first novel, *Us*, was published this year by Poolbeg Press.

AIDAN MATHEWS was born in Dublin in 1956 and educated at UCD, Trinity College, Dublin, and Stanford University, California. He has published a number of poetry collections and has had plays produced in Dublin, London, Boston, Avignon and Paris. Winner of the *Irish Times* Award in 1974, the Patrick Kavanagh Award in 1976, the Macauley Fellowship in 1978/9 and an Academy of American Poets Award in 1982, he has published two widely acclaimed collections of short stories and one novel.

FIONA O'CONNOR was born and educated in Dublin. In 1980 she won an Arts Council Bursary to train as a ballet dancer with the

Dance Theatre of Harlem in New York and since then has been a dancer and actress, performing with the Royal Opera, Covent Garden, and the Royal Shakespeare Company. Last year she won the Hennessy First Fiction Award and now runs an open-air summer theatre at an old water mill in Co. Kerry.

TOMMY FRANK O'CONNOR was born in Currow, Co. Kerry. An accountant and playwright, he won the Kerry International Summer School Short Story Competition in 1994 and 1996. His stories have been published in the *Sunday Tribune* 'New Irish Writing', the *European* and other periodicals and broadcast on BBC Radio 4.

MARY O'DONNELL was born in Monaghan in 1954. Her first stories and poems were published in the *Irish Press* 'New Irish Writing' and she has won the Allingham Short Story Award and the Listowel Writers' Week short story competition. She has published many poetry collections, a short story collection and two novels.

CÓILÍN O hAODHA was born in Galway in 1975. He attended St Mary's College in Galway before studying at UCD, graduating with a degree in English and Philosophy in 1998. His story, 'Her Blood Dripped into Grass', won the 1998 Francis MacManus Award. He lives in Galway.

BRIDGET O'TOOLE was born in Torquay in 1943. She grew up in Cornwall and was educated there and at Oxford and Warwick Universities. She moved to Ireland in 1970, lectured in English at the University of Ulster in Coleraine and now teaches on the Derry campus of the University. Her stories have been published in *The Honest Ulsterman*.

DEIRDRE SHANAHAN was born in London of Irish parents and spent much of her childhood in Kerry and Mayo. She studied English and Drama at University, taught and worked in the theatre and had a play broadcast by RTE. Her stories have been published in anthologies and periodicals in England and the US, and she has won the *Irish Post* B & I New Writing Competition organized by the Listowel Writers' Week.

JOE SHEERIN was born in Dowra, Co. Leitrim. His first poems appeared in the *Irish Press* 'New Irish Writing' in the 1970s and he later had poems in Faber's *New Poetry 5*, while his collection, *A Crack in the Ice*, was brought out by Dolmen Press. He is a lecturer in English and Linguistics at a Sixth Form College in England. 'The Whaler' is his first story to be published.

HOWARD WRIGHT was born in Co. Armagh. He has published two poetry collections and his poems and stories have appeared widely in Ireland, Britain, Canada and the US, and he has also won both the Kilkenny Short Story and Poetry Prizes. He is a lecturer in Art History at the University of Ulster, Belfast.

Short stories, which must not have been previously published, are invited for consideration for future volumes of *Phoenix Irish Short Stories*. Unsuitable MSS will not be returned unless a stamped, addressed envelope is enclosed. Writers outside the Republic of Ireland are reminded that, in the absence of Irish stamps, return postage must be covered by International Reply Coupons: two coupons for packages up to 100g, three for packages 101g to 250g. All communications regarding MSS which require a reply must also be accompanied by a self-addressed envelope and return postage. MSS and letters should be addressed to David Marcus, PO Box 4937, Rathmines, Dublin 6.